INCONVENIENT WIFE

NATASHA BOYD

INCONVENIENT WIFE

By
NATASHA BOYD

Book cover design by Julie Burke
Julianne@hearttocover.com

INCONVENIENT WIFE

© 2018 by Natasha Boyd

ISBN: **978-1732238527**

To stay up to date with new releases, text NATASHABOYD to 31996

KDP Print edition

*For my readers, who always let me follow the story
wherever it may lead*

GWEN

"**W**omen are dangerous and expensive!" Beau's eyes sparkled with mischief and a bit too much to drink.

His brown hair flopped over his brow, and his dusky blue eyes matched his shirt. I was convinced if he let go of the pool cue, he'd lose his balance.

The petite, dark-haired confection in a pink dress who'd just prompted Beau's declaration, unpeeled herself from him and gave me a dirty look as she approached me.

"I was just offering condolences, he doesn't have to be so mean," she said.

I couldn't imagine Beau being mean, so I offered her a small smile. Most of the time he was just honest, which I guess could equate to the same thing sometimes. "Condolences? Nobody's dead yet," I said. "Besides, he's just having a rough day," I assured her. "Better luck when you see him next." She cast one more longing look over her shoulder, a shoulder that seriously only came up to my elbow. Then she flounced away.

"Why, thanks, Beau." I rolled my eyes and took a sip of the beer I dangled between two fingers. "Women are dangerous and expensive? *I'm* a woman in case you missed it." I handed my cue to the guy waiting to take over our table. He was a muscled gym rat with a fake tan, purple tank top, and shoulders wide enough to carry dinner plates.

"You sure are," Gym Rat said, his eyes rising finally from my chest to my eyes. "You can chalk my cue anytime."

I felt sure he'd use me for practice bench-pressing instead. Though he'd probably need two of me to reach his bench weight, despite my solid bones. "Nice line," I said.

"But you're Gracie," Beau said loudly. "You don't count."

"I don't count," I said apologetically to Gym Rat. Gym Rat seemed to belatedly realize some chivalry might be in order and turned. His purple tank top stretched dangerously across his chest. There was hardly enough of it as it was.

"Don't worry about it." I laid a hand on Gym Rat's shiny shoulder in case his steroids accidentally gave him a heart attack and wondered if I could ask him his skin care regime so I could make my legs look as smooth and glossy as his arms. "I don't need saving. I've known that joker for twenty years. I'll just go on and take him back to his momma."

I grabbed Beau round the middle and walked him through the bar. "And you're right Beau. I'm expensive. You owe me fifty bucks, and I'm dangerous because you always owe me when we play pool. Have you not learned by now?"

"Awww, come on, Gracie. Do we *have* to leave?"

I caught the eye of the bartender and our friend Alice, the owner, and waved with a motion toward Beau to explain our sudden exit. They knew one of us would be back in to settle our tab. And if not tomorrow, we were there almost every Sunday. It was our ritual.

"Wait," Beau said, suddenly digging his heels in and squinting at the flat screen behind the bar. "I didn't see who won the game."

"Carolina lost." I gave him a shove to keep moving. "Clemson nailed a three pointer at the buzzer."

"Noooooooo." Beau drew out the word incredulously.

"Jeez, you're drunker than I thought. What's going on?"

"Oh, Gracie."

"Stop calling me Gracie."

"Gwendolyn," Beau boomed in a deep, severe voice, a hand on his chest. "My apologies, fair maiden."

"Beau," I said in warning.

"Fine, *Gwen*," he said with a chuckle. "Gwen getting-on-with-your-life-with-your-fancy-job, *Gwen*."

I frowned. "What's that supposed to mean?"

"Nothing."

"Your dad been on your case again?" I asked, knowing his comment was probably more about him hurting today than anything about me. "I thought you've been working for him. I've hardly seen you. Is he saying you're not doing enough?" I felt indignant on Beau's behalf. Beau considered working in his family business a death sentence. He hated it. The thing was, he wasn't ungrateful. That wasn't it. And he worked damn hard. But as long as I'd known Beau he'd wanted to build boats. He was like a thwarted and tortured artist whose family laughed at his efforts. Unable to work with his hands and create on his own was slowly killing him. He helped my dad when he could, but those boats weren't *his*. I could see the hope for his own business fading over the years as time went on and he realized he'd never get to fulfill his life's passion.

I had to tell him about my dad's news. But now probably wasn't a good time.

"I *have* been working," he said loudly. "I've been working my ass off. I'm there aaaalllll the time. And I hate it," he explained needlessly because I knew. "And now grandfather is in the hospital. And ..."

He trailed off and rubbed his hand down his face. "He's gonna die Gracie, and they're going to ask me to commit full time to Montgomery Homes & Facilities."

I sucked in a breath and didn't correct him on my name this time. "I'm so sorry, Beau." No wonder Beau had been acting strange and with forced joviality all day. And it was probably why little pink confections kept swinging past him "with condolences"—because Beau Montgomery was about to go from eligible bachelor to *extremely* eligible bachelor. *And* he was straight. A unicorn! I could almost hear the morbid squeals of delight over the Charleston City skyline.

"How bad is it? Is he really about to go?" I asked. I'd known his grandfather's heart disease had been getting worse, but he'd always seemed infallible.

"I always had a 'some day,'" Beau went on as if he didn't hear me.

"I know you did."

"I thought grandfather would groom Dad, have him running things so I could step away. At least for a while. But now grandfather's in the hospital. I should be sad I'm about to lose him, but instead I'm so fucking mad, Gracie. He's going to die without ever addressing what I've asked him for. Freedom. I just wanted freedom to forge my own path. I missed my chance to go out on my own and thumb my nose at the money. If I'd just left and made my own way I'd be better off. I was stupid, Gracie. Greedy. And they've controlled every aspect of my life."

Beau saying it all out loud in no uncertain terms pierced me in my chest.

"And our family is so splintered and fucked up. What would it have mattered if I'd left?" he growled and threw an arm out in an empty gesture across the dusk-lit parking lot. "Just one more Montgomery cast to the wind."

I assumed he was talking about his cousin Trystan. I squeezed Beau's lean and hard waist as I guided him across the gravel in the muggy night air, the heat of his skin emanating through his rumpled button-down shirt. It was an abbreviated version of the hug I wanted to give him. I could feel the hopelessness and sadness he wore like a heavy mantle, and I wished I could relieve it. I wasn't even sure he was that drunk, but he seemed to need comfort. So I held on.

"It would have mattered to *me* if you'd left, Beau."

Trystan, or should I say the lack of Trystan, was the reason I had Beau. I remembered that summer clear as anything.

I was fully thirteen, as only a thirteen year old girl can be. Full of sass and the desperate hope to be noticed, but wanting to fade into the wall when anyone did.

Beau and his cousin would run down to the marina every day, every chance they got. They'd offer to do odd jobs and invariably cause trouble when they got distracted and bored.

"Do you remember the summer we met?" I asked Beau, trying to get him to focus on something other than his pity party while I hustled him into my brand new Jeep Wrangler I'd bought after a year at my new job. She was indigo blue and I called her Eliza.

"Yeah. Course."

"No, specifically. Do you remember getting into trouble grabbing a fish from old Dwyer's cooler to try and lure the dock cat closer, and it turned out that was one of his redfish he'd just caught, and he almost skinned you alive he was so mad."

Beau chuckled as I got in on my side. "Yeah. Your dad had to come out there and save our behinds."

"He gave you and Trystan jobs at his boat shop to keep you out of trouble." I snapped my seat belt in and checked my rearview. "You remember what my dad said? Boys with idle hands and no skills—"

"Fall for trouble and cheap thrills," he finished.

I smiled as I pulled the open-air car toward the exit, wheels crunching. "Trystan left soon after, but think about how momentous that was for you, Beau. You may never have known what incredible skill and artistry you had if not for Trystan leaving. Not to mention, you wouldn't have me."

"Sure I would. You're a cheap thrill."

"Oh you are so freaking funny I could die."

"That's me."

"Seriously, Beau. I became your friend because I felt sorry for you. You were lonely. When Trystan was around, you never even knew I existed."

"Not true."

"So true." So painfully true.

"Fine, maybe. But that wouldn't have lasted long. I mean you can't have two teenage boys running around a marina and not notice the hot blonde girl with the flyaway hair. All tan skin and bubblegum lips." Beau sounded annoyed by his memory.

My own voice failed me for a second. "Wait. What? You thought I was hot."

"Stop it. You used to wear those tiny cut off jean shorts, hair like an angel, legs for miles and perky tits. Flitting around all over the place like an exotic bird, fuck, you were a sixteen-year-old's wet dream."

My breath caught in my chest, and as I rolled the Jeep to a stop at the exit onto Coleman Boulevard I had to actually think about which way to turn from a place I'd driven out of a thousand times. I was shook. Had Beau Montgomery had a kid crush on me? It was the first I'd heard of it. "Beau—"

His phone rang and I jumped. That obnoxious, old-timey, shrill ring like an actual honest-to-goodness landline from a 1950's TV show. "God, could you have your phone any louder?" I asked. Why didn't he ever just set it on vibrate like normal people?

"Sorry." He fumbled it out of his pocket, frowning at what I could see was his father's number lighting up the screen. He let the cacophony continue.

"Answer it," I muttered, feeling weirdly annoyed and utterly out of sorts after his revelation.

He sighed and hit the green accept button. "Hello?"

I could hear the sound of his father on the other end but not his words.

"Oh," said Beau. "Yes, I'm—I'm so sorry." His voice caught. "I'll be right there."

He hung up, pressed the phone to his chest, and turned his head out the window. "Can you drop me at MUSC?"

"Of course. Beau is he—?"

"He's dead. He passed away about fifteen minutes ago while I was telling you how mad at him I was." He let out a long breath and continued to stare out the window.

"I'm so sorry."

"Thanks," Beau said, and his hand came over and landed on my upper thigh and gave it a pat. "You're a good friend, Gwen."

So we were back to Gwen now. My thigh burned and my chest squeezed. It occurred to me right in that moment I was a complete masochist. Who other than someone with masochistic tendencies could continue to be friends with someone they were insanely in love with?

I drove over the Cooper River Bridge, the warm spring wind tossing our hair and battering our ears. Neither of us attempted to have a conversation. Beau lifted his face up and watched the suspension cables slip over the night sky. The moon was rising, lighting everything up and leaving a silver path across the black water beneath us.

The bridge tipped us smoothly into the city, and I followed the Crosstown toward the hospital on the other side of the peninsula.

I pulled up at the brightly lit drop off entrance to the hospital.

"You know my condo's right around the corner," I said as he made no move to get out. "You can come over if you need to after." That was me, always there with a shoulder.

"Can you come in with me?"

I glanced at him in surprise.

"I'm sorry to ask. I know you can't stand my grandmother. But I need you."

"I don't hate your grandmother. It's the other way around."

"She doesn't hate you, she's just—"

"Incapable of affection?" I finish off the sentence we'd both said so many times before. "Uninterested in people not of her class?"

But Beau wasn't playing along tonight. "Please, Gwen. She's just lost her husband."

Sighing, I smiled tightly. I was being bitchy. He was right. "I'm sorry. Sure. Let me go and park."

What are friends for, after all?

2

GWEN

*I*nside was exactly how I imagined. Bright, sterile, and full of memories from when my mom died. I stalked alongside Beau as he made his way to the elevators, following the directions we'd been given at the front desk. The doors closed us in the sealed box, and I reached out a hand for the railing, squeezing tight.

"You okay?" Beau's voice broke the silence.

I opened my eyes to his concerned face.

"Oh shit," he said. "I forgot you don't do hospitals. Damn, Gwen. I'm sorry. I'm a selfish fuck."

"It's fine, Beau," I said, my voice weak. "Got to get over it sometime."

"Thank you, Gwen. I mean it. You're a g—"

"Good friend. I know." The doors pinged and opened.

In a small, pale blue and gray grieving room at the end of the hall by the chapel sat Isabel Montgomery. She was wrapped in the arms of her son, Beau's father, Robert. He rested his chin on her not-so-perfectly coiffed gray hair. Despite my long history with her disapproval, my heart broke seeing her so crumpled by the loss of her husband that she'd let someone hug her and hold her up in public. She looked smaller than I'd ever seen her. On her other side sat Suzy, Beau's younger sister who stood up to give him a hug. Opposite them sat Father Peter.

I crossed myself. "Father."

"Gwendolyn Grace Thomas," he said with his slightly Irish lilt he'd never managed to shake. "Good to see you. You haven't darkened my doors in over ten years. How are you?" The guilt. Always with the guilt.

"Fine, thank you, Father." I glanced at Mrs. Montgomery as she extricated herself from her son's embrace and allowed Beau to lean down and kiss her cheek. "I'm so sorry for your loss," I said to her as Beau straightened.

She dabbed at her eyes. "Thank you."

"I'm sorry I wasn't here," Beau said.

His father patted his shoulder. "It's fine. He never regained consciousness after we all left yesterday. Mother sat with him all day, and he just slipped off."

"I wish we could have taken him home." Isabel Montgomery sniffed.

"I know, but it happened so quickly," Father Peter said gently. "It was better this way, leaving him comfortable rather than trying to move him."

I hugged Suzy and then tentatively touched Robert's blazer sleeve to get his attention. "I'm sorry for your loss too," I said. He opened his arms and I gave him a brief, stiff hug. It was the first time I'd ever hugged him. How odd.

"Thank you, Gwendolyn."

He'd put on weight but was about the same height as Beau. Beau got his coloring from his father. Brown floppy hair, Montgomery-blue eyes, a healthy complexion. But Beau had a smile that went from nice to naughty with one wink of a dimple. And where Robert was stocky like his late father, Beau had grown up willowy like his mother, all long lines and awkward angles. He'd finally grown into himself and was now a sleek racing yacht with every part of him beautiful and practical. It was only when they stood side by side like this that you could see Beau was Robert's son.

"Gwen drove me here," Beau offered as a reason for my presence.

"Right," I said, a sharp pinching sensation in my chest. "And now I've done that."

"No wait. Stay, please." He cleared his throat and reached for my hand, giving it a squeeze, a gesture that didn't go unnoticed by the hawk eyes of Isabel. "I need you," Beau told me. "It won't be long, right?" He looked to his father.

Robert shook his head. "Nope. We were just communing with Father Peter and then I was going to take Mother home. It's been a long day. You're staying with us in town tonight, I presume, Beau."

"Actually," I said, years of practice at helping Beau avoid his family obligations tripping off my tongue. "Beau was planning to stay with me because we were going down to the marina to help my dad tomorrow morning."

Beau glanced at me as I made things up on the fly. But then I realized if he came to the boat shop I'd have to break his heart all over again and tell him about my father closing the business.

"But, of course," I said to Beau, "With this new development, you don't have to—"

"No, I want to," he said. "I told Rhys I'd help him, and I will for a few hours." He turned to his grandmother. "Then I can come over before lunch and help with the arrangements."

She nodded, still seemingly shell-shocked and unable to put up her usual resistance to all plans that weren't directed by her.

"And I'll be with you." Suzy patted her grandmother's hand.

"That'll be fine," said Isabel. "How *is* your father, Gwendolyn?" she asked me, shocking everyone in the room.

"F—fine. Thank you for asking." I glanced nervously at Beau. No one said anything so I carried on. "Actually, he's dealing with a cough that won't go away after a horrid cold. But he doesn't let that stop him," I babbled and stretched my lips to a smile.

"See that it isn't pneumonia. He should get an X-ray. Tomorrow if possible. There's a Doc-in-the-box just over in West Ashley who should be able to see him on a Saturday," Isabel Montgomery said. "And send him my regards, will you?"

I looked to Beau, Suzy, and Robert and even Father Peter to see them mirror what my eyebrows were doing. Raised up in disbelief. "Of course," I managed. "I'll let him know."

After some goodbyes and further condolences, I slipped toward the door. "Beau, I'll bring the car around to the entrance again and text you."

He nodded, and I let the door close and took a breath.

"Gwen?" I looked up to see my friend Penny. She lived in my building, as did a lot of the people who worked at MUSC because it was so close and had at one time been reasonably priced because the developer had gone under and had a fire sale of condos. Half of us who bought there hung on for dear life because we'd never get another deal so good. Others had taken the profit and moved on. Penny and I had moved in at exactly the same time. She had finished her qualification to become a physician's assistant, and her parents had bought her the condo as a congratulatory present. I still had a mortgage I was paying off, but I almost owned it free and clear due to my accelerated payments now that I had a well-paying job.

She looked behind me to confirm I had indeed walked out of the grieving room.

"Beau's grandfather," I said to her concerned expression. "Walk me to the elevator."

"Oh. How sad. He still single?" she asked hopefully. "Beau, I mean. Obviously. Not the dead guy."

I laughed at her and felt relieved at the break in tension I'd been holding inside.

"Beau might need some cheering up," she mused. "Right?"

I continued walking.

"What?" she asked innocently when I gave her the side eye. "You know my mother raised me to always be the first over with the casserole to the newly divorced or widowed young man, just in case. That's why I work in a hospital."

"You're like the dating equivalent of an ambulance-chasing lawyer." I elbowed her. "Mercenary. Like half the single girls in this town."

"You can't blame a girl for trying. The dating world is tough. As you know. You've seen the creepers on the dating apps. By any means necessary has to be the mantra. Besides, that man is soooo hot," she whined. "It's a crime. Hooooow have you known him for so long and not tapped that?"

I shook my head. "Keep your voice down."

The elevator opened, and Penny followed me in.

"Never?"

"Never. You've asked me that before."

"Seriously, Gwen. He's straight and single and hot as sin. And clearly *heir apparent*. Are you dead inside?"

"No. Yes. Maybe." I punched the button for the ground floor.

"What? Maybe you think he's hot?" she asked and gave a leap off both feet like an excited rabbit.

"No, maybe I'm dead inside."

She stared at me. "No way," she said suddenly.

"No," I said and shook my head vigorously.

"Oh my God. You *do* like him." Her face went from excited to somber in an instant. "Oh shit."

"Nope."

"Yep."

My shoulders slumped. "Don't say a word."

"Never."

The doors opened and I stepped out. Penny stayed inside.

"See you soon, Penny. And forget what you think you know. I mean it."

She mimed locking her lips and held the elevator door. "You coming to the pool party on Saturday?"

I frowned. "Tomorrow?" How had that snuck up on me?

"No, next Saturday, goober."

"I'll have to see when the funeral is first."

Penny clapped. "You'll need a cute dress."

"For the pool party?"

"For the funeral, silly. It will be the most attended funeral you can imagine. Everyone will be there to support both Beau and his father. *Two* eligible men! You have to get in there first."

"Is this conversation really happening?"

"I'm thinking you should wear navy instead of black. Somber but not morbid. I have just the thing. Pop by this weekend. It'll be fun," Penny went on, holding the doors open. "Oh, and I have next Friday off too. Let's go get waxed and get manis and pedis before the pool party? I have a coupon."

"Sure," I said so I could get going. I'd make an excuse to her closer to the time.

"And buy a new swim suit. A bikini! Make it sexy!"

"Bye, Penny." I rolled my eyes, and she grinned at me as the doors closed. Only Penny could turn a funeral into a social event. I loved her, but she was slightly mad.

The full on beauty regime was just not my bag. My boss, Sylvie, had begged me to get manicures when I first started working at my new job, but they'd instantly get ruined as soon as I spent an evening helping dad in the boat shop. I'd since proved I could sell luxury yachts from glossy brochures with or without a manicure. And anyway, I didn't seem to have a problem being hit on by all manner of men. Although usually, they were married which was unfortunate.

The amount of times I'd had to politely remind someone that

I didn't come with the boat was laughable. And I wasn't under any illusions that it was my beauty, probably more that they thought I might be just desperate enough to say yes or be wowed by their money (since I obviously couldn't even afford a manicure). I wasn't sure grooming myself like a poodle wouldn't make it worse because then I'd look as if I was trying very hard to be plucked out of the yacht showroom and installed in a mistress' apartment.

I'd been blessed with my mother's olive-green eyes and her Mediterranean skin, which held a permanent tan and rarely burned, but I had my father's light sandy hair. It was an interesting mix of features. His at-home-DNA-kit he'd wanted for Christmas had told us he was part Viking and part some tiny isolated Nordic fishing tribe. Someone must have had an interesting encounter up by the North Pole one day way back when.

Anyway, I normally felt completely mismatched in my appearance. Like I was cobbled together from spare parts. And I'd decided young I didn't much care for all the primping and preening the other girls did to try and change themselves. We just were who we were, and that was that.

* * *

BEAU HAD SOBERED up some on our windy drive across the bridge to the hospital, so when I offered him another beer at my condo, he declined. I threw his pillows and blanket I kept in my coat closet onto the couch. "Your toothbrush is under the sink."

"Thanks." Beau wandered around my tiny living room, looking lost.

"You want to watch a movie?" I asked. "Maybe a Disney movie?" It used to be our college hangover cure to sit around and watch kid movies. It started as a joke but had kind of become our thing. Not that Beau would ever admit it to anyone else.

"I *hate* Disney movies."

"Fun fact, Beau Montgomery, you love Disney movies. You've watched them all with me. Multiple times, I might add."

"I felt sorry for you," he said, repeating our age-old exchange. "You're a grown woman who has a collection of animated kids' movies."

"For every situation in life, there's a scene or a l—"

"Line in a Disney movie that can provide guidance," he finished for me.

"Right," I said primly.

"Except for *Bambi*," he grumbled right on cue. "Who the fuck was running Disney when they decided to make Bambi and traumatize an entire generation? No wonder my parents were so fucked up."

"I don't know, I never watched it." Why would I watch a sweet baby fawn sob as his mother slowly bled out after being shot by a hunter?

"I know," said Beau. "But I did. Big mistake. You could have warned me."

One day I'd get him to admit he was an addict like me.

"You take the bathroom first," he said. "I'm going to watch Sports Center."

I bit my lip. Eschewing Disney movies meant he really was feeling terrible.

"Are you sure I can't tempt you with a little … *Aladdin*? Or a little," I waggled my hips, "*Emperor's New Groove*?"

He shook his head. "Sorry."

I patted him on the shoulder and slipped into the bathroom. I rinsed off, brushed my teeth and changed into my sleep shorts and t-shirt.

When I came out, Beau was fast asleep sitting upright. I turned the TV off and gently pushed him sideways. I slipped his boat shoes off and lifted his legs with effort. Pulling the blanket over him, I tucked it behind his back so it wouldn't slip off, then I took a moment to stare at his face so peaceful in sleep. His dark lashes lay gently on his cheekbones, and his chest rose and fell as the deep slow breaths of sleep claimed him. He actually got better looking every damn year. Even the little crow's feet at the edge of his eyes were sexy.

I couldn't resist gently moving a lock of hair off his forehead.

He frowned slightly, then relaxed.

"I love you, Gracie," he said softly on a puff of air.

I stilled. The words were so clear they still floated through the silence.

He let out a deep sigh and then shifted, rolling over to face the back of the couch.

It didn't mean anything, I told myself. We told each other we loved each other all the time. It was just that today had been weird. And everything today had felt weighted and important. Today he'd called me Gracie all day. He hadn't called me Gracie in years. Since I'd told him to stop. My dad called me Gracie of course, and when I was seventeen Beau doing it had felt condescending. I'd wanted to be seen as a woman not a girl, so I'd asked, no *demanded*, that I be called Gwen. Not that it had done any good. He still saw me as his best friend and probably as a sister too. Especially since my father treated him like the proverbial son he never had.

I let out a long slow breath. "I love you too, Beau," I whispered and then headed to bed.

I lay there too wired to sleep. It felt like everything in my world was about to tip sideways. I couldn't put my finger on how or why, but somehow my gut couldn't let the feeling go.

Tossing over to my side, I grabbed my spare pillow and mashed it into a huggable shape. Then I stared out of my uncovered window to the clear night sky. There was a glow from the city, but a few really bright stars still shone through. At seven floors up, I never had to draw my curtains for privacy. I had a gorgeous view over part of the peninsula, the marina, and the confluence of the Ashley and Cooper Rivers.

Beau's words in my Jeep earlier came back to me. I'd been a sixteen-year-old's wet dream? *His* dream? Did that mean at around the time I'd been demanding he see me as Gwen and not Gracie because I was crazy about him, he'd been crazy about me too?

My blinks became longer, and I hugged the pillow tighter.

How had we both missed the boat all those years ago? Why had we fizzled into friendship? And tomorrow, would Beau remember what he'd admitted to me?

Would it even matter now?

3

GWEN

"Gwendolyn Grace! Stop fussin' on me." My dad's voice was gruff from his coughing fits. "I can carry my own dang air."

I stepped back, palms up in innocence, and watched him struggle to wheel the oxygen tank over the lip of the shop floor. "If you say so."

"I say so." He glared at me. He was embarrassed that the doc had told him he needed oxygen in addition to antibiotics after he was indeed confirmed as having a bout of pneumonia.

"You're too proud for your own good, Daddy."

"Been proud my whole life. Served me well." He huffed. "What do you have, if you ain't got no pride?"

"An oxygen tank and a bad attitude. That's what."

"Girl, that don't need an answer. And definitely not one all full of sass."

"Come on, old man," I grumbled at him good-naturedly. "Let me show you our progress."

The interior of the boat shed was dim, and I felt for the switch that would light up the space down a flickering track of fluorescent tubes. The light filtering in through the high windows wasn't enough after a certain time of day and certainly not an overcast morning like today. The clouds didn't stop the heat though, if anything the heat and humidity stayed trapped by the clouds, feeling that much more oppressive. I switched on a floor fan to get the heavy air moving.

"*Our* progress?" He picked up on my use of the plural word. "Does that mean Beau big-for-his-britches has been back in here helping you?"

I rolled my eyes at my dad's nickname for Beau. He'd called him that as a boy, ever since he'd found out Beau was a Montgomery. It was never meant with malice, and while it drove Beau crazy for a while, he soon got over it.

"And how have you managed to take time off from work?" He'd been grumbling about my job since the day I got it. "You can't sell a boat on a high street, you gotta be on the water," my dad had complained. As you can imagine, that just wasn't true. People *liked* to flick through the glossy heavy-gauge catalogs while sipping over-priced beverages and waiting for their wives to finish shopping at Lilly Pulitzer and Boden. It was calm, air-conditioned and serene. They felt like millionaires should feel when about to drop hundreds of thousands of dollars— pampered and appreciated.

The lights of the warehouse shone down on the last boat to ever be made by Rhys Thomas. It was a small vessel compared to the sleek motor yachts I now talked about every day at my job, built in size similar to a Boston Whaler. But this one would come equipped with custom features, a beautifully crafted walnut console and wood accents. It would look like a pristine antique. My dad always told Beau growing up that if you could master the art of building wooden boats, you would rival any master carpenter anywhere. You could build anything you wanted.

My father looked the upside down hull over. He shuffled around it, then ran his palms over the wood. "Great job, Gracie."

Dad could see a rough spot the size of a grain of sand from twenty paces. It was like he sensed them.

I flushed with pride. "Beau hasn't been around the last couple of days. What with the funeral coming up."

"You been doing this by yourself?"

"It's fine, Dad. I know it needs to be done."

"You bent the wood in the steam box?"

"Just like you showed me. Steamed it, bent it, clamped it into shape. I didn't grow up in your boat shop and not learn anything."

"I know. But I know you didn't fall in love with the craft like Beau did. He's like a son to me. You and he—"

"Welp! Glad you approve of my work."

My dad cleared his throat. "I know, I know. I thought one day, you and he might get together. It just seemed like … you might."

"We're friends, Dad. Nothing more." The nothing came out heavier than I meant to sound.

"And he's passionate about boats. So are you in a different way. It was silly of me. Y'all might be best friends, but that boy ain't grounded, blowing through girlfriends at the rate of five a year. Not suited for you at all. That damned dog is the biggest commitment I've ever seen him make." He shook his head.

I wisely stayed quiet. There was no good place this conversation ever went except to the guilt express.

"Did you tell him?"

"Sure," I said and looked anywhere but at my dad. "Hey, did I tell you that pink epoxy stuff you ordered came in from Canada? More expensive than caviar."

"You didn't tell him, did you?"

I walked over to a pillar and picked at the flecks of peeling paint. "It just wasn't the right time. What with the death in the family and all. Are you sure, Dad?" This was my father's whole identity. Who was Rhys Thomas if not a boat builder? Who was I, for that matter, if not a boat builder's daughter?

He shrugged. "Not really. I thought I'd have longer to get my mind around retiring. I thought I'd be leaving a legacy."

Dad saying the word legacy pinched me with guilt again.

"This can't have been easy. Why didn't you tell me? I feel terrible you had to make this decision on your own."

"I've been making decisions on my own since your mother passed on. And one thing I've learned is that there are no good decisions and there are no bad decisions. There are simply decisions. And you live with the outcome. And I've decided to take the money and retire. It's time."

"How very Zen," I deadpanned. "You're not going to tell me you've met some spandex-wearing aerobics instructor at Bingo who's persuaded you to go on cruises and invest in her juice cleansing business, are you?"

My father gave a crack of laughter. "You know as well as I do, you'd never see me on a cruise ship. Now, a spandex wearing aerobics teacher … " he rocked his head back and forth as if giving it serious consideration.

I rolled my eyes, amused. We both knew he was still faithful to my mother's memory. God rest her soul.

"Do you need me to call him right now and tell him?" he asked.

"No. I want to tell him. I will tell him. Just not today of all days. I'm meeting him tomorrow night for a beer."

Just then my phone buzzed loudly. I hauled it out and saw who the text was from. "Speak of the devil."

BEAU: *You're coming to the funeral right?*

OF COURSE.

. . .

BEAU: *Phew. Thank you. I feel like a guppy in a shipwreck being circled by sharks.*

I SMILED at Beau's reference to *The Little Mermaid.* "All right, old man," I said to my dad. "Now that you've seen our progress, let's get ourselves over to the funeral."

* * *

"WHO'S THAT?" I asked Beau as I kept him company outside Grace Cathedral waiting for the hearse. A black SUV with tinted windows had pulled up and was idling on the corner.

I was also running interference. So far I'd counted nine hopeful women who'd come over with or without their parents to commiserate with Beau. And in four cases, actually had to awkwardly introduce themselves to him because he had no idea who they were. I thought at least three had but a passing connection to the Montgomery family, and some probably had none at all.

To an outsider it might all look like the normal paying of respects, but I was close enough to Beau to see him stiffen when a female hand held onto his arm too long or when they stood too close. His eyes would dart toward me, and I'd step in and introduce myself practically forcing them to let go of him.

Finally, almost everyone had arrived and gone inside.

"Your parents got married in this church too, didn't they?" Beau asked.

"Yes, I'm named after a church," I grumbled.

The back door of the dark SUV finally opened and a tall, dark suited man stepped out with a scowl. He exuded boredom and confidence. So much you could almost smell it.

"Holy shit," Beau whispered.

"What?" I touched his black suit sleeve. Beau hardly ever wore suits, and I could tell from the moment I saw him this morning he couldn't wait to get it off and get a pair of khaki shorts on.

"Holy shit, that's Trystan."

My eyes narrowed in focus. "Oh my God."

Trystan walked at a fast clip, his eyes on the entrance and not seeing Beau who'd left my side and was heading to stand right in front of him.

The man was fine.

Tall, hard and dare I say it, cold. His demeanor seemed arctic and I immediately thought of Isabel Montgomery. The apple clearly didn't fall far from the tree. Suddenly Trystan stopped and did a double take at Beau standing in front of him. They were exactly the same height. I wished I could hear their conversation or see Beau's face to see if this was a happy meeting. Trystan's face was unreadable. Oh wait. A hint of shock and a ... smile? No. Maybe not. Wow, so Trystan Montgomery came back.

I wondered if he was staying permanently, though I doubted it.

The hearse pulled up with the coffin inside. I hurried into the church ahead of Trystan and headed to the row where I'd ensconced my dad and waited for the service to start.

"Beau all right?" my dad asked.

"Fine. Trystan just showed up."

My dad's eyes bugged out for a moment.

"Yeah," I said. Then the funeral procession began.

I'd miss the wake and finding out from Beau about Trystan because I had to be back at work by one thirty as we had a "big fish" coming some time this afternoon according to my boss, Sylvie.

It was only Tuesday and it felt like I'd fit four days' work in already.

The service was short which was much appreciated by all. Dad and I snuck out the side door as soon as it was over.

* * *

"THIS MIGHT BE the most professional I've ever seen you look," Sylvie said as I entered dressed in my figure-hugging black sheath dress and high heels I'd bought for hot dates but had so far only ever seen the action of a funeral. I had eschewed Penny's offer of her navy dress.

"Thanks, I think."

She shook her silver-blonde coiffed head. "If you didn't know so much about *les bateaux* … " she trailed off.

"If I didn't know so much about boats, then what?" I smirked, knowing how much she liked to harass me but also how much she enjoyed my company. Originally from Quebec, she spoke French fluently. She affected it sometimes and acted as if she was Coco Chanel.

"*De Rien*. Nothing. Obviously. Just think how many more you'd sell if you primped a little more. You have the looks. With a bit of effort you could be a showstopper."

"Maybe I don't want to be a showstopper."

"Maybe you don't have incentive to be a showstopper."

"Please, what kind of incentive would entice me to add in an extra hour of primping, plucking, painting and preening every day? I'd have to get up at four. I like my sleep, thanks very much."

"Maybe the incentive of a dream man? Surely there's someone out there you might fancy?"

"I'm in a relationship, remember?"

"Oh yes, your relationship." She made air quotes. "With the man who's deployed. That's a bit convenient, don't you think?"

"That's not very nice, Sylvie. He's fighting for our freedom, and you're encouraging his girl to run around on him."

"Well, I'm not *nice*, darling. I'm *practical*. Nice doesn't get you married to a widowed billionaire."

"Well, you haven't found one, so perhaps practical is not working either."

"Yet," she breathed. "Anyway, why do you hide behind your relationship with ... what's his name?"

"Derek."

"Right, Derek."

"I'm not hiding. It's just ... convenient. He's big and manly and ... enthusiastic in bed."

"When you see him only every six months. Darling, a porcupine would be good in bed by then. Your standards are *very* low."

"I'm going to tell him how mean you are about him."

"No, you won't."

"You're right, I won't." Mostly because we really didn't keep in touch much. In fact it was always a surprise when he popped back up on my radar home for some R & R and sex. I should probably make more of an effort to keep in touch. Send him ... letters ... or emails or something. I scrunched up my nose.

"So, the funeral was for your friend Beau Montgomery's grandfather. Does that mean Robert Montgomery, Beau's father might be coming into the money?"

"Sylvie, you don't want to marry Robert Montgomery, trust me."

"Why not dear?"

"Because first of all Isabel Montgomery would be your dragon-in-law. And secondly she controls the purse strings for that family. They're all like little sad marionette puppets."

"Then perhaps they need me going in there like a grenade? Shake things up?"

"They don't."

She huffed and flounced over to the beverage bar stocked with all the things a gazillionaire might need while deciding to buy a luxury yacht: *Nespresso, San Pellegrino, Dom Perignon*. And *Orangina* for the little gazillionaires because Sylvie had heard that's what they served at Le Club Cinquante-Cinque on the French Riviera where these yachts might be parked one day. She'd even had *Caquoettes* imported from France. They were hideous little peanut-flavored crispy balls to put out with *aperitifs*. Why not just serve real damn peanuts for goodness-sake?

"You are right, *ma cherie*." Sylvie waved her hand in a circular motion. "Even though they are Montgomerys, they are but small and provincial. Medium-sized fish in this small city. I'm far too sophisticated. A shark. I would eat them alive. I must spare them."

I laughed delightedly at how she saved face. "You are far too sophisticated, Sylvie. That's for sure."

"Pfff. *Bon*, I need a cigarette."

She pulled out her Chanel compact and powdered her nose and then reapplied her coral lipstick. Then she rummaged for her silver cigarette case. She extracted a cigarette and her cigarette holder and then snapped the case shut.

"This no smoking in public is so tiresome. I will slink into the back alley like a pussy cat and see you in a few minutes."

She stopped and looked up at me.

I raised my eyebrows. "What?"

"*Non*. This will not do." She stuck her cigarette behind her ear and stalked toward me with her purse and pointed to my desk chair. "Sit."

I sat and she spun me to face away from her.

She pulled my emergency scrunchie out of my hair and then pulling a comb from her purse proceeded to tuft and smooth and wrench and twist my hair. Then she jabbed my head with sharp things. Hairpins? "Ow," I moaned.

When she was satisfied with my hair she spun me round again and teased a strand lose to fall down the side of my face in a frame to my chin. "*Bon*," she said again but sounded mildly disappointed.

Scowling she pulled out a pot of makeup and dabbed something on my eyelids, my cheekbones and then my lips. She stood back, and after a moment her shoulders slumped.

"*Bon*," she said again. "Not good. But good enough." Then she shuddered, rescued the cigarette from her ear, and marched out the back door of the showroom.

I glanced over to the dark computer screen that served my reflection back to me. Sylvie had put my hair up in a chignon. A bit more sophisticated than my normal bun, it couldn't hurt to start wearing my hair like this for a bit, see if it sold more boats. I turned the computer on and checked our office-wide shared to-do list to see what I could do before our "big fish" came in. I'd promised my dad I'd get a bit more work done at the boat shop after work every day this week to help keep him on top of his timeline, so I'd need to get out of here on time.

"Oh my goodness, Gwen." Sylvie came trotting back inside, teetering on her high heels with her excitement.

"You will never guess what I heard."

"What?"

"I heard it from Marion next door, whose daughter was apparently told by Daisy Rathbun. You know she works in her uncle's law firm?"

"No, and why do I care?"

"Just wait. They are the estate lawyers for the Montgomerys. Apparently, Beau has been cut out of Montgomery Homes and Facilities." She pressed her palms together, her eyes wide, giddy with being one of the first to know such a scoop. Then she made a slicing motion with her hand. "Completely. Apparently it's all going to the other grandson. The one no one has seen in years."

"Trystan?"

"Yes, that's it! I knew you'd know his name." She sighed, a hand to her chest. "I bet he's so handsome. I remember his mother, Savannah. A looker and a trouble maker that one."

I sat back in my chair. I hated gossip. And bloody Daisy should have kept her mouth shut. But wow. "Wait. It's all going to Trystan? What about Beau? Is he just expected to work there then?"

She let out a deep sigh. "Yes, poor Beau. How tragic."

My heart tripped. This didn't sound right. I thought of all he'd given up to work at the family business. To be cut out of the will was ... devastating.

I checked my phone. But there were no messages from him. I hoped he was okay.

"Apparently he's been left a few bits of dirt, and that's it," she added as she smoothed her eyebrows.

I sat straighter. I knew what plots of land the Montgomerys owned. I'd driven around them with Beau, in fact, as he had to make sure they hadn't become dumping grounds. If that was the case, then Beau wasn't as bad off as the rumor mill was suggesting. A vacant lot on the side of Hwy 17 could easily fetch a million if zoned correctly.

At that moment my phone vibrated.

BEAU: *We still on for that beer tomorrow night? I've got news.*

I BIT MY LIP. I hated that I had to wait until tomorrow for him to tell me news I kind of already knew. And I had my own news to tell him.

YES WE'RE ON. *And I have news too.*

BEAU: *Thank you for coming to the funeral.*

OF COURSE. *Are you doing okay?*

. . .

Beau: *I think so. Taking the boat out this evening to clear my head. Been a long day.*

I couldn't afford to spend time away from helping at Dad's boat shop this week, but I didn't like the thought of Beau going through this alone.

Need company?

Three dots popped up and then disappeared.

I looked up just as a tall man walked into the showroom in Gucci loafers and Nantucket red shorts and a white polo. A navy sweater was loosely knotted over his shoulders. His gray hair was swept back.

Sylvie squeaked out of her chair.

"Mr. Canopolis," she purred as she hurried toward him, her hand out to shake his.

This must be the big fish Sylvie mentioned.

I stood and smiled as he turned to me.

Oh.

But wow. A literal silver fox.

He was gorgeous. No wonder Sylvie was in a tizzy.

4

BEAU

*W*omen *are* dangerous and expensive. I know I say that jokingly a lot, but I think I've come to actually believe it. That's what's passed down on the male side of the Montgomery family. In fact, as I sit at the conference room table in the law offices of Ravenel & Maybank, I can almost hear the words come out of my late grandfather's mouth, his voice all gnarled and rough.

He might not have said this outright, but we all lived our life by these guidelines:

Don't feed the alligators

Sharks hunt in the evening

Never loan money you expect back

Women you sleep with are always looking to trap you.

Especially if you happen to be a Montgomery.

Frankly, I can do without either of those pitfalls; the danger or the added expense. I'm thirty-one years old, and while I don't have a ticking biological clock per se, my what-am-I-doing-with-my-entire-life clock has the frantic countdown pace of a ticker on a bomb.

I drag my fingers through my brown hair, upsetting whatever

effort I made to look put together this morning. Yesterday I was told my dreams might come true: I might get to start my boat building business after all. Today, I'm told what the stipulations are on those dreams.

Unfortunately, as it turns out I need both a woman and a shit ton of money or my life as I dreamed it will cease to exist. That's right, my dreams will die. Dead. There will be no half gasp. It will all be over. No muss. No fuss. No long drawn out illness. Just one long eulogy to the Beau Montgomery with the big plans I once knew.

So even though in life, my grandfather all but told us never to trust a woman, he was singing a different tune from beyond the grave.

Which is why I now have a headache the size of Montana from my forehead crashing in shock to the polished mahogany conference room table within the law offices of Ravenel & Maybank, Estate Lawyers.

I need a woman.

Apparently.

Nope. Let me be more specific.

I need a wife.

A fucking *wife*.

Me.

Beau Montgomery who keeps his non-family, female relationships segregated into two super clean categories. Category one: sex. Category two: girls who are just friends. And never the twain shall meet. I should amend that to *girl* who is just a friend, not girls who I am just friends with. Gwen is the only member of the female friendship category.

Every other woman is in the sex category. If the sex starts giving them ideas about crossing into the friendship box, we just end it. Okay, *I* just end it. Yep. Gwen gets to be in the friend box, by herself. She was there for me when Trystan left and never came back. She was there for me when my parents divorced. Her and her daddy's boat shop were there for me as a second home as I grew up. Her father is *why* I do what I do. Or should I say *want* to do. She is my rarified best friend, took over Trystan's spot pretty damned fast. And she certainly has never tried to get into the sex category. Ever. Although there was a time when … never mind.

Gwen. Gwendolyn Grace Thomas. I used to call her Gracie like her dad did until she told me when she was seventeen and fighting with her dad about college that she'd gotten too old for it. I took it in stride and tried calling her Gwen for a while. Luckily, I still get away with calling her Gracie on rare occasions. Usually when her defenses (or mine) are down. But it bothers me senseless when anyone else tries it.

"Beau?"

My head snaps up to see my grandmother glaring at me. She motions to her left and my eyes focus on Mr. Ravenel, the family's attorney. "Yep?"

"So we'll reconvene tomorrow," Mr. Ravenel says, and I realize he's probably repeating himself for my benefit. "And go over any questions you might have. Daisy can schedule one-on-one time with me if you'd rather discuss the particulars of your disbursements in private."

Damn right I would.

"Sure. Thank you." I glance out the glass doors of the conference room at Daisy, the paralegal and receptionist. She's prim, wears a tight suit, tighter hair, and has a cute face. Pretty. What if I married Daisy? As the niece of Ravenel's law partner, I know she comes from an old Charleston family. *The right pedigree* Isabel Montgomery would say, although I'm sure grandmother would be concerned that Daisy's legal aspirations might interfere with her volunteer requirements as a Montgomery wife and her Junior League membership commitments. It was why my mother ultimately divorced my father, after all. She got tired of living up to Isabel Montgomery's expectations. And tired of my father being too weak to step in.

I dismiss the idea of marrying Daisy and realize I am now going to be sizing up every single woman I know to decide if I can stomach being married to her, or she me for that matter. It will probably be an instant gut check rather than based on any other merits. The problem is my gut doesn't want to be married, not for all the money in the world. But, I think, as I push back from the conference room table and exit the glassed-in room, I want to build boats enough to do it. Anyway, it's not like anyone I've known has ever taken marriage that seriously. Seems like a lot of fuss for a piece of paper no one respects and promises no one keeps.

I stop at the paralegal desk. "Daisy, please schedule me for a one-on-one with Mr. Ravenel tomorrow. I need to know what these ridiculous marriage stipulations are about and what my work-arounds might be." She nods and writes my note down in her notebook. She looks back up. "You know ... I could put the word out—"

"No!" I snap a little too abruptly. "I mean, thank you for the offer. But I need to get my head around this first." I look up and see my grandmother, Isabel, still at the table talking to Ravenel, her eyes repeatedly flicking to me with concern. She'll want to have a fat discussion with me about this later, I'm sure, to see what's in the best interests of the family. I'd rather she just stay out of it.

"Just ..." I look back at Daisy, but she's watching the rear end of a brooding Trystan disappear out the door. "Schedule me for time tomorrow, and I'll give it some thought. Thank you."

Heading outside, I'm so dazed I walk right into someone's back. "Sorry," I mumble. Then I realize it's my cousin who looks as dazed as I feel. "Oh hey, Trystan."

Trystan looks at me blankly, and I can see his mind churning. He just inherited our family's entire business and has been asked to leave New York City and relocate here to Charleston to run it. It looks like we both have a lot of processing to do. But damn, it's good to see him.

"You want to grab some lunch?" I ask him, suddenly needing to reconnect. Yesterday at the funeral was the first time I've seen Trystan in almost twenty years. We were best friends as kids, or so I'd thought. He's changed. His Montgomery-blue eyes, which I always remembered as bright and fervent, seem hardened and icy. They soften though as they look at me.

He blinks and shrugs. "Sure."

I'm at a loss as to where we should go. "I've been living out at the house on Awendaw," I tell him, referring to the old plantation house about forty minutes up the coast, north of downtown Charleston. "I don't know what's good around here anymore. Let's walk and see what we find."

"I know someone who will," he says, pulling out his phone. His mouth has a smirk playing around it as he starts texting. He looks up. "Are we close to Market Street?"

Amused at the way he's looking at his phone and wondering who he's communicating with, I point left and we start walking.

We go into a cool restaurant that's housed inside an old church.

As soon as we sit, Trystan pulls his phone back out. Something about his expression when he texts has me asking, "Your girlfriend?" and nodding at the phone.

He jerks his head up, shocked. "Oh, no," he says. "Just someone who knows the best places to eat in Charleston. I don't know her."

I smirk but stay quiet, waiting. There's a story there, I know it.

"Actually, it's kind of a funny story," he admits with a sheepish expression, and I lean back and settle in. "In the airport when I arrived, I plugged my phone in the charging station and somehow this woman took it." He holds up his phone. "This phone isn't mine, it's hers. We switched phones, and she's in New York now, and I'm here."

Yikes. Someone else having my phone? "Oh my God, that's crazy." I wouldn't even lend mine to Gwen.

He shrugs and shakes his head like he can't believe his own words. "We've been … talking. She's from here so I guess she's been my unofficial tour guide. She's just a tour guide," he reiterates, seemingly for his own benefit.

Somehow, I can tell from the way he smiles when he texts her that he's enjoying their "talking" a lot more than as a mere tour guide, but I decide to keep my thoughts to myself. "And I thought *my* life just took a turn for the weird and wonderful. You have me beat."

He rubs a hand over his face. "I wouldn't say that. So do *you* have a girlfriend? Are you even close to doing what he wants?"

"Getting married? Hell, no. I haven't ever gone past a tenth date to my knowledge." It's not like I keep perfect track, but I'm pretty sure it's around ten. Maximum.

"Ten. That's not bad. I draw a line at three. Four if we haven't … you know."

Sadly, I do know. But unlike Trystan's clearly hard and fast rule, I'm happy to go back several more times if it's good and fun and clearly casual. "I should rein it back to four," I admit. "Getting all the way to ten gets you in all sorts of trouble." Recently, ten dates has seemed to signify it's moving into "let's meet the parents" category. Maybe it's our age. "Lots of women around here looking to trap a Montgomery. Though," I look up at the stained-glass window and cross myself. *May my condom never break,* I pray. "Thankfully, I've been careful."

We order and catch up some more, which includes me reassuring him I'm not the least upset about not being given any part in the family business. It's been a drain on my psyche to be in that office all day every day when I'd rather be on the water and working with my hands. In fact, that's why I've kept my head down, worked hard, and have been staying at one of the family homes—to save money. I've been squirreling away every cent so I can buy the boat building equipment I want. I'd been planning to start my own business come hell or high tide. Our grandfather's last will and testament just made that an *almost* reality. The "almost" because of the tiny catch of having to get married. Jesus, my grandfather was a twisted old S.O.B.

"So who are you going to marry in order to get your inheritance?" Trystan asks as if he can read my mind. Of course the words are out of his mouth right as the waitress arrives to top off our iced tea. I glare at him then glance toward her, my face feeling hot.

She pauses mid pour and gives me a slow perusal. "Well, honey," she says obviously satisfied at what she sees, which must be me naked in her mind's eye, "I'm available if you're stuck."

I open my mouth to say something, my skin is burning. "Uh, thanks."

"He'll keep you in mind," Trystan tells her with a huge grin.

"See that he does. Your food will be right out."

If we were twenty years younger or I knew him better I'd kick him under the table. Suddenly I feel stupidly happy Trystan is back, and he's all but being forced to stay in town. I was devastated when he and his mom left. Back before the days of social media, it was like he just ceased to exist. I've missed him and I didn't even realize it. I hope he and Gwen get along. Then I think of him and Gwen meeting and frown. I really hope this girl Trystan is texting keeps his interest.

We both watch the server walk away.

"She's cute," Trystan says. "You could do worse."

"Probably. What in the hell was Grandfather thinking putting that stipulation on me?" I vent. "Why not *you*?"

"Me? Never. Anyway, I hardly got off scot-free." He grimaces. "It just so happens I'm about to sell my company in New York. I wasn't sure what I was going to work on next, but it sure as shit didn't involve being involved in anything to do with the Montgomerys. No offense. I'm sure grandfather knew if he added in a marriage stipulation to that bombshell, I'd walk."

I try to ignore his jab at the family. I know he was hurt by our grandparents' actions of cutting him out for twenty years. He must be reeling at the apparent change of heart. "Well, I for one, am glad. It'll be good to have you back here more." I push my hair off my forehead. "You can help me narrow down my prospect list." I think of bringing up Gwen as an option, but I know I have to dismiss the idea. She'd laugh in my face. She's always said she'd as soon kill me as date me. Marrying me would result in bloody murder. Even if it was just for convenience. Not least of all, her father wouldn't condone his daughter marrying someone under these circumstances. He likes me well enough, just probably not *that* much. He'd want grandkids.

Our food arrives and I watch with amusement as Trystan pulls his phone back out. "Just a tour guide" my ass. I chomp down on a fry and don't say a word.

Thinking of Gwen gives me a yearning for a salt breeze and the smell of engine oil. I planned to head to the Montgomery home on South Battery, but instead when I head that way after lunch, I find myself passing the house right on by and heading for the city marina.

5

BEAU

*E*ver since I was a boy I've gone to the marina when things get stressful. Of course, the marina has changed a lot over twenty years. In fact, it hardly resembles what it was with all the new development and the mega yachts.

Rhys Thomas Boatworks is one of the last remaining holdouts of what the working marina used to be. Last I heard someone wants to turn Rhys' place into a high-end oyster and champagne bar. Like we need another luxe restaurant in Charleston. And of course, he'd never sell.

But as a kid, down there with my hands full of splinters, my lungs full of saw dust and epoxy fumes, and the calming advice of Gwen's father, Rhys Thomas, I'd found where I belonged. I'd found who I was and who I could be. And today, I need the company of the old boat builder, and if not him then just the boats will do. I glance at my watch, wondering if I'll catch him by himself since Gwen should still be at work at her fancy job on King Street.

Obviously, Gwen would be the easy solve for this marriage predicament, but last I knew she was seeing someone. Daryl? Derek? I can't remember. I do remember he had big hands, and I remember wondering if they were gentle enough for Gwen. Which is ridiculous of course because Gwen is the toughest girl I know. In fact, if you tell her a girl can't or shouldn't do something, she'll go right away and do it, regardless of consequence.

Gwen has never mentioned wanting to get married and be a mom, so maybe it could work. But what if she does want that? Maybe that's why she's waiting on Daryl, David, or whatever the hell his name is.

The thought of Gwen as a mom brings a smile to my face. I wonder if she'd let them run wild about the marina like she and I did. I'd be their "Uncle Beau," teaching them about boats, and carving wood, and fishing. They'd have permanent tans, freckled noses and soft, salt-dusted skin. My insides feel a weird churn, an attachment, and I quickly try to imagine their father but come up short. I can only see Gwen looking at me, smiling widely, her hair catching gold in the sun with love in her green eyes.

Wait, what?

I stagger slightly and catch my step. Uneven sidewalk. And I'm hopped up on too much iced-tea—that waitress would not stop refilling it.

Christ, this whole situation has me thrown. Gwen really would laugh in my face if she knew where my head just went. Besides if we did give it a go and I messed it up for some reason, I'm not sure I'd survive the loss of her friendship. She's tied up in the very fabric of who I am. The cold fear of that is enough to make me reaffirm the vow I made as a teenager never to mess up that friendship line. Even though I'd once had a painfully large infatuation with her, I don't see her that way any more. And haven't for a long time. Thank God.

The afternoon May heat beats down on the back of my neck, and I turn the corner to see the sea of white masts bobbing in the distance set against the backdrop of the Ashley River bridge and the bright blue sky. To my right, I see the hospital Medical University of South Carolina, where grandfather passed away.

But when I get down to Rhys' boat shop, it's not him I find. Nor any of the guys who work for him. The strains of Hot Chocolate's "You Sexy Thing" are audible from outside.

Gwen is there by herself in cut off jeans and a white tank, her blonde hair hoisted high on her head. I take a moment to watch her work. Her skin is slick from sweat, her muscles working hard as she rhythmically planes the joins of Rhys Thomas' latest creation in smooth, long strokes. Her flow is beautiful—a fluid push and pull. She's singing along as she pauses to do a little hip wiggle on each backward stroke, dancing as she works. Seventies classics. That's all her father ever played in his shop when we were growing up. She shouldn't be here on her own, with the place unlocked and unable to hear anyone approach. I'll be mad at her later, but for now I take a moment to appreciate her at work. I know it made Rhys sad when Gwen told him she didn't want to take over the business. To be honest, I never can understand why she wouldn't. She loves boats as much as I do. She lives and breathes them. And she's really damn good.

It's been my life-long dream to do this. To build beautiful wooden boats. But I wasn't born to a boat builder like she was.

Now, my dream is so close I can taste it.

And there's not much I wouldn't do to make it happen.

* * *

"I NEED A WIFE," I say loudly, making Gwen jump and turn with her hand to her chest.

The planer she was holding skitters along the floor.

To her credit she recovers quickly, giving me a scowl after she leans down to retrieve it. "I know you do. Been telling you that for donkey's years." She wipes the dew off her forehead, wisps of her blonde hair are curling and sticking to her damp skin.

"*Wife.* Not life," I grumble. And I'm not sure why I just come right out and say it, but as soon as I do I feel relief that it's out there. That Gwen knows. She's a solver. She'll help me figure this out. Just like she helped me figure out how to take Ginny McKinley to the Magnolia Ball, instead of Lucy Peterson who I'd promised to take six months prior. In fact, I'd really have rather taken Gwen as my date, but she'd refused to set foot in a country club since we were teenagers.

She's still for a second, then she gets back to work without answering. I've shocked her. Hell, I'm *still* shocked.

The muscles in her bare tanned arms flex as she swipes the planer back and forth in a steady rhythm over a join on the hull of the boat. It's better when there's at least two of us working on a boat this size, but I've been MIA the last few days what with all the funeral and reading of the will shit going on. She has her own job and can't afford all the time her dad needs to keep the business going since he's been under the weather.

The boat shop is hot and humid, the stinging smell of swirling wood dust sticking to the insides of my nostrils.

She straightens finally as she gets to the end of the curve, not looking at me but staring unseeing, straight ahead.

Then she casts me a quick glance to see if I'm joking. Whatever she sees on my face hopefully makes it clear I'm not.

"Why exactly?" she asks carefully.

"Fuck knows. Because my grandfather was a crazy old coot. But, Gwen, he left me the warehouse on James Island, the boat slip, everything I need. I think I can finally do it."

She stares at me, a myriad of emotions I can't even begin to name moving through her green eyes. Is she happy for me? I can't tell. A smile finally materializes at the edges of her mouth.

I'm happy. I'm so damn glad I get to share this news with her. She's been with me through thick and thin. And I know, *know*, she's kept a few buyers for her dad's equipment at bay while I tried to raise the money to buy into his business. I may be a Montgomery, but the family is pretty tight with money unless you're dancing to their tune. It's a control thing. Which is what makes this whole new situation as much surprising as unsurprising.

"Are you serious?" she finally asks.

"Deadly." I purse my lips and wait.

"Congratulations. I'd heard a rumor you were cut out of the will."

I roll my eyes. Of course, this is Charleston. Still small enough to have a wicked grapevine. "On the business side of things, yes. In a surprise twist, he left pretty much everything to Trystan. But," and I can't help a large smile as I list out what he left me.

"Wow, Beau." She covers her mouth in delighted shock. "So he believed in you after all. Congratulations."

"But on the personal side, perhaps not congratulations. Perhaps commiserations." I shrug. "The inheritance comes with a stipulation that I have a wife."

"That's the most ridiculous thing I've ever heard. Sounds like Isabel's handiwork to be honest. The question is *why* do you have to get married? It makes no sense."

"I think it was all him, actually. Perhaps it was some twisted way of getting the family back together. Like the way he left Trystan the business side of things, all but forcing him to come back here. He knew we'd all have to communicate if there was a wedding being planned. He's made the same stipulation of Suzy too. Which makes even less sense."

"But that's ludicrous. You could grab a girl and just go to the courthouse. Getting married doesn't mean it has to be a big old Charleston wedding. If it was me, I'd have a captain perform the wedding on a boat, a mile off shore. That way, you can be sure only people who really want to be there would make the effort. To be honest it seems like there might be something else at play."

"Well, he didn't say I couldn't do a simple wedding. He didn't say anything at all about that. Only that it had to be a real relationship and I'd have to provide proof to the lawyer."

"Proof?" Gwen wrinkles her nose with a laugh. "What, like soiled linens? The wet spot? A virginal sacrifice?"

"Christ, I hope not. I'm thinking like love letters, photos, that kind of thing. Maybe friends vouching for the relationship? I'll find out more."

The thought of any one of the girls I know, or any one of the Charleston women I'd met since the funeral, being my wife, makes me feel ill. Physically ill. My stomach cramps with dread and nerves.

And then, all of a sudden I don't want to do this with anyone else.

I stare at Gwen.

She slips an escaped ringlet of blonde hair behind her ear where it had stuck against her glistening cheek.

I haven't prepared this at all. Up until this moment it had been but a fleeting possibility. But, I throw out every argument in my head about why asking Gwen is a bad idea.

I'm dead serious and sweating bullets. "Will *you* marry me, Gwen?"

She stiffens and then tosses the towel onto a pile of waxy tarps, her green eyes catching a shaft of sunlight. "Um, what?"

My palms sweat and I rub them down my khaki pants I'd worn in an attempt to be formal for the meeting this morning. My mouth is dry. "I know I have no right to ask, what with Derek and everything."

"Derek?" She looks thoroughly confused.

Shit. I knew I'd forgotten his name.

"What *about* Derek?"

Thank Christ, I got his name right. "Look, I'm not sure how serious you guys are, or when his deployment ends, but I haven't seen you date anyone else recently so I assumed maybe you were waiting on him. And if you are, that's cool. Just thought I'd ask. Just in case."

Gwen is staring at me, her mouth hanging open, her green

eyes wide. Her eyes are my favorite feature on her, I can always find a temperature gauge for any situation; amusement, comfort, honesty, or daring. They're like my mood compass. Right now might be the first time I haven't been able to read them in twenty years. It makes me feel unmoored. But at least she isn't laughing at me.

"Look." I exhale. "I need a wife. And not someone who's going to make things complicated by trying to seduce me and get pregnant as fast as possible. And frankly someone who I don't want to seduce."

Her green eyes narrow.

"Wait, that sounded wrong," I amend quickly. "But you know what I mean. Someone I don't want to sleep with."

"Right. Naturally, that would be me."

"Naturally." I shift my weight and slip my hands into my pockets. "So?"

"I have no idea what to say," she says, her voice stiff.

"I've shocked you."

She chews her lip, her face unreadable.

"There's no animated movie line for this?" I smile feeling grim now.

"I can't even get my thoughts together enough to wonder if there is. But yeah, I doubt it." She leans down and swipes up the towel she dropped earlier. "How about: *Most everyone's mad here.*" She cleans the planer and hangs it upon a wall hook. Then she walks back to the boat and rubs the wood with the cloth to clean off the wood dust and shavings.

"Alice in Wonderland," I guess.

Her hand is shaking. I've really, really shocked her this time.

"Okay, run this past me again? For some reason known only to your dead grandfather you need a wife and you think *I'd* like to leap at the chance?" She puts her hands on her hips and faces me. "Ooooh, wait! A chance to join the Montgomery clan and deal with your cold fish grandmother." She lets out a chuckle that borders on a deranged cackle. "Oh my God, she'd freak out! Can you imagine? Her precious Montgomery grandson marrying a scrappy little nobody from the docks."

"She has another precious Montgomery to worry about now. Trystan is back. So the heat might be off you and me."

"You're making it sound more and more enticing," she says, sarcasm oozing.

"And you're not a scrappy little nobody," I tack on, albeit a bit late.

"This is *so* messed up." She folds her arms. "I need a damn drink."

"Now that's a good idea."

She laughs, but not in my face.

That's a start.

And she hasn't said no yet.

"And the answer is no."

"What? We're not going for a drink?"

"No, I won't marry you."

"Gracie—"

"Let me go get cleaned up. Stay out here and inspect my handiwork. I'll be quick as I can." She all but sprints into the office.

"Just don't say no yet!" Shit.

6

GWEN

I closed myself in the tiny bathroom behind the office. The space was a six-foot by eight-foot box clad in stark white tiles with grout I struggled to keep clean. It contained a showerhead and drain, toilet, and porcelain sink with rust stains that were at least fifty years old. I took a quick glance into the aged rectangular mirror. My green eyes were bright with shock. There was too much to process, I felt like a deer in the headlights. I had to think fast about how to react or I was going to be hit at sixty miles an hour and go through a windshield.

Hurriedly stripping down, I stepped under the spray to rinse off the sweat of working on the boat. The water pressure was like opening a fire hydrant, and I winced as it stung and battered my skin. I always promised myself that one day, I'd install one of those large dinner plate sized shower heads to distribute the velocity. Maybe upgrade the sink too while I was at it. But I'd been promising myself that for at least ten years, and now I wondered why I should bother since the boat shop would all be gone as soon as we'd finished this last boat. I tilted my head back, letting the water beat up my scalp for a moment, then I quickly shampooed, soaped up, and rinsed. Any longer under this shower head, and I'd look like I'd gone a few rounds with Mike Tyson.

I toweled off and dug out a Ziploc I kept in my purse, containing spare underwear, a spare toothbrush and a rolled up peasant blouse , just in case I ever had a one-night stand. I was morbidly fearful of showing up at work in the same clothes as the day before. Sylvie was like a bloodhound for gossip. I also kept a bag in the safe in the office and three spare tops in the locker next to the work overalls.

What it really boiled down to was rather than a healthy sex-life or a hope for one, I was actually too busy for one. I always running from here to the next place, or work to here, and Rhys Thomas Boatworks had filled every free nook and cranny of my life since I was born.

It had broken my dad's heart when I told him I didn't want to study boat building at a technical college. I'd informed him I wanted to study marketing and business administration at a real university, and you'd have thought I'd told him I was secretly murdering people and hiding the bodies. Not even the fact I'd gone to College of Charleston so I could stay close to him and been the recipient of a partial merit scholarship to help with tuition had thawed him any on that score.

I stuffed the Ziploc back in my purse, deciding instead to use the clothes I stored here. Wrapping the towel back around me, I opened the door and stepped out into the office in a swirl of steam, my eyes on the lockers, and darted across the industrial carpet. My damp feet picked up wood dust because it had been two months since I'd last vacuumed for my dad. I had to use two hands to wrench open the metal door, so I tucked my towel together firmly, braced a bare foot on the adjoining locker and pulled hard on the door, almost losing my balance.

"Can I help?" Beau's deep voice came from the desk area behind me.

"Shit," I yelped in surprise, lost my balance, and as my hands lost their grip, the force of my pushing leg tipped me backward. I felt the towel pop free of my breasts and slither to the floor just as two strong arms caught me.

The next few moments were a frantic scramble as Beau almost dropped me, presumably in shock at my nakedness. Or because I was still slippery and wet from the shower and trying to jack-knife away from him while reaching for my towel at the same time.

"Argh! What are you doing in here?" I yelled, wrapping myself back in the towel.

He let go and moved away quickly.

My cheeks felt like they were on fire. Luckily, I didn't blush very visibly.

Beau was already with his back to me, against the desk, one hand still covering his eyes, which was now pointless since he was turned away.

"I was waiting for you," he huffed, annoyed. "Obviously." His shoulders were bunched and tense beneath the stretch of his navy tee. His tanned neck was tinged pink like he'd spent the day fishing. Beau *did* flush easily. Always had.

Of course he was waiting for me. I'd just assumed he was still out on the shop floor where he always stayed. He couldn't leave a bare hull alone. I thought as soon as I'd abandoned sanding to go get ready, he'd have picked it up and kept at it like he always did. He liked to keep his hands busy. They were always doing something. It was lucky he hadn't turned out to be a smoker.

"Never known a woman who could shower so fast," he grated out. "I just thought I'd wait in here and check my emails." He waved his phone that was in one hand.

I abandoned the spare clothes and backed up into the bathroom. "You can turn around now," I said and closed the door.

Mortified.

In all the many, many years I'd been friends with Beau Montgomery, we'd never seen each other naked.

Not that I hadn't imagined it, of course. It would be hard not to. Especially as I got older and couldn't help but notice how women, and men for that matter, watched him.

The man was stunning. Not that he was aware of it. He was the perfect mix of cultured and disheveled. Rigid and devil-may-care. He could dampen and comb his hair, but that cowlick over his brow would spring up in defiance. He could act like he was a lazy slouch, but his constant thrumming energy would always be expended working with his hands, handling heavy equipment that sculpted his muscles and tendons. He could act serious, or mad, or sorry, but his eyes would always sparkle with mischief and boyish naiveté. There wasn't a vain bone in his body. It had been a while since we'd even seen each other in swimsuits out on the water, but every now and again he'd strip his shirt off while working on a boat, and I'd have to concentrate hard not to let my eyes linger lest I gave myself away. I closed my eyes and replayed the moment my towel got loose, and my memory heard his sharp inhalation.

I swallowed with a thick throat and finished pulling my clothes on. Not for the first time, I wondered where we'd be now if I hadn't been oblivious to his sixteen-year-old boy crush.

Who was I kidding? I knew where we'd be. We wouldn't be in each other's lives at all. It would have been all flash, bang, and smoking, but unidentifiable remains.

I combed my wet hair and braided it so it would dry smoothly.

And even if our relationship somehow survived teenage angst and hormones, it wouldn't have survived Isabel Montgomery.

His grandmother, Mrs. Montgomery didn't like me. I almost laughed out loud right now, thinking of how she'd react to Beau's harebrained proposal. She certainly wouldn't stand for a marriage.

I was in another, separate part of Beau Montgomery's world that she tolerated and ignored. A parallel universe he visited when he wasn't at his cotillions and country club lunches.

I'd once made the mistake in my senior year of filling in for a friend who had a special events catering gig at a golf club in West Ashley and had to come face to face with Beau and his fellow classmates from his private school celebrating one of their birthdays. To his credit, Beau really didn't hang out much with that crowd toward the end of high school except when he had to. My ill-fated foray into the service industry being one of those times. His friends had turned their noses up in distaste when he acknowledged knowing me, and I hated that I may have embarrassed him. But he'd found me as soon as dinner was over, and it didn't take long for him to persuade me to ditch work so we could break into the driving range and compete for who had the longest drive while we got drunk on the contents of his monogrammed silver hip flask. It was the last time I ever waited tables at a country club. It also cemented our friendship.

"How long are you going to be exactly?" His voice called from the office. "That beer's calling my name, and it's beginning to sound pissed."

I shook away the memories. His grandmother had forbade us seeing each other for the rest of the school year that year. It hadn't lasted long. "Hold your horses." I did a light coat of mascara and a slick of lip gloss. It was so easy to hang out with Beau because it never occurred to me to care what I looked like. But suddenly, I felt unsure. What did marriage material look like? I stared at my reflection and wondered if Sylvie was right that I should make more of an effort. My makeup for work consisted of tinted moisturizer to even my complexion, heavier eye make-up than I liked, and the same nude lip gloss I always wore. Screw it, why was I overthinking this? It was Beau. At least the pale green of my peasant top made my eyes stand out.

I stuffed everything back into my purse and hung up the

towel to dry and pulled open the door. Beau was at the desk with his hands over his eyes again. "Is it safe?" he asked.

"Dork. Yes, it's safe."

He lowered his hand and leaned forward, his biceps filling out his shirt sleeves, tanned forearms resting on the metal desk top. "So I told you my news, what's yours?"

I snorted a laugh. "I can't remember," I lied. "I think your news was the doozie to end all doozies. How can anyone think of anything else?"

He shrugged and bit his lip. "Yeah."

I couldn't help the way my heart warmed to blazing at the sight of my friend. Everything in my life seemed to be changing all at once, and I wanted it to stay just the same. I couldn't marry this man. It would slowly break me knowing he didn't love me romantically, and I'd forgone my chance for happiness with anyone else. "It's not going to be me, Beau," I said quickly, going with my gut before my stupid heart convinced me to make the biggest mistake of my life. "But I'll help you if I can."

His smile wavered, and he swallowed thickly and nodded. "I—I just can't imagine what this new future looks like. I don't want to marry some stranger. I guess I just always wanted everything to stay the same."

"Get out of my head." I smiled ruefully. I wanted Beau to remain my dearest friend, my safe zone, the pillar of stability and reliability in mine and my dad's lives. Beau, who was about to get married. I couldn't deny panic was starting to take up residence inside me. I felt off-kilter. Jeez I was getting choked up. I was sad I might lose my best friend. Actually there was no *might* about it. It was probably inevitable. Already his panic proposal tonight had shifted everything off base. If he married someone else, where would that leave me?

"Are you all right? Are you going to get over me seeing you naked?" he teased.

I blinked, snapping out of my funk. "What? Oh yes. Wait, how much did you see?"

He chuckled and sunburn pink climbed up his throat again. "Let's just say, I know you're a healthy C-cup, though I'd always suspected. But now I know the color of your nipples and that you are extremely thorough with the razor."

My heart thumped like a stone into my stomach sending out a ripple of heat that seared the air from my lungs. "Wax," I wheezed.

"What?"

I cleared my throat and went for a bored tone. "I don't shave, I wax. No razors involved."

"Oh."

I replayed my words and felt further mortification. Why had I told him that exactly? "So anyway, I am over it. Shall we go?"

Beau remained seated behind the desk.

"Beau?"

"Yeah, need a minute. Really, it's fine. Just um …"

Was he still checking his emails? He wasn't even holding his phone. His hands were clasped in front of him.

"*I'm* not over it apparently." He pursed his lips and looked pained, embarrassed and apologetic all at once. "Not quite."

"Oh." I swallowed. "Ohhhhhhh. Right." I turned and burst out the office door. "I'll wait for you outside," I called over my shoulder.

I fast-walked past the boat, skirting a few pieces of machinery and aimed for the door where there was air. Beau needed a minute? I damn well needed a minute. Did he just admit that seeing me naked gave him a stiffy? So maybe I wasn't his sexless best friend after all.

Okay. I didn't know what to do with that. Not in light of everything he'd just told me.

How long did an unexpected erection last anyway? I'd gone

back in the bathroom to get changed after all. Or maybe it was the talk of nipples and Brazilian waxing that sent him over the edge. That must be it. Not me, at all. More of a concept. I burst into the outside and dragged in a lungful of sea air, then blew it out on a long breath and blinked in the setting sun.

7

BEAU

*A*lice's Bar is not quite crowded yet with the mid-week crowd, so we can find two spots at the bar. I nod to Euan who's pulling a pint. He sees me and his eyes slide past me to Gwen, and he grins wider. He arrived last summer on vacation from England with his family and totally overstayed his welcome. By overstayed, I mean it's eight months later and he still hasn't gone home. We all know he's underpaid and lives on cash tips, but he's entertaining and brings in lots of girls. They can't get enough of his accent.

Gwen has a theory Euan had a very sad nerdy existence back home and being in America gives him a whole new identity. Looking at the attempt at a man bun and beard he's been working pitifully on for the better part of six months, I have to agree. It's like in that movie, *Love Actually*, where the nerdy British virgin goes to America to get laid because the girls all love his accent.

Maybe I should do the reverse and go to England for a wife. Do British girls like American accents? Probably not as much as we like theirs.

I pull out a stool for Gwen.

She gives me a look.

"What?" I ask.

"Nothing." Frankly she looks shell-shocked.

I realize I probably should have taken a moment to explain my predicament to her. The chances were we may have come to the decision *together* to get married so I could get the inheritance, as opposed to my ridiculous, fumbling request. As it was, I can tell she's still reeling. And her knee jerk reaction is obviously to say no. I mean who says yes off the cuff to such a crazy plan?

Things are beyond weird now. We need to get them back on to regular territory. What the hell had I been thinking? In shock myself, I'd panicked. And then there she was, my Gwen, so familiar, so … capable. And yeah, I'm not above admitting I think she's freaking gorgeous and there she was all sweaty and busy and taking care of shit, and I just thought … she should take care of my shit too. Utterly selfish. Of course, I'd been quick to assure her I wasn't remotely tempted to sleep with her and a weird look had crossed her face. It almost looked as if she'd been … offended.

"Hey, hey, Gwendolyn." Euan the bartender greets her with a wink. "Was hoping you'd be back in soon. What can I get you, beautiful?"

Since when were Euan and Gwen so chummy?

"Hey, Euan," she returns his greeting and leans over the bar to give him a kiss on each cheek.

I scowl.

She smiles at him. "I'll take a pint of Caffrey's and—"

"And I'll take a double Jamisons," I interject and they both swivel their heads to look at me. "Rocks, splash of soda."

Gwen raises her eyebrow. "Everything all right there?"

"Peachy."

"Caffrey's and a whisky coming up in a jiffy," Euan says in his flat British accent.

"Oh and bring our check from the other night to Beau here so he can settle up," Gwen says.

"Why me?" I ask Gwen. "It was your turn."

"You owe me for pool. I beat your ass."

"Oh, right."

Euan nods. "Right-o. How's your three-legged dog, Beau?"

"Eileen? She's doing great, thanks."

"Such a cute little mutt. I still don't know why you gave it a *poncey* name like Eileen, mate."

I level a look at him, working out if he's serious. But I see nothing but an earnest expression. "Sorry. How about that whiskey?"

Euan scratches his head.

"What was that?" I ask Gwen when he leaves.

"What was what?"

"That kissing thing?"

"Isn't that adorable? It's how the British greet each other. A kiss on each cheek. Did you know in France it's three?"

I lift a shoulder. "In Belgium, it's four."

"It's not. How do you know that?"

"Watched a Dutch porno once," I deadpan, trying to shock her because I'm suddenly feeling irrationally annoyed. And I don't know why. Actually, I do know why. I hate that she's flat out refused to marry me. I need her, Goddammit. She should help me as a friend.

"You did not."

"I did," I argue. Okay, maybe not specifically a Dutch one. "I'm sorry to burst your bubble, Gracie, but I do watch porn occasionally."

"Ok, you probably did, but I doubt there was any kissing. Let alone four cheek kisses in a row," she snaps.

"You don't know that."

"I do. Why waste valuable screen time on chaste cheek kisses or even romantic kisses when you can use that time to show someone ejaculating?"

My mouth drops open.

She glares at me, daring me to contradict her. I guess she's annoyed too. Touché on the trying to shock each other tactic.

But I'm more stunned at how her words just launched a heat wave through my gut. I lean across the bar and pick up a toothpick from the work station, casual as can be, and stick it between my teeth. "Fair point," I admit, pretending I'm totally cool with our topic. "Been watching a lot of pornos have you?" Stupid, stupid question. My pants are having an uncomfortable moment. Surely not caused by Gwen.

My friend, Gwen.

Friend. Friend. Friend.

Friend who I said I'd never have any interest in sleeping with. I literally said those words out loud to her less than an hour ago. Although, I still need to analyze what the hell happened earlier in the office. And also, why the hell I'd admitted her naked body made me hard, I had no idea. I couldn't have been thinking straight since my blood had all vacated to my groin, leaving my brain starved for oxygen.

"I was curious." She shrugs.

Fuck, I was hoping she wouldn't answer. But she goes on, oblivious to my reaction to the thought of her watching porn. *My* Gwen watches Disney movies, not pornos. Do they turn her on, or is she disgusted? It's hard to get a read from her tone.

I mentally slap my own face. Why do I care?

"It underscored the fact that the porn available is made *by* men *for* men. Where's the porn made by women for women I want to know?" she asks.

"Honey, I've got the book," Alice, the bar owner's voice cuts in as she delivers the drinks Euan has made. He's gotten busy down the other end of the bar serving a large group of girls. "Yeah, it's got pictures of buff, shirtless men doing housework, reading books, changing diapers and cuddling kittens. Now that's some porn right there."

Of course, it'd be a book. I roll my eyes.

Gwen lets out a hoot of laughter and they high-five. "Hey Alice. Good to see you. I notice you haven't fired Euan yet."

We all look down the bar.

"It's a risk keeping him on, but he sure is good for business. If only I could get him one of those 'extraordinary people' visas they save for celebrity chefs, Slovenian first ladies, and the like." She shakes her head slowly from side to side. "It's quite fascinating really. If he spoke like he was from upcountry South Carolina, he'd be barely tolerated for being such a slut."

"Aw, he's a sweet kid. Don't be so hard on him," Gwen says.

Alice laughs. "Yeah, yeah. You're right. I feel like the Dread Pirate Roberts. Every day, I'm like, good night Euan, sleep well. I'll most likely fire you in the morning."

"You could always marry him and keep him here," Gwen suggests.

"Marry him? He's half my age! Try proving that to the authorities. Anyway, never marry for convenience, it always leads to disaster."

I manage to keep my eyes off Gwen and swallow hard on a sip of whiskey. It goes down the wrong way, making me cough.

Euan chooses that moment to glance down the bar and wink at Alice.

She goes beet red. "Christ," she snaps and whirls away to busy herself with another customer.

I cough again, my eyes watering and Gwen thumps me between the shoulder blades.

"Ow."

"Huh," says Gwen, an eyebrow raised. "Looks like I might have accidentally poked a yellow-jacket nest."

I pick up my whisky and hold it out to Gwen.

She closes her hand around her thick pint glass and swivels her barstool to face me. "What are we toasting to?"

"Me starting my own boat-building business?"

"Getting a bit ahead of yourself, aren't you? Let's toast to finding you a wife. Hey, what about Alice?"

"No."

"No?"

"No."

"Look, beggars can't be choosers." She goes ahead and clinks her glass with mine and takes a sip of her ale. Her eyes close and she makes a small moan of satisfaction before licking the cream off her top lip. Her jade colored eyes pop open, and I quickly look away.

What is going on right now? I've drunk a thousand beers with my best friend, and never once have I found it sexual in any way. I must be too long between hook ups. I sip my whisky and revel in the bite of it giving me another sensation to focus on. What were we talking about? Oh yeah. "I'm not a beggar."

"Not yet."

"Ever." I form an expression of disgust. "Please. Plenty of women would jump at the chance." Except *you*, obviously, I want to say out loud.

"What are we talking about?" Alice is back.

Gwen looks to me for permission.

I shrug. What the hell?

"Still on the subject of marriage," says Gwen to Alice. "And this one will shock you."

"Okay," says Alice. "I'm fifty-five years old and run a bar. I can promise you nothing will shock me. Shoot."

"But you can't say anything to anyone," I add.

Alice looks affronted. "Aaaaand I hear a lot of things, I'm a bar tending therapist. And they stay right up here." She taps her temple.

I think how best to explain my predicament.

How to word it the least salaciously.

But Gwen cuts me off. "Beau asked me to marry him," she says, tossing the conversational live snake onto the bar top.

Alice reels back, and is in fact, speechless.

"Jesus," I hiss. "You don't have to put it out there like that."

Gwen turns to me. "But that's what happened, isn't it? You were offered a dream come true with the stipulation of marriage, and you came running to your dear old dependable Gwen." Then she turns back to Alice and shrugs. "That's me, isn't it? A dependable good friend. Actually, this Caffrey's isn't quite doing it for me. Can I get a shot? I'm thinking Tequila."

Alice is frozen for a second more and then seems to snap to attention. "A shot. I could do with one of those myself." She reaches for two shot glasses and a bottle.

She holds up the bottle to me. "You too?"

I shake my head and motion with my glass of whiskey. I learned at around age twenty not to mix brown and white liquor.

Alice pours two shots, and she and Gwen clink glasses, knock them back, and slam the glasses on the bar top. Gwen's mouth twists with distaste.

"You hate tequila," I remind her too late.

"Desperate times," she says cryptically.

"So," says Alice to Gwen. "What did you say?"

I chuckle humorlessly because obviously I'm the butt of the joke here. "No," I answer instead of Gwen. "She said no. *Obviously*."

"Why obviously?" Alice asks.

"Alice," Gwen says in a warning tone, but Alice looks unperturbed.

"Actually, I'm not sure why it was an *obvious* no." And sensing I may have an ally in our friendly bartender, I turn to Gwen. "So, Gwen. Why did you say no?"

Gwen's expression changes from startled to distracted. Then she looks down and pulls out her cell phone.

I see the name Derek flash across the screen.

"You should answer that," I say, even as it annoys me he's interrupted our evening. But I have to say I also feel relieved.

She looks at me for a long moment, then bites her lip and accepts the call. "Hello?" She hops off the barstool and heads toward the door.

I turn back to Alice.

"You want to tell me why you have some harebrained notion of getting married? Because I gotta tell you, it's not a state of affairs I recommend."

"Believe me, I agree. But I have to." I proceed to tell her about the will and my dreams to open a custom boat business and the ridiculous marriage stipulation. Alice listens without judgment.

Then she says, "I'm sad."

"Why?" I frown.

"Because I enjoyed you two coming in here. And this is going to change everything."

"It doesn't have to." I lift a shoulder, my expression hopefully conveying my confusion at her reaction.

Alice rolls her eyes. "Honestly, men are so dense sometimes."

"What am I not getting?"

"If you haven't figured it out, then I can't tell you." She taps her temple. "A vault, remember?"

Gwen comes dancing back into the bar, beaming and fairly leaps onto the barstool. "Derek's back this weekend."

"Ohhh, lucky you," Alice croons. "Nothing like sex with a sailor back in port after a dry spell. They can go all night. I hope you get around to actually talking."

"What the hell, Alice?" I frown. Do I have to be included in the girl talk?

"What? I'm excited that our gorgeous girl here is going to get a much needed *shagging,* as Euan would say … nothing inappropriate about that."

I swallow the taste of acid in my throat.

Gwen is busy texting and smiling and not paying the slightest attention to me.

Alice leans toward me. "Unless you're *jealous*."

"What? No. Of course not." My voice sounds strangled.

Jesus. I'm not, am I? Why should I be jealous of Gwen having sex? I can have sex whenever I want. Although I suppose when I have a wife, and I'm trying to keep it uncomplicated, I'll have to find some other work arounds.

"Okay, cool. All set." Gwen puts her phone down and looks up at us with happy eyes. "Derek is so sweet. I really should text him more. Oh, I almost forgot, Beau, are you coming to the pool party on Saturday?"

"Yeah, I said I would."

"Great," Gwen says. "My friend Penny will be there so you don't have to feel left out if I'm with Derek."

Alice smiles sweetly at me. "Penny will be there," she confirms as if I hadn't just heard it for myself. "So you don't feel left out."

I scowl. Penny is the mad chick who lives in Gwen's building. Wife material? I shudder. No, she's a definite no. Not that Penny isn't pretty. She is. I'm not sure why she's a definite no. She also talks a lot. A *lot*. That must be it. I just ... *no*.

Alice flicks my forehead and hands me the tab.

"Anyway," says Gwen and beams at me in a somewhat maniacal way. "We need to start making a list of potential marriage partners."

"There's no rush, right? Although we could fix this all tomorrow if you'd just say yes."

Gwen takes a long gulp of her beer, her eyes getting shifty.

"What's going on?"

"I've been looking for the best time to tell you this, and then after your, you know," she clears her throat, "proposal earlier, it completely slipped my mind."

"Yes?" I prompt.

"Well, uh. So ..."

"Gwen."

"The thing is … my dad … well, he sold the boat shop."

I slowly lower my glass to the bar top. My breath seems not to have filled my lungs.

"But …"

"I know you were going to buy into the business." She winces, pity painted all over her face.

"Yeah, I've been saving …" I say, telling her what she already knows. "I … there's no way. It's too soon. Who'd he sell to?" How could he?

She lays a hand on my wrist, it's warm and comforting and I wish she could fix everything. "He didn't sell the business. He sold the real estate. And I don't know who bought it."

Blinking rapidly, I manage to expel a breath without making it sound like I'm about to cry. I'm not obviously. I'm shocked, that's all.

"He wants you to come and talk to him about buying the equipment and setting up on your own. He wants to retire."

Retire? That doesn't sound like Rhys. But I know he's had some recent health problems. But setting up on my own? I've always thought it would be a partnership. Not that I don't think I'm capable, it's simply that I love that old man. He's like a bonus father to me. And working with him has been one of the privileges of my life, and I know he would have told me. "Retire? Are you sure?"

Gwen chewed her lower lip. "I know. I never saw it coming either."

"He's sure?"

"Extremely."

God, and I am so close to getting an inheritance that would let me set up on my own. Just not close enough. "How long do I have to come up with the money?"

"A month."

My mouth drops open, and my stomach falls.

Gwen's nose crinkles with a sympathetic look. "A month, or he's selling the equipment at auction because it needs to be out of there before the closing."

I pick up my glass and down the rest of my whiskey.

A month to find the money to buy myself into the boat building business.

A month to find a wife.

8

GWEN

"Omigod, omigod, omigod," I whined aloud back in my condo. I dumped my purse and flung my phone onto the couch.

I wasn't really sure how I got through that bombshell. Beau asking me to marry him out of the blue. And then having to tell him about my dad. Holy shit, this was the kind of thing I'd pick up my phone to immediately text Beau about, but of course it had everything to do with Beau.

What in the hell was I going to do? The feeling of everything slipping away from me ignited some deep panic instinct within me, making my heart race and my gut churn. I felt like a fish desperately trying to avoid a shark. I paced back and forth around the room, which started to make me dizzy as it was so small, I was literally walking in circles.

My instinct had been to reject Beau's marriage idea outright. I know that was borne of shock and surprise. But it was also self-preservation, I was instantly terrified my feelings for him would be broadcast all over my face and I'd blow up our friendship in one fell swoop. But the alternative, imagining him married to someone else felt like being gutted with a fillet knife.

This was the problem with having a best friend you were stupid enough to fall in love with, there were no allowances to freak the hell out to them when they told you they were getting married.

Okay, breathe, I told myself. I grabbed the TV remote and went to my streaming service to find a movie.

And then I'd had to tell Beau about Dad selling the boat shop. He'd looked like he might pass out for a second. "You sure?" he'd asked with eyes that looked at me like I'd just run over his dog. Damn my dad for making me do it.

My phone chimed. I snatched it off the couch.

Beau: *Hey.*

Hey back. You doing okay?

Beau: *I'm feeling weird about earlier. About my ham-handed proposal.*

I blew out a breath. Well, if that wasn't calling the sea wet.

Why? I evaded. Better to leave my answer open-ended or answer with another question.

Beau: *Because I shocked you and made you feel uncomfortable.*

Why would you think I was uncomfortable? I could be a politician.

There was a long pause, and I congratulated myself on being able to chat with him without revealing I was completely thrown.

Beau: *So you're not uncomfortable?*

Well played, Beau. What in the heck did I respond with now? Lying to my best friend didn't sit well. But there was no way I could say I was either.

Didn't say that ... ;-)

Beau: *I knew it. I can always tell what you're feeling.*

Even in my agitated state, I burst out laughing. Oh, Beau. I would have been busted ages ago if that were true.

I hope you're not texting and driving, I texted instead.

Beau usually had about a thirty-minute drive home out to the family place at Awendaw. It was beautiful out there, but it was a real pain for him to go back and forth. Hence why I normally let him crash on my couch a few nights a week as long as his dog had someone to look after her. He preferred my couch to the Montgomery family home on South Battery.

Beau: *Home already. Eileen's mad I didn't take her into town.*

What she do this time?

Beau: *I need to install a webcam. She tipped over her food bowl (It was still full - hunger strike too, maybe?) and spread it all over the kitchen floor. Sending pic.*

The phone buzzed again and an image loaded.

It was of the old black and white kitchen floor at the planta-tion house with little pellets of food spread evenly from one end of the room to the other. It was almost perfect. No big piles in one spot over another. Beau's dog was a perfectionist in mess-making, that was for sure. In the foreground sat Eileen, her gray and white shaggy head cocked to the side looking as innocent as you please.

Beau: *There's even a piece in each corner of the room.*

That must have taken her hours. She's a three-legged genius. Let's take her on the road and get rich.

Beau: *Let's not change the subject. Are you okay?*

I took a deep breath. *Fine. Why?*

Beau: *I don't want things to be weird between us.*

Weird how?

People have marriages based on less than the kind of friendship we have.

What kind of friendship do we have?

Beau: *?? Are you serious ??*

Beau: *Gwen, you're my best friend. You know that. Are you saying you don't feel that way.*

I do.

Beau: *Then I don't understand ...*

Oh, Beau. I stopped pacing and detoured to the kitchen and flipped on the electric kettle. Maybe some chamomile tea would help calm me before bed. Because as it was I was too jacked up to even contemplate closing my eyes. How did I explain to Beau why I said no when I didn't fully understand it myself? With my father selling the business in a month, Beau must feel desperate and also totally confused as to why I wouldn't help him.

Don't you want more? I asked him. Then bit my lip with nerves at all the ways that could be interpreted if someone was looking for meaning. But Beau never looked too deeply for hidden meanings. He wasn't shallow per se. He was just straightforwardly honest and expected the same of others.

I pressed send. Then I typed out another quick text.

Night, Beau.

Beau: *What do you mean more?*

Beau: *Gwen?*

Beau: *Hello? Please txt back.*

My phone rang.

Beau.

I ignored it and went to pour boiling water on my teabag. Then I slipped my laptop out of its case and started working up some specs for our new client, the handsome Mr. Canopolis. Someone may as well make use of the fact I wasn't going to get to sleep anytime soon.

An hour later, after I'd completed the outline of the specs and interior offerings I thought our client may like based on his interests (music and overnight guests) and his budget (healthy), I was back in my inbox weeding out junk mail. Timeshares in Hilton Head, pharma from Canada, singles in my area …

Wait.

What if I ran an ad … then *I* could weed them out? I'd told Beau I'd help him find someone. I didn't really hang with "his set," or anyone his grandmother would deem suitable. But if he let it be known he was in the market, he'd be fed on like a wounded seal. If I could weed out the ones who were looking for other reasons over the ones who were looking for love or money, maybe I could keep us both sane.

But what if, deep down, Beau actually wanted to fall in love? Who was I to deny him that?

I needed to have a difficult conversation with myself.

But I couldn't face it right now. Beau asked me to help him and help him I would. However, I was going to need help with the helping.

* * *

"Sylvie, I need help," I said as soon as I swung inside the doors to our showroom the next morning.

Sylvie looked up from where she was blotting her red lips in the mirror above the beverage station. "*Cherie?*"

"I need to find Beau a wife."

Sylvie's perfect red lips in Chanel's *Rouge Irresistible* dropped into an O shape.

"Someone I can stand," I went on. "But who's not nice enough that I'll lose him." I raised my eyes to hers, owning my words.

She turned, her eyes bright. "Ah."

"Yeah." I dropped my gaze and busied myself stowing my purse under my desk.

"So finally you admit you have feelings for your handsome Beau."

"I do." My shoulders slumped.

"It's about time."

"Which is a damn nightmare right now."

"*Pour quoi?*" She lifted an eyebrow. "This is a blessing, no? He needs a wife. It's perfect!"

"No, you're not hearing me, Sylvie. He doesn't want anything real. He wants to marry to get his inheritance. He wants to divorce in a few years, and he definitely doesn't want to down-grade his dating."

"Did he say that?"

"Basically, yes. Actually ... exactly."

"That's what he *thinks* he wants." Sylvie huffed.

"No, that's what he wants."

"Knock, knock," a voice called from the door.

I jumped around, immediately feeling the heat in my cheeks thinking someone may have heard me tell Sylvie about Beau.

It was Daisy, Beau's friend. Sylvie mentioned she worked in the law office, that she started the rumor about Beau being cut out of the will. I narrowed my eyes with suspicion, even as she smiled tentatively. "May I come in?"

"Daisy, *alors*," Sylvie cooed. "How are you, *ma cherie*?"

Um, since when did Sylvie know Daisy that well and why did Sylvie look guilty?

Daisy's eyes darted from Sylvie to me. "Gwen, hi. I'm not sure if you remember me, we've met through Beau a few times." She held out her hand. Her face was open and friendly, even while her outfit was taking no shit. She wore a royal blue sheath with a black jacket and black high heels. Perfect for her job as a paralegal. "In fact, I'm friends with Penny too. You live in her building, right?"

I gave her a tight smile, not quite sure where all this was going. "I do."

"Penny and I went to Ashley Hall together. Prep school," she clarified as if I'd never heard of the elite private girls' school. Beau's sister had gone there too but several years below Penny and Daisy.

"Oh, right. Okay," I managed. "You in the market for a luxury yacht?"

She laughed and smiled at me like I was the cutest thing ever.

Sylvie waved her to a seat. "Our dear Gwen has admitted she has feelings for Beau."

"Sylvie!" I gasped.

"It's all right," said Daisy and clapped her hands together.

"Actually, I already suspected, and I asked Sylvie if she could find out because I want to help."

"You did? You do?"

"Ha. I've been *shipping* you two for years."

"But I thought … didn't you start the rumor Beau was cut out of the will?"

"Of course, I did! I wanted to protect him. Give you both a chance. Can you imagine if people found out he was looking for a wife? Far better to think he's cut out of the will."

"Fair point," I conceded.

"I offered to put the word out for him and he balked. You should have seen his face. Besides, the stipulation is for Beau's sister too. She also has to get married. And she's also become a good friend of mine. I figured I'd help them both out."

"Beau did mention Suzy had to get married too." God, Beau's dead grandfather was crazy as sugar in grits.

"Well, she's not in any hurry."

I thought of Beau's ticking timeline. "But Beau is in a hurry. He has a really short deadline." I proceeded to tell them about my dad and how Beau needed to buy him out within a month. If he had a wife, he could get his inheritance or at least borrow against it.

"Who else do we trust who can help?" Sylvie asked when I was done.

"Alice of Alice's Bar knows."

Sylvie raised her eyebrows.

"I didn't tell her, Sylvie. You know I would have told you first. She guessed ages ago."

"And remind me why you won't just marry him," Daisy asked. "Surely, if you have feelings for him …"

"And he doesn't know. He can't know. It would ruin everything."

"But how? I mean. Have you ever thought he might have feelings for you too? Are you sure he doesn't?"

I hated the stupid kick of hope that hit me against my ribs before I let common sense remind me of where I stood. "Nope, Beau told me just yesterday when he asked me to marry him—"

"He asked you?" Daisy jumped up and down with her hands together. "This is great, we're much farther along in the plan than I—"

"He asked me because he wanted someone he wasn't remotely attracted to, didn't want to seduce, nor be seduced by, and who he had no intention of ever wanting to sleep with."

Daisy's face fell. "He said that?"

"He actually said all that," I assured her.

"In those words?"

"Those words exactly." More or less.

"Oh."

"Right." Then I replayed something she'd said earlier. "What plan exactly?"

"What do you mean?"

"You said we were farther along in the plan than you hoped."

Daisy glanced at Sylvie. Sylvie shook her head slightly then smiled brightly at me.

"What's going on?" I asked. "I thought the plan was to find Beau a wife. What am I missing?"

She grimaced. "The plan was to help Beau realize how he felt about you. It was to get *you two* married."

There were several beats of silence where I felt lightheaded as my brain dropped into my lower stomach.

I took a seat opposite Daisy.

"But, yes," Sylvie said glumly. "I guess now the plan is to get him married off *tout suite* to a convenient wife."

"A wife who's not you," Daisy added and scrunched her nose as if the words pained her.

Well, they pained me too, but I kept my mouth shut.

"So, I mean, do you want to find him a real wife then?" she went on.

"No," I said and then slammed my mouth closed. "I mean obviously I want him to be happy. But since it has to happen so quickly, it's probably best to keep it simple. A business transaction. That's what Beau wants anyway."

"Call Alice then," said Daisy. "And who else do you trust?"

"Penny?" I ventured.

"Great. The five of us ladies can put our heads together to try and solve this problem."

"Why are you doing this?" I asked her. "To be honest, I thought maybe you'd want Beau for yourself."

"Ha. Not gonna lie. He's gorgeous, and yeah, I could definitely go for him."

"But?" I pressed.

"But, when I get married it will be for love and babies. That biological clock is ticking after all."

"Tell me about it," I muttered.

"And of course, no one can stand the grandmother, darling," said Sylvie.

Daisy shrugged. "I know you think she doesn't like you," she said to me. "But frankly I'm not sure she likes anyone. Anyway, I've always gotten the impression Beau is somewhat … taken."

"By who?"

"You, darling," said Sylvie.

"But—"

"*Oui, oui,*" Sylvie talks over me. "You think he doesn't see you that way. Everyone else thinks otherwise."

* * *

I WASN'T GOING to lie, hearing both Daisy and Sylvie suggest Beau may actually have feelings beyond friendship for me felt both exhilarating and agonizing at the same time. I'd trained myself not to hope, dream, or read anything into anything, and in one morning they'd opened up enough pressure fissures in my psyche to have me close to losing my shit.

Daisy had gone back to work, and I'd left Sylvie looking over the proposal I'd drawn up for Mr. Canapolis as well as making a list of potential candidates for Beau. If we were going to find him a wife, he needed to be willing to go all in on the effort.

The next day, I decided to text Beau during my lunch break walk to the juice bar and pretend I hadn't avoided his texts and calls for a few days.

Hey, you in town today?

Then I texted Penny. *You free tonight?* Firstly, I urgently needed to make a new bestie, and secondly I'd promised Daisy and Sylvie I would corral Penny's help.

Penny texted back immediately. *I have a date! His profile is normal at least, but you never know.*

Thumbs up! Can't wait to hear about it.

I navigated the sidewalks of Meeting Street and cut up Broad to King Street. The heat of May already felt damp and heavy. This summer promised to be another scorcher.

My phone buzzed.

Finally.

Beau: *Coming in this afternoon. Bringing Eileen.*

Meet you at the boat shop? Can you spare some time to help Dad?

Beau: *Was planning on heading there today anyway.*

To my relief, it seemed Beau was also going to pretend I hadn't ignored his texts and calls. Either that or he was just waiting until we were face to face.

9

GWEN

"How's the plastic boat business?" my dad called out as soon as I entered the boat shop later that day. My father was coating pink epoxy (affectionately known as pink shit) across the hull of the boat. The smell was strong and acrid.

Eileen came hopping over to me, yipping and squeaking. Her entire small gray and white body vibrated with excitement. If she wasn't careful, she'd lose her precarious balance.

"Lucrative. Thanks for asking." I crouched down. "Hey, girl," I crooned. "These men boring you to tears? So sad Mr. Thomas doesn't know the difference between plastic and fiberglass," I added in a baby voice.

Seeing Eileen always made my heart pound because that meant Beau was here. How had I never paid attention to what my body did when he was near? Perhaps I'd gotten used to it, but today felt like I was feeling everything for the first time.

Eileen barked in response, and I heard Beau chuckle from wherever he was busy inside the boat. A warm, rich rumble that made my arm hair stand.

It was my dad's and my standard fare of ribbing each other.

Of course my dad used fiberglass on some of his boats too for certain things—the outer hull for instance. But he loved to think that because the boats I sold were mass-produced versus hand-crafted they were inferior in quality. Perhaps they were to some people, depending on what they were looking for in a boat. I had to admit that some of Rhys Thomas' vintage-inspired fishing boats, and the incredible antique boat he restored when I was a teenager, were without parallel. But I'd never admit that aloud now that I worked for a sort-of competitor.

I rose from petting Eileen.

A noise had me looking just in time to see Beau stand up from inside the boat. "Hey Gwen," he said as he peeled his t-shirt over his torso and over his head. He proceeded to wipe the sweat from his face and body, then he tossed the shirt over the side of the boat and disappeared back to whatever he'd been doing.

I blinked and swallowed in an attempt to work some moisture back into my mouth. Checking to see if anyone had seen me gawking, I clashed gazes with Eileen who sat with her head cocked to one side regarding me.

"What?" I mouthed.

My dad still dragged his squeegee back and forth. One couldn't stop when doing this part or the whole finish would end up streaked and uneven that no amount of sanding could fix. I was happy to see he was wearing a mask to protect from the fumes.

"So Jimmy and the guys have left already?" I asked as I headed to the office to change.

"Yeah, there was a job starting this week up in North Carolina, so I sent them on their way. It's just us now."

In the office I hurriedly removed my skirt suit and pulled on my jean cut offs. I left my tank top on and tied up my hair with a bandana to catch the sweat sure to afflict me within minutes of work. Just being in the office reminded me of Beau seeing me naked the last time he was there. He'd been a gentleman not to mention it, but the thought of it right now made my skin flush and my belly heat. I wondered if Beau still thought about it, about the fact he got aroused. Not that it meant anything necessarily. Some men got hard when the wind changed direction, some … not so much.

"You guys mind me putting the radio on?" I asked as I headed back out to the shop floor. "How about some Blondie?" I stuck a dusty cassette tape in the machine and pressed play.

A sponge came flying through the air and hit my head. "Hey!"

"Hey!" said Beau. "What if I didn't want to listen to Blondie?"

"What do you want to listen to?" I crossed my arms.

He winked and shrugged. "Blondie."

"Loser," I said and threw the sponge back at him.

He chuckled. "You coming up here to help me?" He knew how much I hated dealing with the pink shit.

"What are you working on?"

He held up an oddly-shaped and gleaming piece of wood. "Trying to get this one-of-a-kind hand-carved Beau Montgomery masterpiece of a console fitted, but I need someone to clamp it from the other side."

I climbed up the ladder and stepped into the boat.

Beau grinned his boyish grin that had melted the hearts and panties of girls far stronger than I. I tried to keep my eyes away from roaming down his chest, naturally chiseled and tan from a lifetime of manual work. One would think I'd be used to it by now, but well, I hadn't seen much of his chest recently, what with my new work schedule and his helping with his family business.

His eyes snaked down my form for such a brief second I almost missed it. Almost.

"You made this?" I asked to distract myself. He'd hardly been here, so I doubted it.

"I did. I set up a small woodworking shed out back at Awendaw. I built it there and brought it in today."

"Wow, it's really beautiful."

Beau gave a smile of pride. "Yeah, well let's make sure it fits. It's my first time building something this intricate completely off site and from your dad's measurements and drawings alone. Normally, when I'm working in here I can come and fit and adjust several times before I'm done."

"My measurements are spot on," my dad called. "It's going to be fine."

Beau and I glanced at each other and grinned. "It's beautiful," I said again as I admired the long lines and smooth curves. It rivaled any piece my dad had made over the years. I thought of Mr. Canopolis and his request for some one of a kind interior finishes, then shook my head. That would be really complicating things.

"Ready?" Beau asked, and I walked around to where he indicated, and we began working it into place.

"So you guys talked?" I asked him as he put a tiny wooden shim like a toothpick between his teeth to hold it while his hands were busy.

He grabbed the shim out of his mouth and worked it under the edge of the console. "Your dad and I? Yeah." The console fit perfectly, and it was truly stunning.

"You okay?"

He cut his eyes up to me and held them.

I swallowed.

"Yeah, I'm fine," he said finally. "Gonna do my best to get the money together. Just press it down more on your side, will you?"

"So I was talking with Sylvie, and ... Daisy."

Beau frowned. "Daisy Rathbun? Didn't realize you two were friends."

"I don't really know her well. But she seems nice. Anyway, Sylvie and Daisy are going help me find you a wife."

"Christ."

"And Penny. And in full transparency, probably Alice too now that she knows."

"Fuck it." Beau stood up. "I appreciate you are doing this as a favor, but I think I'm going to find my own wife, thank you very much. The last thing I need is a … posse of … of …"

"Of what? Nice women who understand your predicament and want to help?"

"Why would they want to help me? They hardly know me. Those are the least likely group of women I can imagine knowing each other, let alone trusting to help me. Wait, don't tell me. One of them wants the position?"

My eyebrows peaked upward. "No, actually, you self-absorbed jerk."

"There's bound to be an ulterior motive, and I don't want to be a part of it."

"They want to help *me*," I said by way of explanation.

"How is helping me, helping you?" Beau asked.

Okay, when he put it that way, I was treading on very thin ice.

"I said I'd help you." I shrugged with what I hoped was nonchalance.

"Well, the only way you could help me right now you've declined, so thanks but no thanks. Anyway, I have other things to worry about first."

"And what way is that?" My dad called up.

I'd almost forgotten my dad was right below us.

"What was what?" I asked, dragging my gaze away from Beau.

"Beau said the only way you could help him, you've declined. What was it?"

I locked eyes with Beau again, my jaw tight and my eyes trying to convey how mad at him I was that he mentioned it in front of my dad. "Noth—"

"I asked your daughter to marry me, sir," Beau said loudly, holding my gaze and folding his arms across his bare chest. The muscles flexed.

My stomach dipped.

There was the sound of something dropping and a scuffle. "Goddamn it," my dad said.

I held Beau's look for five long seconds. "You're playing dirty," I hissed.

GWEN

*A*fter our long evening helping my father with the boat, we were back at my condo. We'd spent most of the time cleaning up the pink shit my dad had knocked over in his surprise. Beau had apologized profusely.

I'd offered Beau and Eileen my couch again because the alternative was a long drive home or to send him home to discuss potential wives with his grandmother.

"I'm sure we can help you narrow the field down to one of those Charleston girls who'll be the least high maintenance," I told him as we entered.

Beau was currently sporting a massive beer belly as he smuggled Eileen into the building under his windbreaker. "Please, you'd never give them the time of day. Let alone be able to pick one out you approve of. You still have some pale ales in the fridge?"

"I think so. Help yourself. Look, I know I've been judgmental of some of the girls you grew up with." I slung my purse over the corner chair and pulled my hairband out to finger comb my hair. "That's only because I've been judged *by* them. Often. I know it's been a long time since high school and I'm not saying they're all the same, but—"

"They were young. We all were. Can I get you one?" He held up his bottle.

"No thanks."

"And take Suzy for example," he went on. "My sister is officially a Charleston debutante. You like *her*."

"Of course, but she's different."

"So if she can be different, there have to be others, right?"

I sat down and patted the couch next to me for Eileen.

She bobbed over to me and managed to have enough spring in one back leg to jump up. She loped around in a circle five times before sinking into a donut shape next to my thigh. "Do you realize you are arguing the point for marrying one of them?"

"Damn, you're right," he said, taking a sip of beer. "God. This is a disaster."

"It's not a disaster. It's just a challenge."

It was a huge challenge. How did I find someone I actually approved of for Beau, who was in no danger of falling in love with my best friend, or worse, him falling in love with her? Not that I didn't want him to be happy.

God.

Of course, I did. What was I saying? Why was this where I kept mentally tripping up? I had to keep reminding myself of the fact I wanted all good things for my best friend.

This was ridiculous. I'd turned down marrying him myself. I'd dismissed it for the bad, crazy, stupid idea it was. But it didn't stop me regretting that fear-triggered reaction.

"You said you talked to Trystan," I said. Maybe Trystan would tell him to marry someone he knew and trusted. Beau trusted me. Maybe I could get my head around it. "What did Trystan say?"

"He said it would be easier with a stranger and a contract than with someone I know. Less chance of complication."

I nodded, even though inside my stomach sank in inexplicable disappointment at having that confirmed. "Makes sense."

"I just can't fathom that kind of transaction. Someone who's cold enough to embark on this thing ... for what? What do they get in return?"

"Money?" I suggested redundantly. *You*, I wanted to say instead.

"I have nothing to offer. The inheritance is the real estate involved in running a boat building business. But without clients there isn't a business, and with no business there's no money. I'm hardly in a position to pay someone to marry me. And at this rate, if I can't buy the boat equipment in time then even if I get my inheritance, there's no business. I'll have to start from scratch. This is hopeless."

"It's not hopeless. It will work out, I feel sure. And you don't think some of these debutantes will hold out hope you'll fall madly in love with them? They'd do it just for that chance." How could they not? Some of them were probably already half way there. I mean, Beau was well-known in Charleston. He moved in the same circles most of them did. He was smart and funny and well-liked. He'd been on the track and sailing teams in school, he volunteered for everyone's causes and fundraisers, and went to everyone's parties. He was talented. And he was a Montgomery. Probably the nicest Montgomery ever produced.

And he only got more and more attractive with age, which was my cross to bear.

"Christ, you're scaring me," he said. "And no. I don't. And that's the exact person I need to avoid if I'm doing this right. I've already had women texting me asking if it's true that Trystan Montgomery, the long lost Montgomery bachelor, is back permanently and if he's single. Can you imagine what would happen if people knew I was actually, actively, looking for a wife?" He gave a shudder. "It would be even more of a feeding frenzy if they knew it was for purely convenience purposes."

"So you need to find someone who needs something. What about someone who might be gay but doesn't want to tell their conservative parents ... I wonder where we can find some of those conservative types?" I tapped my chin thoughtfully.

"Stop it," Beau grumbled with a reluctant smile.

I shrugged. "True though. I mean, there's got to be someone. How to find out though ..."

"Impossible. There's no way to ask that question discreetly. It would be around town in minutes."

I snapped my fingers and Eileen raised her head. "Which is why I've brought in reinforcements."

He rolled his eyes and sipped his beer.

"Beau, how do you live in this day and age and know the amount of people in Charleston you do and not know of someone who might be gay and hiding it from their family? I can think of at least three people right now."

"I do actually. But they're guys. I either don't know any gay women or maybe they are better at hiding it."

"Fair enough. I still can't believe you told my dad you asked me." I picked up a couch throw pillow and tossed it at him.

He caught it, mid-air. "Pay back for telling Alice. Are you *sure* you won't do it?" He looked me in the eyes again, and my heartbeat seemed to increase exponentially. "I know you think I'm an asshole to even ask you. For some reason." He shook his head. "But please marry me, Gracie."

Damn him calling me Gracie. The sound of it always hit me beneath the ribs. But along with the question he asked, it was as if all the air left my chest too. Then I remembered he did get turned on the other day. I could talk my way out of that every which way, but the reality was people didn't get turned on by things they found unattractive.

Maybe there was a chance.

If I was brave enough.

This was my moment. The moment where I could take a leap

of faith. Faith that I could marry him and make him fall in love with his wife. *Me.*

Taking a deep breath, I looked into his eyes. Those beautiful, soulful, playful, mesmerizing eyes. "Beau—"

"Because it would make this all so much easier. I mean we could still date other people. Have sex. Whatever. We'd have to be discreet obviously but hey, no one said we have to spend every second together. So feasibly we wouldn't have to give that up. And I'll find out how long we'd even have to keep up the pretense. I'm thinking a year or two?"

Ouch. I blinked rapidly and looked toward the window, acting like I had an itchy eye. But I could see his reflection, the features I found so dear, and they stabbed my heart.

"You could still …" he paused like he had a bad taste in his mouth, "sleep with Daryl."

"Derek! His name is Derek. For fuck's sake," I said abruptly, and I grimaced at my reflection in the window.

"Sorry. Derek. So what do you think?"

"I think, *Beau Montgomery*, this might be the most selfish thing you've ever asked of me." I glanced at him in time to see him wince. "And the answer is no. Absolutely, categorically, no." How could I do that to myself? The punishment of being in unrequited love with my best friend had gone on long enough. Too long.

"Fair enough. I guess you really meant no when you said it the first time." He shrugged like it was no big deal, but I could see his shoulders slump in disappointment.

Argh.

How did he get to be upset about this? Did he even realize what he was asking of me?

Of course he didn't.

I folded my arms and clenched my jaw, then let out a long breath. How had I never realized how dysfunctional this friendship was? And it was my fault for letting it go on like this. "I'm annoyed, I think you should go."

Beau chuckled and took a sip of beer. "Come on. You don't mean that. I'll do you a solid—we can watch *Beauty and the Beast*."

"I'm serious." I turned fully toward him.

He dropped his feet from the coffee table and sat up straight, his eyes shifting into an expression of confusion. "Oh. Right. That time of the month or something?"

"Argh! Fuck you, Beau Montgomery."

Eileen whimpered and slunk off the couch to sit on my feet.

"Why is it that men can behave like jackasses, and when their behavior pisses a woman off, they immediately assume it's nothing to do with them—that we're hormonal or something? You are being a selfish prick. And I don't feel like having a selfish prick in my condo tonight. Or any night. I don't need a better reason than that. So ... please ... leave." Realizing it might be Beau who needed protection, Eileen loped over to him, her tail lowered. She paused once to look over her shoulder accusingly at me.

Et tu, Eileen?

Beau set down his beer bottle, his brow furrowed. "I'm sorry. You're right. That was an asinine thing to say. I was joking, obviously. I just didn't know you were actually mad at me."

"Well, I am."

"I can tell. But why?"

"Christ, Beau. Because my best friend thinks I'd like to waste my last few remaining child-bearing years married to someone who doesn't love me." I began counting off the reasons on my fingers. "Doesn't want to sleep with me and then wants to divorce me in time for me to be a childless spinster for the rest of my life. Thank you, but don't mind if I don't. That's kind of a dickish move, don't you think? Certainly not something a best friend would ask of me. At least I didn't think so." I dragged in a breath. "But maybe we're done being best friends too. I mean with a friend like you, who the hell needs an enemy?"

My chest was heaving, and I was about one second away from

bursting into tears. And that was a totally cliché and lame last word in my argument, but whatever. It was true.

Beau watched me rant with his mouth parted in shock. Then he swallowed heavily. "I'm sorry I asked you, I just couldn't think of an alternative. I still can't. There's no one who'd agree to something as big as marriage without there being an obvious pay out at the end of it."

"God, you are completely missing the point."

"And no one would do it for love, I'm not that stupid."

"Wow, you really think poorly of my gender, don't you?"

"No, I—"

"How have I never noticed what a sexist pig you are?"

"Gracie, please."

"Don't fucking call me Gracie!" I yelled. My outburst was loud and shocking and ricocheted around the condo. Eileen whimpered again.

"Sorry, Eileen," I told her sincerely. As a rescue dog, it was obvious she didn't like being around shouting humans. "I'm sorry, girl."

Beau stared at me, a muscle ticking in his jaw and then picked up Eileen and stalked to the door. After one long look at me, he wrenched the door open and walked out.

How dare he feel hurt right now?

The door slammed behind him.

"Good riddance," I shouted.

And then I burst into tears.

GWEN

*B*eau was right, it *was* a night for *Beauty and the Beast*. I made myself some herbal tea, my eyes stinging from the salt in my tears, and sank onto the couch. I couldn't believe how I'd fallen apart. I never did that.

Beau must be reeling from the way I acted. But if I was honest with myself it was a long time coming. I couldn't believe he would assume I'd just go along with a sham marriage! It wasn't like asking me to be his stand in date or his plus one. Marriage was a seriously big deal, or it should be. It was to *me*. He was so cavalier about it, like it was no big deal to ask me. "Ugh!" I growled aloud.

It was time I stood up for myself and created some distance between us.

After this marriage debacle, I was going to have to be officially done with Beau Montgomery. How would I ever find someone else to think about falling in love with when he was so intertwined with my life?

I wasn't even that excited about seeing Derek this weekend. Had I really ever been, or was it just convenient? I mean, a girl had needs. *I* had needs. And those needs included being touched by a masculine hand once in a while. Male-induced orgasms instead of the merely satisfactory ones I could give myself. Though, to be honest, sometimes I had to help myself along anyway, even when I was with Derek.

But the thought of having to go online or something to start dating again made me shudder. Penny had shown me some of the profiles and messages people sent, and I knew I probably didn't have the stomach to wade through that pool of toads.

Also, I was going to have to go out there and get a new best friend.

A knock sounded at the door. I frowned. It was late. If Beau was back to apologize, I wasn't sure I was ready. I pinched my cheeks and hoped my post-crying face didn't look like I'd been stung by a swarm of yellow jackets and swung open the door.

"Penny!" I exclaimed.

She held up a pint of ice cream. "Caramel," she said. "I bumped into Beau downstairs. Seemed like something happened between you two? You look like shit."

"I—thanks. I honestly don't even know what to say about it."

"You don't have to tell me anything, but I was on the way back from a really bad date. Thought we could commiserate? I need some girl time."

I managed a smile. Truly, I could probably do with some too. I opened the door wider and retreated to the couch.

"Spoons in drawer to the left of the cooktop."

She headed to the kitchen and then joined me on the couch. I muted Mrs. Potts singing about whether there could really be something there that wasn't there before between the Beast and Belle.

"So Beau looked upset, huh?" I couldn't help asking. "How was he acting?"

"Um ... smacking the door of the lobby open into the parking lot and nearly plowing me over as he stalked out without looking to see where he was going?" She held out a spoon and when I shook my head she laid it on the coffee table and dug in with her own. "That poor dog of his looked ready to make a run for it."

"Oh." I picked up a throw pillow and started picking at the corner stitching. "We got in a fight."

Penny paused with the spoon midway to her mouth. "You and Beau? In a fight? What on earth about?"

I shrugged. "It happens." It never happened. Not like that. But I went with my little lie for now. "So how bad was your date? Make it bad, make it really awful so I feel better."

"On a scale of one to I actually excused myself to go to the bathroom and didn't return to the table?"

"Noooo!" I covered my mouth. "You didn't."

"I did." Penny sighed and dug the spoon back in the ice cream. "I'm bummed too, I've been dying to eat there." She gave me the name of a new restaurant that had been all over my social media recently.

"Oh, I saw that on Instagram. What's the name of that restaurant Instagrammer? I always follow that girl's recs."

"Right?"

I took the carton from her and scooped up some for myself. "I'm reluctantly impressed you didn't feel like you had to sit there and be polite."

"Girl, do you even know me?"

"So what happened?"

"He starts talking to me about umbrellas, right? So he's all like, Jesus is the big umbrella, he takes care of all of us. We're all under his protection. Fine, right? I'm like okay, he loves Jesus enough to mention him on a first date. A little weird but I can roll with that."

I sucked in another spoon of ice cream and shrugged. "Sure. I got you. He's spiritual."

"Yeah. Then he's all under the Jesus umbrella comes the husband umbrella, and it's the husband's job to protect the family, blah blah, be the leader of the family, to provide, blah blah."

"Sure. People like a protective father figure."

"And of course to love his wife like Jesus loves the church."

"I'm not sure ice cream is going to cut it for me. Should we pour some rum in the container? And tell me that last part again?"

"He thinks a husband should love his wife like Jesus loves the church," she said patiently.

"Wait. Like asexually?" I was confused.

"I guess. I was starting to get super uncomfortable at this point because I'm all like, what does it mean?"

"And, like, was there even a church when Jesus was alive?" I mused out loud. "Didn't that come later?"

"And it gets worse."

"It gets worse?" I shoveled another massive mouthful of ice cream in without thinking, like I was watching an episode of *Riverdale*, my eyes pinned on Penny as she flipped her dark corkscrew curls out of the way dramatically.

"Beneath the husband umbrella there's another umbrella," she said. "It's smaller because it has to go *under* the husband's umbrella."

I gasped. "How small?"

"Small." She shuddered.

I recoiled and set down the ice cream. "And pray tell... what's this tiny umbrella's job?"

"To ... wait for it ... sub—" she coughed. "Sub—" Her cough turned into a choke.

I handed her my chamomile tea.

She took a sip. "Thank you."

I placed it back on the table and picked up the ice cream.

She took a deep breath. "To submit to her husband's authority," she managed finally, and we stared at each other for several long seconds.

Then I couldn't help it. A hysterical snort climbed up past my closed mouth. And another, and then I was giggling madly.

"You should have all the ice cream." I thrust the carton at her.

She was laughing so much, tears began rolling down her cheeks.

And when we could finally breathe again, let alone talk, she said, "Jesus probably damn well hates these fake money-driven mega churches formed in his name. So I guess that man is gonna hate his wife. And for the record, the bathrooms were by the back entrance to the restaurant. In case you ever need to escape."

"Good to know. It sucks when you have to climb out a window," I deadpanned.

"Right? I ruined my red silk skirt that way once. I loved that thing. So you want to tell me why Beau was stalking out of here like a raging bull?"

"Because I won't marry him."

There was dead silence. "Um, what?"

"Yeah. So. Apparently he has to get married."

Penny's mouth hung open. "I didn't even know he was dating anyone. At least no one serious. Has he *ever* done serious?"

"He's not. And no, he hasn't. I don't think he's capable of a long-term commitment," I grumbled in a sour tone while I dug the spoon in to scrape up some of the last drips of the sweet, creamy contents.

"Except with you."

"*I* don't count. Our friendship doesn't count as a relationship commitment. And since he's not dating anyone and you know, I'm always there for him through thick and thin, and whatever, he thought I'd jump at the chance." I rolled my eyes.

"Sorry, I still don't think I understand."

"Apparently it's a stipulation of his grandfather's will," I explained. "And you can't tell anyone."

"And why don't you want to marry him?"

"Penny."

"Seriously. You like him. Marrying him seems like a gift from his dead grandfather."

I sucked on the cold spoon, letting it soothe my hurt.

Penny watched me. "You really love him."

"I think I do. I think I always have." I savored the words being out there and felt relief and pure terror at the same time. "For a while in high school I just had a crush, a huge honking can't-sleep-can't-eat crush, then I thought it had morphed into the love of a good friend. A really good friend. And now at the sad old newly-minted age of thirty-two, I've realized I am quite literally *desperately in love with him.* And it's the saddest fucking thing in the world." My eyes stung again. "And being married to someone who's simply *fond* of me while he looks over my shoulder at other women might kill me. It *will* kill me."

Penny wisely stayed quiet.

"And we're out of damn ice cream." I sniffed.

"Okay, look," she said. "We have to make sure he doesn't really have feelings for you before we get him married, otherwise you'll regret this forever."

"Why does everyone keep saying that? He told me—"

"What he said, and what's really going on inside are two different things."

"Stop, seriously." My stomach churned uncomfortably. "You don't understand. There's just no way he's been friends with me for almost twenty years and not once has there been an inkling." But then suddenly I remembered the things he said the other night about thinking I was hot when we were teenagers. But that was eons ago.

"Gwen, in my experience, guys are pretty damned good at compartmentalizing. They're liable to stick whatever compli-cated feelings they have into a box and fight like hell to keep it sealed. Hermetically and airtight. It's a survival mechanism. I'm sure it's been honed from eons of hiding weaknesses from predators."

"I guess I'm the predator in this scenario?"

She laughed. "But seriously though, but the greater the danger, the tighter the seal. Think about what opening that box might mean for him. Probably along the lines of how you feel about hiding your feelings. Terrified you'll lose your friendship."

"God, Penny. You're like the third person today to try and convince me he might have feelings for me when the man himself has made it abundantly clear it's nothing more than friendship. And the simplest explanation is usually the correct one. The simplest explanation being that Beau is telling me the truth. I'd be a fool to listen to you guys over him. And worse, we don't have time."

"Every girl I know who's run into Beau doesn't even bother going for anything more than sex—"

I winced.

"No, Listen. They don't bother going after him for more than sex because they all know or suspect you have his heart."

"But that's natural, isn't it? If a guy has a female friend, we always wonder if there's more there. I'm telling you there isn't."

"And by the way, not that you've asked. But rumor is the sex is good."

"Penny," I whined as a Bunsen burner lit under my belly.

"You have two options to try and prove my point. One, make him jealous. He's coming to the pool party, right. Derek will be there. He'll get to see you as someone desirable, and you can totally play it up."

"He's been around Derek before and wasn't jealous. What's option two?"

"Option two is you make a move on him and see what happens." Her eyebrows raised.

All the organs in my upper body seemed to float down through my legs to my feet. I opened my mouth to talk and a squeak emerged. "How?"

"The usual way ... kiss him maybe? You'll figure it out."

I realized I'd been shaking my head back and forth for the last solid minute.

She shrugged. "Well the alternative is the love of your life marries someone else."

"But a fake marriage of convenience," I protested.

"It may start that way, sure. But are you willing to take that gamble and end up losing him anyway? Coz I'd call that pretty damned *in*convenient."

BEAU

*W*hat in the hell just happened? I stumble out of Gwen's condo building, Eileen at my heels. By a stroke of luck, the front desk is empty with no one to complain I've had a dog in the building without permission.

As I hit the humid air outside, I inhale deeply and shake my head.

I left my truck down at the marina, but I don't want to tackle the long drive back to Awendaw. I need my best friend, dammit. I need Gwen's opinion, but she's the one who's just kicked me out. She's the one I need to talk about. Which is unfathomable. Maybe I should get more guy friends. I have some, sure. I just don't spend a whole lot of time with them. Especially after they started getting hitched one by one.

The next person I think of is my cousin Trystan, and I wonder if it is too late to call him up in New York.

I lope up South Battery toward the Montgomery home. I always keep a key just in case. Magda and Jeremy who spend half their time out at the plantation house in Awendaw usually keep a room for me here made up.

Eileen takes a last squat in the bushes and then we make our way up the stairs of the antebellum home. The smell of the blooming jasmine that grows around the wrought iron railing adds a heavy sweetness to the humid night air.

I unlock the front door and swing it open. Eileen hops inside and I type in the code to the silent alarm and then rearm it. Grandfather had had an alarm at this house as long as I could remember. It made sense given the value of some of the art and 18th-century family silver inside.

"Beau."

I jump about a foot in the air. "Christ," I say as I spin around to see my grandmother like a ghost in the opening to the library. She's wearing her long white nightgown, her hair in curlers and carrying a candle. A fucking *candle*.

Eileen hops over, panting madly, her tail wagging so fast it's about to knock her off her three legs. "Shoo, beast. Shoo." My grandmother flutters her free hand wildly. "Why do you bring this—"

"She's not going to hurt you," I mutter. "What are you doing up?"

Her hand goes to her throat. "I couldn't sleep, so I came down to read my letters to Savannah. Then I remembered I'd given them to Trystan. I used to do that a lot. It helped me keep my mind off your grandfather's illness."

I frown. "I'd have thought you'd do something that upset you less if you were trying to keep your mind off grandfather."

She lifts a bony shoulder. "When you get to my age, you start to wallow in the scope of your life and all the things you regret, didn't do, meant to do…" she waves her hand down an invisible list, then trails off. "I don't—I don't think I created enough happy memories."

I walk toward her. "Come on, let's go make you some of your special tea, then you'll sleep better."

She lets me lead her to the kitchen and takes a seat in her small adjacent sitting room as I turn on the under cabinet lights.

"You know," I say. "You don't need to wander around the house in the dark, it's just you here, you can put a couple of lights on."

"I always worry they'll be too bright and wake me up too much."

I light the gas burner under the tea kettle. "True, but if you set the house on fire with those candles that wouldn't be the best alternative."

She makes a *hmmph* sound behind me, but then I hear her blow out her candle.

Smiling to myself, I pull down two mugs, the chamomile tea, honey, and the small bottle of brandy ("for cooking!") she always tucks into the spice cupboard.

"Where were you this evening?" she asks.

I hesitate. "Gwen's."

"I wish you'd stay here more."

I don't know if she means she wishes I'd stay here more because she doesn't like Gwen, or if she wants me here more because she's lonely. It's probably a mix of both. "I'm thirty-one years old and basically still living at home." I grin at her, not getting drawn into her comment. "We don't need to make it worse."

"I've seen how much you're doing to restore the plantation house. I don't know what we'd have done with it without you."

"Spent money on it, I imagine."

"Exactly, so I don't call that living at home. I call that paying rent."

I pause momentarily as I stir the honey and brandy into her tea. "I'm glad you feel that way."

Actually, it's a huge relief she feels that way. I mean I know how much people charge to restore these historic homes—a friend I've known since high school now works with the Charleston Historic Foundation. When I started working on the house, repairing rotten wood and restoring some of the original carved stair rails and such, I realized pretty quickly I wasn't going to be able to have time to get any real work done on the place unless I was on site. Working for Montgomery Homes and Facilities, as well as in Rhys Thomas' boat shop means my time is pretty thin.

I hand Grandmother the cup and saucer, noticing Eileen is curled at her feet, chin resting on one of grandmother's fluffy slipper-clad feet. Then grabbing the mug I made for myself, I join her. Looking at her now, she's so different from the domineering matriarch who's presided over the family for so many years. Grief and age have done their work. She's definitely changed since my aunt Savannah died, but I can only see that in retrospect, having been in my teens when we heard. But losing my grandfather has made it all clearer. She does look lonely.

"Any luck wife hunting?" she asks, a smirk playing around her mouth.

I sigh. "What on earth were you and grandfather thinking?"

"Me? I had nothing to do with it!"

"Sure."

"No, really. Your grandfather did begin to lament that you didn't seem to be settling down or have any kind of steady girl-friend. I agreed with him, but that's as far as I went. He thought it had something to do with you being such good friends with Gwendolyn. You had no need of a companion like most do when they are seeking a mate."

"A mate. You make it sound like we're animals."

"Well, humans are animals. And we have need of companion-ship. If you can find your life companion and your romantic partner in one, well, then that's the prize, isn't it?"

"Like you and grandfather."

She inhales deeply. "Your grandfather and I ... we had a mutual respect that, yes, grew into romantic love. It didn't start out that way. I wouldn't call it an arranged marriage, but you know how Charleston families are about who's who and bloodlines. Our families were friends. It was always assumed we would join the two. It was the way I'd been brought up—to worry about pedigree and reputation and being connected with the right sort of people."

"And now?"

"Well now I'm here—a lonely old woman. My daughter died on the other side of the world without me. My son, your father, is unhappily divorced, which I fear is partly my fault. My grandson, *other* grandson," she clarifies, talking about Trystan, "hasn't spoken to me in almost twenty years. I'm tired Beau. And I really just want you all to be happy. I want Trystan to be happy."

It occurs to me if I move or even lift my mug to my mouth I might wake up from whatever dream this is.

Isabel Montgomery laughs bitterly. "I know I'm disliked. Feared. I cultivated that as a way of respect. But as the years go by, I find it harder and harder to remember why it all seemed so important that you all went to the right schools and knew the *right* people and didn't consort with the *wrong* sort of people. For what purpose? To make my *ancestors* happy? Ha!"

There's that word that no one should ever use in real life because it's completely ridiculous, but I find myself thinking it fits perfectly—I am *gobsmacked*.

Grandmother sniffs and takes a sip of her tea, wincing at the bite of brandy and then sighing contentedly. "Perfect," she says.

"Just so you know," I manage when I find my voice, "I respect you because you are my elder and my grandmother, but I don't make my decisions based on what I think you'll approve of."

Isabel snorts. "Don't I know it."

"No offense."

"None taken. Anymore. But Beau, if you do find a wife to fulfill your grandfather's request, please don't marry some stranger for convenience. Find someone to love. Who loves you in return."

I sip my own brew and enjoy the heat of the brandy in my

chest. "That sounds idyllic. But actually, I'm in a bit of a hurry. I need to buy Rhys Thomas' equipment and machinery before the end of next month. Someone bought his building at the marina. He's been resisting offers for decades, but suddenly right now when I need time the most, he's gone ahead and decided it's time to sell. If I don't get the money together, he's sending it all to auction."

Her brows furrow. "Surely he'd sell it to you with financing."

"Maybe, but I hate to ask him. This is his retirement."

"Beau, go speak to Mr. Middleton."

I sigh. "I already have an appointment." Visiting the family's banker has been something I've been trying to avoid out of some misguided feeling it would mean I wasn't doing things on my own. But I know I'm shooting myself in the foot by not going. He's been dealing with Montgomery Family finances so long that he is, quite clearly, the best person to talk to about my options. "I wanted to do this on my own. I should have left to do this on my own years ago."

Isabel leans forward and reaches for my hand. "It would have killed your grandfather. He needed your father and he needed you. Especially close to the end when he would handle less and less of the day to day. Thank you so much for staying. But now, yes, it is time you followed your dream."

"Who are you? And what have you done with the fearsome Montgomery matriarch?"

Grandmother blinks and grimaces. "I told you, she's tired. And sad. She's reassessing some things."

Quite clearly. I've never had a conversation like this with her.

"How's Gwen doing?" she asks.

At her question, my evening comes rushing back to me. Gwen's teary-eyed anger and her kicking me out.

"I don't know," I answer, honestly. "She's upset with me."

"Why?"

I swallow. It's been no secret my grandmother has never had

much time for Gwen. I know it, Gwen knows it, everyone knows it. But I honestly don't care right now. If Gwen had said yes, I still wouldn't care what grandmother thinks of her. I'd be sad of course. More for Isabel than Gwen, at what an incredible person Isabel would be missing out on.

"I asked Gwen to marry me."

Isabel, to her credit, doesn't gasp like I half expect her to. She does pause with her cup halfway to her mouth and redirects to set it on the table instead, her hand unsteady. "And she turned you down, of course."

"How do you know?"

"Because she's smart."

"Thanks," I say offended.

Isabel raises an eyebrow. "It's true. Ask yourself what she gets out of it."

"I would have thought you would have answered that yourself. I'm sure you'd think she gets the Montgomery name and family and all that might entail. Not that those things have ever interested her."

"No, they haven't. And maybe in the past, I found it irritating that she was unimpressed by our stature. In fact, at times I thought it was a ploy. But over the years, I've learned family and name don't really deserve automatic respect. People do. And most people have to earn it. I think I like the way Gwen looks at life. Close your mouth, you look like a guppy." She sniffs and reaches for her tea. "So what do *you* think she gets out of a marriage to you?"

"Apart from my sparkling personality?"

"She already enjoys that without having to marry you."

I shrug and replay my conversations about marriage with Gwen, especially all the things she'd said tonight, and I start to imagine what being married to her would be like. Not much different. Maybe I'd stay at the condo more. In a flash, I see myself not on her couch but waking up in her bed.

Wait.

Hold on. I shake my head, and the brandy from my tea burns through my insides. Okay, it's not the brandy.

Isabel is looking at me with interest. "So she doesn't gain anything from marrying you that she doesn't already have. Unless ..."

"Unless what?" I grouch, feeling out of sorts.

"Unless you were offering her more." She finishes her tea without looking at me. "Well, it's late. I believe the tea has done the job. I think I'll sleep like a baby."

More. That's exactly what Gwen said. *Don't you want more?* Had I misunderstood what she was saying?

"Wait, what do *you* mean by more?"

Grandmother gently shifts her slippered foot from underneath Eileen's shaggy head so as not to wake her up, then she levels me with a look. "Really, Beau?"

Oh. "But that's not ... she's not ... I don't ..."

"You don't what? Think she's attractive?"

"She is, of course. I mean—"

"I'm tired. Turn off the lights when you're done down here." She pats my forehead twice in a rare and warm display of affection. "Night, Beau."

13

BEAU

 *ost & Courier Newspaper*
PERSONALS

SEEKING *fine pedigree Southern lady to wed*
  Someone looking for prestige of a name
  Prenup
  No romance
  No children
  Marriage within three days (depending on background check)
  Divorce guaranteed within three years
  No alimony
  Bonus on completion

WHAT THE ...?

I set down my coffee with a thud.

Isabel wafts into the kitchen in a cloud of Givenchy perfume and Aquanet hairspray. "Good morning, Beau. Picked up my newspaper from outside, I see?"

"Did you know about this?" I snatch the paper off the counter where I've laid it out while I have my coffee and toast. I hold it up.

My grandmother pats her chest for her glasses she hung there on a string and then fumbles them onto the tip of her nose and peers at the paper.

I hold it patiently, my molars grinding.

"Since when do you read the newspaper? Don't you do everything on that phone you carry everywhere?"

"Not the point."

"And you're reading the personals?"

"I wasn't reading the personal ads, I was reading the classifieds. I always do to see if anyone is selling woodworking or boating equipment. And this is kind of hard to miss, don't you think?" I jab the offending piece with my finger.

The ad is right in the middle, in its own box, about three times the size of all the others, and in bold type. There's an email address at the bottom. *Inconvenientwife* at a well known webmail service provider, where it says to send head shot, measurements (measurements!), and reason for responding.

"Hmm. How ingenious. It wasn't me. And are you sure it's even about you?"

"Huge coincidence if not, don't you think?"

"Have you asked Gwendolyn?"

She wouldn't. Would she?

I fish my phone out of my pocket.

YOU WOULDN'T HAPPEN to have placed an ad about my situation in the paper would you?

GRACIE: *I'm still annoyed with you. I'm not talking to you right now.*

· · ·

GREAT. So text me. Did you or did you not place a personal ad about me in the paper this morning?

GRACIE: *No. And isn't there a Carly Simon song about that? And for the record I count texting as talking.*

AND YET HERE YOU ARE "TALKING" to me. And I'm not being vain. I add to her Carly Simon reference. *You'll know what I mean when you see it.*

I SMIRK.

WHY ARE you mad at me again? I forgot.

GRACIE: *Argh. Stop texting me.*

WHY? I ask, knowing that at this very moment she is probably flinging her phone onto the couch and hiding it under the cushions, which is what she does when she's mad at something someone said or sees something online she wishes she didn't.

"What's so funny?"

I snap my head up. "Oh, nothing. I don't think it was Gwen."

"Hmmph," my grandmother says.

"Can I leave Eileen here while I go to the bank this morning? I have an appointment with Tom Middleton in a couple of hours, and it's too hot to leave her in the truck."

Eileen lifts her head on cue and looks pleadingly at Isabel Montgomery.

Grandmother sniffs. "Fine," she grumbles and then addresses the dog. "But don't go barking at every squirrel who dances past the window. I have things to do today, I don't need to be jumping out of my skin every few minutes."

"Eileen accepts your terms," I say, fighting a grin.

I think my grandmother is growing a soft spot for Eileen.

*   *   *

ENTERING the bank building at 16 Broad Street is a step into history. As the oldest continuously operated bank building in the United States, they take their heritage seriously. I'm immediately greeted, offered something to drink and ushered into a waiting area while I wait for Mr. Middleton.

I've pulled on my least rumpled pair of khakis that I left stuffed in a drawer in the guest room on South Battery and raided my grandfather's wardrobe for a seersucker bowtie and Sunday blazer. Luckily, I'm also the same shoe size as he was, and I can't stop tapping the brogues on the polished marble floor. My toes feel like they're in a straight jacket.

I don't know why I'm nervous, I've known Tom Middleton my entire life, but suddenly I feel the need to impress, to fill these Montgomery shoes and show him I'm worth something. Worth investing in or taking a chance on.

My hand slips into my pocket to text Gwen even as I remember she's still mad at me. I don't like that things aren't right between us, it makes me feel unsettled and off-balance. She's always been there. I know who I am when I'm with her, and to think she's somehow found fault in my personality makes me feel like I might not believe in myself anymore. I examine that train of thought. Is Gwen that tied up in who I am and who I believe I am? The thought is unsettling. And today, of all days, I need to believe in myself.

If I can get a loan based on my business plan, and not a wife, then maybe, just maybe, I can table the marriage thing until I'm ready. And maybe piece my friendship with Gwen back together while the damage is still superficial.

Before I talk myself out of it, I slip my phone out of my pocket.

I'M SO SORRY. What can I do to apologize?

THOUGH I'M STILL HAVING a hard time figuring out what I'm apologizing for. I consider myself fairly smart, and obviously I now know she was offended I assumed she'd give up all her hopes and dreams of marriage and family just to help me out, but last night she'd been more than offended. In the almost twenty years we'd known each other, Gwendolyn Grace Thomas had never thrown me out. I'd like to say I've never done anything to warrant it, but I doubt that's true. Something about what I said last night really got under her skin, and I'm going to have to replay that conversation in detail, or at least as much of it as I can remember, and figure out what triggered our fall out so I can try and fix it.

"Beau?"

I look up from absently staring at my blank phone. "Mr. Middleton." I greet him as I hastily get up.

He smiles and stretches out his hand, and I shake it. "Call me Tom, please," he says. "Come on through."

Tom Middleton is tall and lanky. Close to retirement age himself, I imagine. He absently finger-combs his thinning gray hair that doesn't have even a strand out of place.

We head down a short corridor with mahogany paneling and a plush rug that makes everything suddenly hushed and reverent. Several oil portraits adorn the walls.

"Past bank presidents." Tom waves at them, then points to a

grand one at the end. "And the founder of the first bank to be housed here in 1817, John C. Calhoun."

I give a silent acknowledgment and follow him into his office.

"Have a seat." He motions to one of the two leather chairs opposite his massive desk. "I'm sorry about your grandfather."

"Thank you."

"How is Isabel doing?"

"She's … fine," I answer automatically. "Thanks for asking."

"And you?"

I nod. "I'm good. It's an adjustment not having him around. My father and I had taken on a lot of his day-to-day work and now Trystan, my cousin," I added to Tom's nod. "Trystan will be taking a lot of that on, which is … good."

"It will allow you to get back to what you love best, I assume." He smiles at me again. "Well, he'll be missed." He pinches the end of a pair of bifocals out of his breast pocket, puts them on his nose, and peers at some paper in front of him. "Isabel had the estate attorney fax over the relevant page of your grandfather's last will and testament but without explanation. Your grandfather sure had an odd sense of humor. I assume that's why you're here? How can I help?"

I sit straighter. "Well, as you know I've worked for Rhys Thomas since I was a teenager. I've studied his craft as well as having my own boat-building certification from Cape Fear Technical College." I clear my throat and proceed to explain my predicament and outline my idea.

"Can you get me a copy of your business plan?"

I pull out my phone and forward an email to him immediately. Oh, it's only a little project I've been working on for the last ten years. It is the most detailed business plan covering market conditions, threats, opportunities, sales goals, and growth plans I'll bet he's ever seen. "There you go. It's in your inbox. I apologize for not having printed copies with me, I've been staying with Grandmother."

"Please. It's fine. I don't miss the clutter on my desk. I love this new era of electronic mail." I watch his eyebrows rise as he reads through it, and I concentrate on keeping my foot still.

"Well," he says finally. "This is certainly impressive. How much have you saved?"

I tell him the amount and he purses his lips together in thought. "A respectable amount," he says and taps some things into his desktop calculator. "And I've been assured by Ravenel and Maybank that they don't foresee any issues of clear title or probate in the inheritance assets. A loan against those future assets should be no problem, and you'll be good to go."

He smiles, then stands and holds out his hand.

"Wow," I say on an exhalation of relief. "I'm getting the loan? That's incredible. Thank you so much."

My entire body hums with relief and elation. I get to my feet and grab his hand in return, pumping it up and down vigorously. I can get the business started and worry about this stupid wife hunt later when all the inheritance stuff finally gets wrapped up. I have to admit since Gwen said no, the thought I may have to marry a complete stranger without enough time for due diligence has been freaking me out, and I've tried not to think too hard about it.

"You're welcome, Beau. I'm so happy we could help." He comes around the desk. "I'll present it to the board and we'll agree on terms and the interest rate. Simply come on back in here as soon as you have the marriage certificate and we can close the loan paperwork."

I pull up short. Wait, what? I thought ...

"Who's the lucky lady?" he asks, oblivious to my reaction. "Say, what about the sweet little girl you always run around with. Rhys Thomas' daughter? And gorgeous too, though you didn't hear this old codger say that."

"Gwen? No, I don't think so."

"No? Goodness, I felt sure you two would end up together

anyway. And wouldn't that have just worked out well—the aspiring boat builder marrying a boat builder's daughter. A match made in business heaven. Are you sure it wouldn't work out? I could foresee the board of the bank being very generous on terms if they knew your new business was going to have an alliance with such a well-known name in the business."

"I'm afraid it will just be me. Though Rhys Thomas and I will always remain friends, and he will always be my mentor. I don't have to marry his daughter to maintain that," I add stiffly.

"Of course, of course. Oh, before I forget. I saw an interesting personal ad in the newspaper this morning." He chuckles and shakes his head as he ushers me to the door. We step into the hall. "That wouldn't be your handiwork, would it?"

"Um, no," I grind out my response.

"Huh. What are the odds?" He smiles and shakes my hand as he leans in with a wink. "Good luck, son. I know you won't have a problem finding a lucky lady. Liable to be spoiled for choice, I'm sure."

"Thanks," I mutter. "But if you could keep it to yourself, I'd appreciate it."

He chuckles. "I'm afraid my wife said all the ladies at her bridge club last night were already talking about it. You know how these things go. Take care, Beau."

I say goodbye, hoping I'm imagining the interested looks the various bank tellers and staff give me as I walk through to the main lobby, the majority of whom are female. Of course, a familiar looking girl with vibrant red hair winks at me as I pass her desk. "Hey, Beau," she says.

"Claire." I nod and keep moving. I think I slept with her year before last. I don't look back, even though I know it's rude, but my collar is suddenly too tight, the bowtie like a noose. I can't breathe.

I burst onto Broad Street and blink in the sunlight.

The phone in my pocket is buzzing. Trystan. I breathe deeply, relieved for the distraction and answer. "What's up, cousin?"

"I think putting an ad in the newspaper was a little dramatic, don't you?"

"What the hell, why does everyone think I did it?" I make quick work of untying the bowtie and stuff it in my pocket, then undo the top two buttons on my shirt.

"You didn't? Thank God."

"Where are you? You back in town? I need advice."

"Ha. I do too, if you can believe it."

"I can't. Montgomery advice or relationship advice? Because I'm shaky on the former and a disaster on the latter. Even my best friend isn't talking to me anymore."

I look into the windows of Oak Steakhouse next door to the bank and see the bartender polishing glasses as they prepare to open for the day. An ice-cold beer would be spectacular right now.

"I just landed and bought the Post & Courier on the concourse."

"I hope you'll stay on South Battery. Grandmother ... well, let's just say she's lonely. I think it would mean a lot to her."

There's a sigh down the line. "Yeah, all right."

"So what do you need advice on?"

"Relationships."

"The tour guide?"

Trystan chuckles. "Yeah."

"That escalated quickly."

"You have no idea."

My phone beeps with an incoming call. "Hang on." *Gracie.* "Apparently, my best friend *is* talking to me after all. I'll see you at Grandmother's?"

"Sure."

I clicked over. "Gra-Gwen?"

14

BEAU

"Beau? Oh my God. I'm so sorry. I had no idea they'd place an ad. They didn't run it past me."

"What are you talking about?"

"The ad in the classifieds. The personal section. The one you saw this morning looking for a wife."

The blood drains from my head, and I sway in the humid heat. "Oh shit." Standing on the street outside the bank, the phone to my ear, I can feel my blood pressure creeping up and embarrassment rising like a tide. "If it wasn't you, who the hell placed an ad then?"

Gwen blows out a breath, and I imagine her grimacing. "Look, that's not important. I'm so sorry."

"Not important? Are you at work? Never mind. Of course, you are. See you in a second." I hang up and start up Broad toward King Street. I need answers. This whole thing is blowing up, and if I'm not careful it will scatter me like flaked fish food all over the city.

It takes me less than ten minutes to get to the showroom, and when I swing open the door the conversation inside freezes with the air-conditioning that pours over me.

I must look like a beast out for blood because the five women huddled around a computer monitor instantly quail. Only Alice stands up and folds her arms across her chest in an expression of being far from sorry.

"Beau—"

"Who did it?"

"Ooh la la," Gwen's boss, Sylvie says, her eyes raking over me like a hungry jungle cat.

"We all did," says Alice at the same time and motions to everyone, including Gwen.

I raise my eyebrows.

"It's my fault," Gwen says. "But—"

"For fuck's sake. Can you all just back off?"

"So you don't want help?" Alice asks.

"No."

"Really? Who do you have lined up?"

"Not like this! I even had Tom Middleton asking if I'd placed an ad. You think you're being discreet, but you're making it worse. Can't you all find something better to do? This is *my* problem, and *I'll* sort it out."

"I'm sorry," says Gwen. "It's totally my fault. I mean we talked about it as an option. I didn't think ... well, it doesn't matter. I take full responsibility."

"But we got some applications, *cheri,*" Sylvie says and tries to wave me over to where they were all peering at a computer screen.

"I'm not interested," I snap.

"What are you going to do then?" Alice asks. "At least come over and read a few."

"I'm not getting sucked into this." Then I give Gwen a long look where I try to convey how betrayed I feel, but instead I see a strange set of emotions flickering over her face that I can't name. Before I can try, they melt away and she bites her lip and turns her head. Her hair is wound up in some intricate shape on the back of her head, accentuating the line of her neck and jaw. I never see her with her hair up. She stands then, and she's wearing a form-fitting floral dress. I guess I always see her at the boat shop and in shorts in summer and jeans in winter. Or naked. The image hits me like a slap in the face, and I have to literally shake my head to clear it.

She's looking past me, eyes growing wide and then lighting up.

The door opens behind me, and I step aside for a tall man with silver hair.

"Ahh, lots of beautiful ladies today," the newcomer says, addressing the gaggle of woman at the desk. If he's weirded out by them, he hides it well. He looks at me, his eyebrows raised. I note that he's much younger than his silver hair suggests, and he's extremely good-looking which is annoying to notice on many levels. "And gentleman?"

I clear my throat and hold out my hand. "Beau Montgomery," I say and then some instinct has me adding. "I was just here to visit Gwen."

"Ah. The beautiful Gwen." He takes my hand and squeezes it a touch harder than a normal handshake. It makes me want to laugh at him. "I should have known she would not be without a suitor."

Suitor? "No, I mean—"

"Something more serious." He bows his head slightly. "Of course."

I shake my head bemused, half expecting him to say something about muskets at dawn, but then I see his eyes stray to Sylvie.

Gwen is eyeing the two of us with a raised eyebrow as she approaches before she transfers her full attention to the older gentleman. "Mr. Canopolis. Thank you for coming in again."

"Welcome, Mr. Canopolis," interrupts Sylvie, steering him away from Gwen and me. "We were just wrapping up a meeting.

Gwen has been working on your proposal. She'll join us in a moment. *Vien ici,*" she adds, motioning to the small conference table. "May I offer you something to drink?"

Alice, Penny, and Daisy look between me and Gwen, and then huddle back around the computer.

"What the hell, Gracie?" I whisper. "An ad in the paper?"

"I know," she says in a low voice. "I'm sorry. I mean it. I didn't know they would go so far."

"I thought maybe you did it to get back at me."

Her eyebrows knit together. "For what?"

"For, how did you put it so succinctly the other night, being a 'selfish prick'?" Up close, I can see her eyes are slightly bloodshot, the lids a bit puffy. In a flash I know it's because she cried recently, and something twists uncomfortably inside me. What am I not seeing in this picture? I feel like I'm looking at all the pieces of a puzzle but can't quite put it together. I shake my head.

"Look, Beau. I'm so sorry. Can I buy you a beer later?"

"Trystan's back in town," I hedge. "Not sure what my plans are, but I'm planning on seeing him."

She nibbles her bottom lip again. "Okay. I'll be working on the boat tonight. Dad can't make it, and we're running out of days. So if you find yourself at a loose end, I'll be desperate for a cold beer by then. I'd like a chance to explain and apologize."

She doesn't ask me to help. And I would, but right now I think maybe I need to get some distance and perspective. Something is going on in our friendship and I'm not sure I like it. The rules are changing. The field is changing. "I think ... well, I think we both need to take a breather. This marriage thing seems to have blown everything up. I ... can you just leave this alone? I thought when you said you'd help me, it would be discreet. Now I feel like everyone knows, and it's ..." I looked over at Sylvie and Mr. Canopolis and lower my voice even further, "it's freaking humiliating."

Gwen flinches.

"Like I'm a circus animal," I whisper, my temper rising now that I'm giving voice to my feelings. I realize how angry I sound, but I don't change my tone even though I'm in danger of causing a scene in her work place. Good. Let Mr. Fuckopolis think we're having a lover's spat. For some reason that gives me great satisfaction and focuses my irritation. "I'm a Goddamn grown-ass man. If I can find someone to fuck anytime I feel like it, I can damn well find someone willing to marry me if I have to."

Gwen's expression is indecipherable, but her green eyes are glowing so hot I fear they could scorch lines across my skin. It's breathtaking. "Let's take this outside," she all but growls at me. Then I'm following her through the showroom and past the women at the computer who are pretending not to listen. "Don't you all have jobs?" I mutter, but don't wait for a response as I continue out the back exit into a cobblestoned service alley.

Gwen spins around as the door closes behind me, and I'm suddenly speechless, staring at her.

She's reacting all right. But just not in the way I want.

She's not sorry, she's raging.

"I think I'll text you later," I grind out. "Maybe when we're both calmer we can talk."

"You know what?" she hisses back at me, her eyes darting to the door, up the empty alley, and then back to me. "Don't. Don't text me if you're going to act like the animal you purport not to be. You're being ridiculous. The ad was a mistake, obviously. But the sentiment was valid. We were trying to help you. But good luck, Beau Montgomery. Between the shit you said the other night and now today? I'm done. You're on your own."

I don't know what I want from her. But not this—her eyes are blazing, her pulse kicking wildly in her throat. I could touch it with my fingertips and calm her down, I think, but as the thought crosses my mind, I blink. Where did that come from?

I've never seen her so on fire or so beautiful. In a flash, I remember her naked body again and maybe it's the damp

Charleston heat, but if what's holding her back from marrying me is that she wants sex, I can damn well give that to her. With pleasure.

Alarm flickers over her face as I reach for her. "Beau, what are you—"

"Sorry." It's my last word before I reach my hand around the back of her head and my lips crash down over hers. My other arm yanks her slim, athletic body to mold firmly against mine.

Her pale pink lips are stiff in shock and just as suddenly give way, and then I'm tasting her.

A shudder rips through me and *Oh shit, I'm kissing Gracie* is my last coherent thought.

Sweet.

More.

Her tongue. Christ.

A hunger like I've never known claws through me, and I'm not in control as I angle her to taste more, to feel her better. In seconds I have us turned, and I'm pressing her against the metal exit door of the office. My skin flashes from cold to hot and back as her hands rake through my hair making goosebumps race across my entire body. "Fuck, Gracie," I whisper, suddenly hoarse with want. I've never—

"Get off, Beau." Those hands are thrusting me away from her. "No."

I stumble back, blinking.

She swings away and turns her back on me, hands against the door, chest and shoulders heaving. "Don't touch me," she rasps and I drop my arms that were already reaching for her without my noticing.

She lays her forehead against the cold metal door.

I'm blinking, short of breath and painfully hard.

"What the hell, Beau?" she says quietly.

"I—I don't know," I say. It's all I can manage. I have no idea what the hell just happened.

Blowing out a harsh breath, I shove my fingers through my hair.

She presses her cheek against the door and looks at me over her shoulder.

I touch her shoulder, wanting her to turn, and she flinches. "Don't."

But she does turn then, also short of breath like me. The anger in her eyes has returned, this time with unimaginable hurt.

My arousal evaporates instantly. Dread, sick and dark, rumbles through me. What have I done?

We stare at each other, and I truly don't know what to say. I've never been one to fill a silence just because it's there, and I don't start now. I wouldn't even know how to begin to explain what came over me or why I did what I did.

Before I even register what's coming, she raises her hand and smacks me across the cheek.

Stinging, sharp pain flares and my face snaps to the side. It feels fantastic. I should have done that to myself five minutes ago.

"I deserved that," I tell her.

Her eyes are shining with unshed tears and she shakes her head. "I'm sorry."

"Don't be. I'm the one who's sorry. I shouldn't have done that. Thanks for smacking some sense into me."

Gwen's lip trembles then, but she takes a deep breath, clears her throat and nods. "Right." She pulls some kind of chopstick out of her golden hair and it falls softly around her face. Then she lifts her arms and twists her hair around at the back of her head before shoving the stick back in. I have a bizarre urge to take the stick back out.

She wrenches open the door behind her and swings it wide as she enters. I can almost feel the smile she pastes on her face like a knife in my gut as she disappears inside. "So sorry to keep you waiting."

The door slams shut with a clang of metal.

15

BEAU

I stare at the steel door that Gwen just disappeared through, then spin on my heel and walk down the cobblestone alley, wanting to yell.

Everything is fucked up. *I* have fucked up everything.

What in the hell just happened? How had Gwen and I gone from decades of friendship to an unstable and explosive few days that ended up with me kissing her?

I fucking kissed her.

What the hell, Montgomery? Get your head on, man.

I'm back at square one. No scratch that. I'm at less than zero. I have a ticking time clock to find a wife and instead of my best friend helping me, I've managed to get to the point where she wants to smack my face.

God, I am so glad she slapped me.

I reach up and touch my cheek where it still throbs.

By the time I get to the end of the alleyway, I'm stalking around the corner to the same route I took, not twenty minutes ago, and cursing every step. Because I'm going to need that list of potential wives. I cannot believe I'm going along with this, but what choice do I have?

Christ, what has my life turned into? I ask myself as I yank open the showroom door again.

"Uh, deja vu," says Penny.

I don't hazard a look at the conference table where Sylvie and Gwen are showing plans to Mr. Canopolis.

"Not a word," I say to Alice, Penny, and Daisy. I grab a pen and scribble my email address onto a bright pink Post-it from her desk and slap it on the computer screen. "Send the least crazy sounding ones to this email address," I say through gritted teeth.

All three of them are fighting smirks.

"Any key preferences? Dog lover? Masseuse?" Penny asks and bats her eyes innocently.

"No. Fine. Just … no weird sexual things." I shake my head. "Fuck my life," I mutter and turn back to the door.

"Uh, a thank you would be appreciated," Daisy calls as I'm leaving.

I blow out a breath and pause, a hand on the door. "Thank you," I manage painfully through tight lips before I exit.

"How weird is weird?" I hear Alice asking.

"Sexually? Hmm. I don't know."

The door swings shut.

I raise my eyes to the sky. "You old fucker," I say aloud to several loud gasps of pedestrians nearby.

* * *

I SLIDE into a barstool at Alice's at four in the afternoon. I'm mad at Alice too, but there's no other bar I like to go to. It's casual, it's cheap, and watching Euan amuses me. Plus, if my friendship with Gwen is over, and we're going to divide up assets, I'm not just handing Alice's Bar over to Gwen. She can go find some-where else to drink if my being here bothers her. Besides, Trystan is coming to join me. No sooner do I think it, than the man himself steps into the bar. He's tall, intimidating and more than one head turns as he walks toward me. The man has presence.

I spin to face him and he greets me with a hand shake and a pat on the back as he grabs the seat next to me.

He glances around.

"It's my local," I explain.

"It's nice," Trystan responds.

"I wouldn't say that. But they don't judge. Especially not today when I show up here at four."

"Everything okay?"

"Not really. But you go first. How does it feel to have officially sold your company?"

"Pretty damn scary. I wake up thinking of all the things I'm supposed to do that day and then I realize it's not my problem anymore. It feels ... odd. Good in a way, but odd."

"I can imagine. There won't be many more days of waking up with nothing to do though, now that you're taking on Montgomery Homes and Facilities."

Trystan gives a chuckle. "I know. I have some work to do there. No offense." He slaps my back.

"None taken. So tell me about the tour guide." I'm desperate to talk about Gwen, but I don't even know where to start, so I may as well help Trystan with his girl issue since he brought it up first. Suddenly, I'm just so freaking happy he's back. I lay my hand on his shoulder and squeeze.

"I need a drink first," says Trystan. "And it's Emmy. Her name's Emmy."

I flag Euan down and after a brief introduction where Euan and Trystan bond over England, I order us both a local craft beer.

"So I'm assuming things progressed between you?" I ask when we have our drinks.

Trystan takes a sip of his beer. "You could say that. I find myself in an unfamiliar situation though. I want ... more." He grimaces. "And I don't know how to go about getting it."

There was that word again ... *more.*

"I mean, I thought I was the one who could stay detached, not get in too deep. But now I find myself wanting to dive in, and maybe she doesn't."

"Do you think it's got anything to do with you moving here? I mean, maybe it's just a temporary feeling?"

I almost flinch under the look he shoots my way. "Jeez, sorry." I put my hands up, laughing. "Okay, okay."

"Okay," he says and rakes a hand through his thick, dark hair. "Let's just move forward on the assumption this is different than anything that came before. Ever."

He looks slightly pained, and I suddenly realize Trystan might actually have fallen for someone. I've never actually seen it happen in anything but an over-exaggerated Disney movie. I feel like my eyes might bug out of my head, and I'm instantly quite moved by the realization this actually happens to people in real life. I feel like saying "wow" out loud but settle for taking such a large slug of my amber ale I almost choke.

Trystan slaps my back. "Relax, it might be terminal, but I don't think I'm going to die."

When I can breathe, I manage a cough to clear my throat. "So this ... *more* thing. What do you mean when you say more?"

He shrugs. "I mean there's hanging out, and sex, obviously. But, I guess, more means I want to see her every morning, I want to discuss pretty much everything with her. She's hot as fuck of course, but I want to know everything about her. What pushes her buttons, what she likes to eat, watch, do, feel. And I want to be there for every second of it. And I think more means I don't see an end to that. More means it'll keep being ... more. Keep growing into ... more."

I stare at him.

"Look, I know I sound like an idiot. I don't know how else to explain it."

"I think you did just fine."

We sit quietly for a second.

"I don't want to scare her off," he says.

"Why would you do that? You don't think she feels the same way?"

"I think she does but either doesn't realize it, or it freaked her out. She hasn't had the best experiences with people wanting her around. She was in the foster care system for most of her formative years. But despite that, she's the least bitter person I can imagine coming out of that. She's so grateful for the people she has. So positive. But maybe she thinks she doesn't deserve more than that? I don't know."

"Sounds like you need to tell her you understand why she's scared and that you'll make allowances for it. I mean you're nervous too, right? I would be."

He nods. "I am and I'm not. I can't explain it. I feel so damn sure about it, that there's no room to feel nervous. Except if I thought she didn't feel the same."

"Does she have some friends you could maybe find out from? Or who could put in a good word for you?"

He grins. "Since she had my phone, I do have a few of those numbers she put in there. I could reach out." Then he frowns. "At least I hope they saved to the cloud because I smashed my phone the other day in New York. Some asshole ran into me and sent my phone and my coffee flying. Anyway, I'm giving her a few days to think, then I'm going in."

"Used to getting what you want, huh?"

"You could say that."

We order two more beers, and I notice a table out on the deck has opened up. I'd rather talk about my situation with Gwen out of the wagging ears of Euan, or Alice if she shows up. She's probably still ogling the wife applications.

I convince Trystan to move with the promise of a view.

"So what's the latest on finding a wife?" Trystan asks, popping some peanuts into his mouth as we settle in.

I get him up to speed on as much as I can, including the argument I just had with Gwen, and the stack of potential wives I probably have hitting my inbox as we speak. I hesitate to tell him about the kiss though. For now I keep it to myself. When I get done telling him *almost* everything thoroughly and honestly, Trystan is quiet and contemplative.

Finally, he takes a long sip of his beer and sets it down.

"Beau," he says. "I think Gwen is in love with you."

16

BEAU

I laugh so hard my eyes begin to prick with tears.

"God, you are priceless, Trystan," I say when I can finally find my breath. "Now that you've been hit with the love stick, you're seeing it everywhere."

Trystan throws a peanut at my head. "Just calling it like I see it, arsehole."

"Gwen and I have been friends for a long time. I promise you, I'd have picked up on something if she felt that way. Besides she's been seeing some guy in the military for a few years now."

"Serious, are they?"

I shrug. "I don't know. I don't think so because they hardly ever see each other, but he's coming in town this week. She seems ecstatic about it."

"That doesn't mean anything."

"Whatever, Dr. Love."

"So are you going to check out these women that responded to the ad?" He nods at my phone.

"I want to, but I'm a bit nervous. What if one of them is a hulking, three-hundred-pound, ax-wielding murderer named Trevor, who's cat-fishing me?"

"Read a few to me. I'll see if I pick up on anything dodgy."

I swipe my phone open and click open the emails. "How about you actually come with me as protection."

"Um, no." He sips his beer. "I have plans to rearrange my sock drawer. But thanks anyway."

"I'll remember that, asshole," I grumble and pull up the emails. Daisy has very kindly put a name of the applicant in the subject line of each forwarded message. "Delilah," I start.

"Not bad. It's a cute name. Like that song. Go on."

"Let's see. Delilah, sixty-seven years ol—no."

Trystan barks out a laugh. "Come on. Don't be ageist. I know some smoking hot women who are in their sixties."

"Would you bang them?" I ask, unamused.

He lifts his shoulders, smirking at me.

"This isn't funny. And no you wouldn't."

"It's fucking hilarious. And neither are you going to be banging them, right? Isn't that the point?"

I cast my eyes back to my phone and frown. "True. But I can't bring someone home to a family dinner who's closer to Grand-mother's age."

"Why?" He laughs again. "You were just telling me how lonely she is. You can bring her a friend."

"Stop punching holes in my case. You should have been a lawyer. Okay. Moving on. Sandra, no age given, feels like she'd be doing a good deed, and God told her when she was a child that one day she would devote her life in service to someone she didn't know. And that it would change the world."

Trystan snorted.

"Yeah, I think not."

"And these are the vetted ones?"

"Yep."

"I can't believe you are taking these seriously."

"I don't have much choice. I need a marriage certificate." I don't tell him about getting a loan from the bank because I'm worried he'll feel pressured into giving me a loan himself. And if there's one thing I know never to do, it's borrow money from friends or family. Trystan and I have only just found each other again after his mother was ostracized from the family when Trystan was a teenager, I'm not doing one thing to upset the balance of our newly rediscovered friendship.

"Are you sure you don't want to reexamine your feelings for Gwen?"

"Shut up about Gwen already."

"I'm just saying … she wants sex and kids, right?"

"Yeah," I say patiently.

"So give those to her. You want kids eventually anyway, right?"

I hate the sensation that snakes through my gut at Trystan's words. I rake my fingers through my hair and blow out a breath. "I've already pissed her off. Apparently I insulted her by asking. I'm not doing it again."

"But have you offered her sex? I mean is she still cute? Could you go there?"

Cute? She's gorgeous. I instantly replay our kiss from earlier, and before I can stuff that ill-gotten memory into the tight vault where it needs to forget the light of day, it has my pulse racing and my cock hardening. In public. Christ. I should never have found out what it was like to kiss her. *Get a grip, Montgomery.* "She's fine," I say tightly. "Just drop it."

Trystan takes my phone and starts scrolling through the emails. "This one," he says. "Call her right now and tell her to come down here. Look, she even sent a picture."

I look at my phone. "She looks seventeen. No."

Trystan takes the phone back. "No, she doesn't."

"Fine. What's her story?"

"Needs a place to live so she can move out of home while she studies." He looks over the top of the phone at me. "She's twenty-two, has a small dog who's house-trained, would be willing to cook and do laundry too."

"God. Basically, I'd be married to my housekeeper."

"There are worse situations. And this will make me sound jaded—"

"You are jaded."

He rolled his eyes and went on. "But having someone younger might mean *she's* less jaded and easier to get along with."

"You've had some bad relationship situations with older women, have you? The sixty-year-old?"

"Fuck off. And I haven't had *any* real relationships. Not really. Until now."

"And you're not even in one yet. Okay, hand the phone over."

Trystan types out something on my phone.

"What are you doing?" I scowl.

"Texting her. She left her number."

"Give me that. I can do it."

He holds it out of the way. "I don't trust you. You're stalling."

"I'm not." Okay, maybe I was for a few days, hoping Gwen would help me out. But now I am all business.

"What are you saying?" I ask.

"I'm asking if she's free to meet tonight."

I make a lunge, but Trystan is too fast. "Christ, what are we? Twelve?" I complain.

"Incoming," Trystan says as he stops and stares at the phone. "*This?*" He holds up the screen to face me, his eyebrows raised. "*This* is Gwen all grown up?"

Last year, when I got my new smart phone I set up a profile picture I had of Gwen when we were out on a boat her dad had just finished in the fall. We had to deliver it down to the port in Savannah. The weather was cold, and she was all bundled up in a pale cable-knit sweater, her hair flying in the wind and laughing at something I'd just said. It's a great picture, I admit. The call goes to voicemail, and she disappears as the screen goes back to normal.

"Jesus, Beau," says Trystan, shaking his head incredulously. "I'm so sorry I wasn't here to advise you growing up, because dude, you basically got friend-zoned by the hottest girl in town."

"Advise me? You're only, like, less than a year older than me."

"Oh my son, so much experience can fit into but a few months," he says, shaking his head in mock dismay.

"Shut it. Did you text that girl? And is there maybe a faint chance I can get my phone back anytime soon?" I'd really like to know why Gwen is calling me for a start. I thought she wouldn't be speaking to me after what happened today.

Trystan hands my phone to me reluctantly. A text pops up.

GRACIE: *Your grandmother came by the shop and left Eileen with me. Said she was tired of her. There's a special place for her, I'll tell you …*

I GLANCE UP AT TRYSTAN. "Give me a second?"

"Go for it. Heading to the can."

A SPECIAL PLACE FOR WHO? Eileen? What she do?

GRACIE: *Your grandmother!*

I KNOW. Kidding. And sorry. I told Isabel I needed her to watch Eileen while I went to the bank. That was this morning. Whoops.

. . .

So are you speaking to me after today? I send another text before she even answers.

GRACIE: *No.*

I growl.

I'm so sorry.

GRACIE: *Just come and get Eileen before ten.*

UNKNOWN NUMBER: *Sure, I know where Alice's is. I'll meet you there in about an hour.*

I almost drop the phone. "Trystan, Godammit."

He slides back into his seat as if summoned. "You called."

"I don't even know this woman's name and you invited her here? Tonight?"

"Beau, I love you, man. But quit stalling. Let's work through the list and find someone. What? You want to plan a fancy romantic date for two weeks' time? No. You need to just weed through them and get this done."

"You're right. I know."

"I'm always right. You make a decision, you act on it. Done. If I'd run my business the way you're acting about this, I'd never have made it."

"This isn't business in the true sense."

"Yes. It is. Don't muddy the waters, Beau."

"I know." I sigh.

"In all seriousness, I know I was jerking you about Gwen, but it's better that you don't go there. Too many emotions. Keep it clean and all business. I'll have my attorney draft you a prenup and marriage contract."

"I appreciate it." I nod, but in agreeing with him about keeping it clean, I'm also acknowledging what I've been denying non-stop, that there actually is something there more than friendship with Gwen. But taking the lid of that box to examine it, scares me shitless.

GWEN

I was hot and tired. It was almost nine, and I wanted to go home and go to bed. Working by myself on the boat was not fun at all.

I'd told my dad to take it easy while he was recovering from his pneumonia and working late into the night every evening wasn't helping him get better. He didn't put up much of a fight over it either. Which was … out of character. Maybe he thought Beau would have been here with me.

Eileen whined from her spot curled by the door to the office. I think she would have preferred to be inside the office with better air-conditioning, but she also wanted to keep an eye on me. Or so I wanted to think.

The better guess was she was wondering where Beau was.

"You know what we need, girl?" I asked the dog, taking a break from rubbing and vacuuming every inch of the boat to get ready for varnish. "What's that you ask? Well, I think we need a long drink of water and maybe …" I tapped my chin thoughtfully, "Something to wake us up. Put a little spring in our step. Give us a second wind. Nope, not drugs, Eileen. Ha. I can't believe your mind went there. I'm thinking Abba! Sorry, what did you say? You love Abba? I knew you had good taste."

I drifted over to the dusty boombox and fingered through the shoe box of cassettes. "Here you are. Abba's greatest hits. It's a little whiny on track two. But the rest is gold. Gold, get it? It's called Abba Gold?" I sighed. "Yeah, never mind. No one even knows what a cassette is anymore. Granted, *I* shouldn't ... but they are just so cool. So deliberate. There's no skipping to the track you want. Can you imagine the thought the musician and the record execs put into the order of tracks?" I shook my head. "No one really gets that anymore. Not really."

I pressed play and the upbeat strains of "Dancing Queen" started up. I spun around. "Time to dance, Eileen," I called with a laugh.

Eileen hauled herself up onto three legs and hopped around yapping at my game. I think she thought I was certified crazy, but I didn't care.

"Knowing me, knowing you," I yelled during the next song and pointed at her with the vacuum hose as I marched back and forth down the length of the boat, working inefficiently but having infinitely more fun.

Eileen eventually got bored by my weird human behavior and sat down to watch me, her head cocked to one side.

It was while I was crooning "The Winner Takes It All," which I admitted to Eileen got me choked up at times, that she leapt up and raced, barking, to the door.

We had company.

Beau entered and crouched down, greeting Eileen who practically tried climbing up his body.

Oh Eileen, to be so free to express your devotion.

Typical that Beau would show up during this one song. I jogged over and turned down the volume knob on the boombox.

"Hey," I said.

"Having fun?" He grinned at me, his eyebrow raised and his

eyes twinkling. He looked so happy to see me for a moment, I forgot we'd argued.

I smiled back. "Oh, you know I like to show Eileen a good time. In case she ever wants to come live with me." I lifted a shoulder.

"'The Winner Takes It All'? This song gets you moody. You okay?"

Before I could answer, a weird sound started up, like a tiny whining motor. I looked around.

"Oh shit," Beau said just as a small brown furry rocket darted into the boat house so fast, Eileen yelped in fear, and I started in surprise.

"Hiiiiiiiiii!" The high-pitched greeting followed the fur ball in. A young woman dressed in a bright orange shorts romper and strappy white high heels teetered in. Her dark hair cascaded to her waist, and she'd taken make-up application to an art form. She had perfectly bronzed skin, smoky eyes, and pale glossed lips. "Hi, you must be Gwen, yeah?" Her eyes were wide and excited. Her voice sounded like it came from a kewpie doll.

I glanced at Beau, who seemed at a loss. "Um, she offered to drive me here to pick up Eileen since it was on her way. I left my truck here."

I turned to the girl, since Beau's explanation didn't explain who she was. I was vaguely aware from the sounds coming from the back of the boat shop, Eileen was not happy.

I held out my hand. "Yes, I'm Gwen. Hi."

She giggled. "I'm Amanda. I'm interviewing. A wife-er-view!" She giggled again.

Suddenly, there was an unholy sound of howling, growling, snapping, and snarling.

Eileen came bolting as best she could on three legs from behind the boat, making a sound like I'd never heard.

But not just Eileen.

My mouth dropped open.

I think we all stood in shock for a few seconds processing the view of a shuddering brown pom pom attached to Eileen's rear like a small parasite. The small brown Chihuahua was affixed to Eileen and humping her like crazy.

I'd never seen anything like it.

"Oh my God," Beau said, leaping forward at the same time Amanda shrieked.

"Buster! No! Bad boy! Bad doggy!"

Beau and Amanda waded into the assault.

Buster, clearly in mid-thrust was not interested in being interrupted and tried to bite Amanda.

"Get him off," Beau yelled as Eileen tried to crawl into Beau's arms.

"I can't!" Amanda cried.

Apparently Buster finally finished because Amanda managed eventually to peel him off a whimpering Eileen. The whole thing took less than a minute.

I watched with my hands covering my mouth and caught sight of a lipstick the size of which had no business being attached to such a tiny dog.

What the hell just happened? "I think I just witnessed a sexual assault," I managed out loud.

"Oh my God, I'm so sorry," said Amanda, clutching her dog, the ensuing silence almost deafening after the preceding cacophony.

Beau held a quivering and still whimpering Eileen, his expression shell-shocked.

I cleared my throat, seeing the need to take charge.

"Amanda." I stepped forward. "Thanks for your interest, but I don't think this is going to work out. Good luck with all your future endeavors."

She glanced at Beau, then back at me. "Um, okay."

Beau snapped to attention. "Yes, sorry. Thanks for your interest."

"Can I call you a cab?" I offered.

She shook her head. "I have my car. I'm so sorry. So sorry. He's not normally—"

"Bye, Amanda," I said.

"Bye." She bit her glossy lip. "Bye Beau."

I watched her teeter out of the boat house with her tiny monster crushed to her chest.

"Jesus Christ, Eileen, you poor girl. I'm so sorry." Beau held her tight. "I'm so sorry."

I headed to my father's office and opened the bottom drawer of his metal desk. I pulled out the bottle of brandy he kept there, along with two shot glasses. I'd give one of them to Eileen if I thought it would help.

I poured two generous shots and took them back to the boat shop floor.

"Here," I said.

Beau balanced Eileen with one arm, who was licking his neck like a lollipop. He took a glass, practically throwing the liquid down his throat.

"So," I deadpanned. "How's the wife hunt going?"

We stared at each other a few seconds and then burst out laughing. Luckily Eileen had calmed down with Beau's large hand caressing her against his chest.

Inwardly, my stomach clenched to see him being so tender to the little needy animal. He was going to make a good father one day. That thought killed my mirth, but I tried to hide it.

"Does she need the morning after pill or something?" I joked.

"She's fixed. At least, I think she is. The shelter told me she was."

"How did you find Amanda and her crazy little rapist dog?"

"She was on the *vetted* email list y'all sent me."

I held up my hands. "I have nothing to do with it. Neither do I want to. You asked them to forward you the emails."

Whatever good mood Beau was in evaporated too. "Well, I don't have much choice, do I?"

"Stop it."

"Well, I don't. I'm not blaming you. I realize now I was thoughtless. And maybe approached it wrong."

"Approached it wrong?"

"You know what I mean."

"I don't actually. What's the right way to ask someone to give up dreams of being a mother? I mean I know I'm getting up there, but I'm not quite ready to close the door on the idea yet, okay? I don't even know if I can have kids, but I'd like the opportunity to try."

"There's no right way, I know that. I just meant …" He looked nervous. His skin slowly flushed and he cleared his throat. "Trystan said …" He cleared his throat again and shook his head as if answering something in his head.

I raised my eyebrows, waiting.

"Is there a … could … do you …"

"Beau," I grumbled impatiently. "Just go. I'm tired and Eileen needs you to take her home."

GWEN

*B*efore I knew it, it was Friday lunchtime and I had no idea how I got through the week. It was a blur. I ate, *barely*, I slept, I went to work with Sylvie, and I helped my dad on his boat. If anyone mentioned Beau, I shut them down fast. And if they wouldn't shut up, I left the room.

Penny had come by every evening she wasn't working to check on me, and I found having a good female friend was pretty awesome. I didn't know what took me so long to get close to her. We'd lived opposite each other for years, and I guess I had simply been all about Beau. We laughed about her bad dates, and she shared with me that there was a radiologist in the hospital she had been pining after ever since she first started. For the first time, I began to think that actually cutting Beau out of my life might not be the worst thing that could ever happen to me. I'd miss him, of course, but maybe I'd been missing out on a whole lot more.

Sylvie called me over to read through the latest batch of wife applications that had come in to the temporary email address. They ran on a sliding scale from crazy to not quite as crazy.

There were claims of being secret princesses of undisclosed

European nations, one lady said she'd marry a gentile just to avoid hearing about her single status from her crazy Jewish mother one more time, and a few normal sounding people who thought it might be nice just to have a companion even if it was strictly business.

Of course, there were a few outliers—major nut jobs. One woman detailed explicitly that her fetishes precluded meeting anyone "the normal way" and that she would do and say whatever was required if she could just have half an hour a day with the man-in-need-of-a-wife's feet to do with as she pleased. He didn't even have to participate, he could read the paper, nap or whatever. The mind boggled. I almost felt like forwarding that to Beau so we could have a laugh over it.

Then I remembered we weren't really speaking.

Finally, there was another normal sounding one from a local physician's assistant whose long hours had made meeting someone impossible, and she would love to be able to take a husband home for the holidays even if it wasn't real.

I frowned. "*A*, I've read too many romance novels to believe that one isn't looking for love and *B*, she sounds like Penny."

Penny chose that moment to breeze into the showroom. "Hello chickadees. Half day, right?" she asked me. "Don't forget today is my day off, and I am not wasting it. Pool party tomorrow."

"Penny, you didn't apply for the job of Beau's wife, did you?" Sylvie asked, looking at her disapprovingly.

Her chin bobbed back. "Er, no."

Sylvie showed her the email while I packed up my stuff for the day. "Any idea who it is?" I asked.

"No. But certainly intriguing. Forward that one to Beau."

I swallowed and stayed looking busy. The girls were following Beau's instructions and forwarding any applicants that seemed vaguely normal. Granted these women were applying to marry someone they'd never met for no discernible reward, so where the line of "normal" began was anyone's guess.

Beau hadn't responded to any of the emails, but that didn't mean he wasn't reading them. Nor did it mean he wasn't contacting them directly like he had the girl who came by the boat shop with the horny Chihuahua. Time was ticking down for him after all.

"Why don't you make sure Beau is coming to the pool party tomorrow," Penny asked me. "You two have to bury the hatchet sometime. I can't believe he's still so mad."

I hadn't breathed a word about the kiss to anyone, so they all thought Beau was still upset about us placing the ad. They had no idea both of us were avoiding the other or why. If I told them, it would be adding fuel to their ridiculous conspiracy that Beau had secret feelings for me.

I knew Beau better than that.

Beau did sex easily. In his mind, kissing me had been an ill-thought out, harebrained whim. Maybe it was brought on by panic we were fighting. Our normal, happy-go-lucky chemistry had been jarred sideways ever since he'd proposed. It was no wonder we were both acting weird.

For me though, that kiss had wrecked me thoroughly. I'd been mad at him one minute for blowing everything out of proportion, and the next I was skewered in place by a lightning bolt. I'd had fantasies of what it might be like to kiss Beau, but nothing had prepared me for the utter, and all-consuming, hot violence of it.

Just thinking of his mouth on mine now sent a sharp echo of the sensation rippling through me again. Like I'd barely pulled my hand off a hot plate before getting third degree burns.

I closed my eyes and counted to three, waiting for the memory to pass, then pulled my cell phone out of my purse and opened a text message to him. We couldn't go on like this. For the first time in our friendship, I had no idea what to say. But I had to break the tension somehow. Did I acknowledge our stand off or pretend nothing was amiss?

As I thought it through, Sylvie and Penny kept reading through the emails and giggling. My cell phone suddenly buzzed with an incoming text.

DEREK: *Landed last night late. Slept like the dead. Can't wait to see you, babe. What's the plan for tomorrow?*

DEREK. Oh shit. I hadn't even thought of him the last few days. I didn't want to cancel on him, but I suddenly felt so conflicted. On the one hand, I really needed the distraction of another man, on the other ... was it fair to see Derek with the brand of another man's mouth still burning my lips?

"Oh, here's one," said Penny suddenly. "Can you hear me, Daisy?" she asked, and I realized Daisy was on speaker phone at Sylvie's desk.

"To whom it may concern," Penny read aloud. "I don't even read the paper anymore, let alone the classifieds, and certainly would never respond to an ad ... but I find myself in a predicament. Perhaps this unique proposition is, indeed, fate. Let me preface by letting you know I'm in the military. I'm currently stationed in Stuttgart, Germany, though will be shipping to the Middle East in a few weeks."

"Well, that's never going to work with Beau's time frame," I said. "She's not even here." In my head, I said a silent blessing for her safety.

"Wait," said Penny. "Just listen. I have a special needs brother," she read on, "who is currently being cared for by another relative near Charleston. For reasons I don't want to bore you with I will soon be awarded custody of my brother. I've been trying to get on the military families housing list for some time, but regardless of my needs, those service members who are married usually, and understandably, get to the top of the line. Given that I am not in a relationship, and no where near marriage, I have until now been resigned to patience as far as the housing situation goes. The changes in my brother's circumstances have obviously changed everything for *me*. I'm taking a huge risk even putting this in writing, and believe me when I tell you it pains me to be trying to skirt the rules or the law or worse and ask someone else to join me in doing just that. But this is where I am. I have given this a lot of thought, too much, and know all the next steps we'd need to take. It's a long shot, I know, but if *my* situation seems like something that would suit *your* situation, please let me know and we can continue talking. Yours sincerely, Lt. Marjorie Smith."

There was silence as Penny got to the end.

Eventually, Sylvie sat up straight. "*Mon Dieu,*" she said and raised her hands as if she was beat.

Daisy cleared her throat on the other end of the speakerphone. "Shit," she said.

"Why shit?" said Penny. "This sounds perfect."

Daisy cleared her throat again, and Penny looked at me. "Oh right. We were hoping we *wouldn't* find anyone. Sorry."

"Oh, please." I huffed as I realized what they meant. "Still with that, ladies?"

"*Mais, oui,*" argued Sylvie. "We are all romantics, no?"

"Yeah, well. Sanity prevails and the jokes on you. Because this does actually sound perfect." Maybe the fact this was doing a wonderful act of service for a woman and her special needs brother would soften the blow of Beau marrying someone else and being forever off my table of possibilities. It didn't feel like it right now, but I was sure the feeling would come.

"Is this even legit, though?" asked Daisy. "I need to do some digging and see if this would work."

"You could ask Derek," Penny suggested, looking at me. "He'd know if people get married to get on the housing list."

"I can ask him. Don't share it with Beau yet."

Penny lifted her hands off the keyboard. "Sure thing."

"Fine," echoed Daisy. "Let me know if you want me to look into it. Right now, I gotta go. Bye ladies."

"Bye," we chorused.

"Come on," Penny said to me. "I've got us a series of beauty appointments to get *vagazzled*. We're going to be late."

"Oh hell no. You're joking, I hope."

She slung her arm through mine and dragged me toward the door as Sylvie waved us off.

19

GWEN

*P*enny was joking about getting our *hoo-has* adorned with sequins and glitter, thank God, not that I would have gone along with that anyway. But we still went to get "bikini-ready." We got our hair done, our bodies waxed and exfoliated, and a mani-pedi, and we shopped.

The following morning by ten, we were sitting with mimosas in our hands and our feet in the swimming pool. The pool deck was slowly filling with residents, and the DJ for the party was still setting up.

The blue sky was clear and it promised to be scorching.

"Okay, we need a game plan. *You* need a game plan, and I'm going to help you. Time is running out."

"What are you talking about?"

"We are going to refer to Lieutenant Marjorie Smith as our Plan B. We can still keep working on Plan B, but Plan A needs to be activated, like, now."

I sipped my champagne and orange juice, which of course, due to Sylvie's coaching I recognized was actually made with sparkling wine and not champagne, but I wasn't one to burst a bubble. No pun intended. "Elaborate."

"Derek knows you aren't super into him long term, right?"

"I don't know, actually." Derek was arriving in about an hour. "We've always been super casual." I got the impression he had more than one option when he was back for R & R. Maybe that should have bothered me, but it never had.

"Hmm. Okay, well we don't want to string him along anyway, so maybe you should tell him? Why have you been seeing him so long anyway?"

"Convenience." I shrugged. She raised her eyebrow as if she didn't believe me.

"Believe me, it's been the same for him."

"That all?"

"And also acrobatic sex," I admitted with a wink as I took another sip of mimosa.

"Do tell."

"The guy is so damn strong, he can just, like, maneuver me around, you know? It's quite impressive. I feel so … feminine."

"Oh my God, that's definitely worth hanging on to." Penny bit her lip, her eyes gleaming. "That is so hot."

I shrugged. "Meh. Do we really need to try all the positions though? I mean I'm not unadventurous, but if something works …"

"Ha! I know what you mean. I dated a guy once and sometimes I felt like we were a demonstration team for the Kama Sutra."

I giggled. This was fun, this *sharing*. I'd *never* have told Beau any of this. Obviously.

"But meh?" Penny asked incredulously even though she was laughing. "I don't think Derek could be meh."

"Seriously, beyond the acrobatics, and believe me it became a bit old—there's only so many times you want to be moved around before it starts messing with your mojo if you know what I mean—we didn't really have a whole bunch in common. I love books, he doesn't. I keep up with politics, he says if he did it might mess with his military convictions. I love movies, he plays video games. He *hates* seventies music."

"Nooo. You love seventies music!"

"I know."

"Hmm," said Penny. "But he's military, so he must be so buff and hot."

I thought of Beau and then pictured him next to Derek. It was Beau's lean, disheveled beauty next to Derek's hulking, testosterone-built body that won every time. "If you like that sort of thing."

"I just love men's bodies. I'm not sure I have a type."

"And then the big one, he has no interest in having kids. And well, I do. Someday." I took a large gulp of mimosa and it tickled my nose, making my eyes water.

"When was the last time you saw Derek?"

"Last year sometime." At her raised eyebrow, I filled her in on my theory that he had other "ports of call." "Look, honestly, if he never called me again, I might not even notice for a while. You'll understand when you see us together."

"Huh. So you're basically friends who just sleep together?"

I shrugged. "I guess so."

"And you never slept with Beau like that?" Penny asked.

As soon as the words were out of her mouth, I felt myself flush from head to toe. I was instantly back to our kiss in the alley. My stomach flipped and heat flared. I shook my head vigorously to rid my mind of all dangerous thoughts. Heck, if simply thinking about kissing Beau turned me into an unstable incendiary device, God knew what sleeping with him would do. Beau was *definitely* not the sort of friend one casually slept with.

"Wow," said Penny, her jaw dropping open. She tugged her sunglasses down her nose and revealed her blue eyes that were wide and pinned on me. "What the hell was that?"

I opened my mouth and closed it again.

"You slept with Beau?" she asked. "When?"

"No!" I exclaimed so loudly my voice cracked and the volume drew several curious glances. I dropped my face into my hands. "Nobutwekissed," I mumbled.

She drew my wrists away. "Say that again?"

"No, but we kissed." I squeezed my eyes closed. "This week. He freaking kissed me out of the blue. In the middle of an argument about that stupid ad. It was just, holy shit. It was ..."

"Some kiss, apparently," Penny said when it was clear I wasn't able to articulate anymore. "Wow. For a moment there it looked like you were about to float off like a Japanese lantern."

I snorted a laugh, then slotted the rest of my mimosa down my throat. "God, Penny. I'm so screwed."

A whistle sounded from across the pool. It was one of our neighbors who lived a few floors below. "Looking good, ladies," he called. "Let me know when you need more sunscreen, happy to oblige."

Penny laughingly waved him off. "Sure, sure." Then she fixed her eyes back on me. "Okay, plan A is *definitely* on. Tell me everything."

"And Plan A is?"

"You and Beau, of course."

* * *

THE POOL PARTY was in full swing. The DJ was playing summer beats and reggae, and people were dotted around in clusters on pool floats and loungers. The smell of hot dogs, chicken wings and sunscreen permeated the air. I checked my phone for the fifteenth time when it was clear neither Beau nor Derek had shown up.

"See," I'd said to Penny an hour ago. "This is what happens when you're just friends with the one you're sleeping with and in love with the one you're supposed to be just friends with." I sighed. "Neither of them show up and you end up a lonely old maid."

And maybe I'd had a few too many mimosas. They were refreshing though. And I was having a great time, I assured myself.

It was such a relief to be able to discuss how I felt about Beau with someone.

Penny had decided that if Beau arrived, she would distract Derek, with my blessing, and I would … I didn't know what. Penny said I should "take him upstairs and bang his brains out." Her words, not mine. I was leaning more toward simply talking about why the hell he'd kissed me out of the blue.

At any rate, it looked like our plans were for naught. But at least I was getting a great tan.

I heard my phone faintly from my beach bag.

It was Derek.

"Hello," I answered loudly and stuck a finger in my other ear to drown out the sounds of the party.

"Babe, it's me. I'm so sorry—"

Someone squealed nearby, and I looked over to see a group of girls surrounding a guy that looked suspiciously like Euan, the bartender from Alice's. "I didn't hear that," I told Derek. "Hang on, let me get somewhere quieter."

I waved to Penny who was chatting with some friends of hers she knew from the hospital. I pulled on a linen cover-up over my new navy halter-neck bikini.

"Hey Gwen!" I looked over to see it was indeed Euan in the pool and he was waving. I waved back and motioned to my phone. He gave me a thumbs up and turned his attention back to his harem.

"Derek?" I asked as soon as I was back in the cool air-conditioned lower lobby of the building that housed the gym and pool access.

"Yeah, babe. Can you hear me?"

I sat on an upholstered vinyl bench. "Yep. You okay?"

"Not really, had to fly up to Ohio to see my mother. She's not well. So I won't make it today."

"Oh no, I'm so sorry about your mom."

"Really wanted to see you, but yeah, I had to be here. Sorry I didn't call earlier. Was on an oh-seven-hundred flight and came straight to the hospital. She's going to be fine though. A heart attack, but they got it in time."

"I'm so glad you were back and able to be there for her."

"Yeah, me too. Look, I, uh, I'm not sure how long I'll stay up here."

"It's fine, really. You should stay as long as you can."

"Hey, so about what you asked me to look into yesterday?"

"The housing lists?"

"Yeah. I asked around. Turns out I have a couple buddies who got married for that. And get this, one of them got married by proxy."

"What does that mean?"

Derek laughs. "It means he never even had to show up for the wedding."

"What? Are you serious? How?"

"Apparently there's a law in Flathead, Montana that allows a minister to marry someone by-proxy. He gets stand-ins for the bride or groom if they're deployed. Sometimes both. He does a lot, *a lot*, of military weddings. You can find him online."

I sat there frowning. "And this is legal?"

"Hundred percent."

It really would be a great solution for Beau.

"You there, babe?"

"Yeah, sorry, I was just processing. That's crazy."

"I know, right? It sounds made up. But hey, getting on the housing list sounds great. Any chance you feel like getting hitched?"

"Ha," I let out the half-laugh, half-shout. What was up with these men acting so cavalierly about marriage? "No. Sorry. Beau's already asked me to be a childless spinster, thanks, and I turned him down." I'd explained Beau's inheritance predicament to Derek when we'd spoken yesterday.

Derek chuckled at my response. "Worth a shot. I'm still surprised you turned him down. Totally thought you two would end up together."

"You did?"

"Yeah. How come you'd be childless?"

"Because Beau said he'd have no interest in sleeping with me."

"Bullshit."

"Excuse me?"

"You heard me. It's a good thing I'm a confident guy because not many would be able to handle the love fest between you two. I always thought it was only a matter of time before you both realized how you felt. Always knew I was borrowing you, babe."

"Seriously, what is up with everyone thinking that?"

"What's up that you haven't?"

I laughed at the ridiculousness of this conversation. "Please."

"Just telling it like I see it. No hard feelings. So who's the Marine?"

"I can't tell you!"

"Of course. I don't want to get anyone into trouble. I have honor you know? But if I know her, I may be able to make sure she's on the up and up. For Beau's sake."

I chewed my lip and crossed my free arm over my body. It was chilly inside after the heat of the sun. "Fine. Lt. Marjorie Smith."

There was dead silence on the other end. I looked at the screen to make sure we were still connected.

"Derek?"

"No shit."

"You know her?"

He cleared his throat. "Yeah. If it's the same one. Nice girl."

"Derek? You being facetious?"

"No. I, uh, no, I really mean nice girl. Kinda had a crush on her back in basic. Shut me down, completely."

"Huh."

"Yeah. Beau should be good. Guy has all the luck, seriously. Tell him not to fuck it up. Listen, I've got to go."

I frowned. "Okay. I hope your mom's all right."

"Thanks, babe. See you." The line went dead.

I stared at the phone long after he'd disconnected.

Then I went to the inbox on my phone and pulled up the email from Marjorie Smith I'd asked the girls to forward to me.

I sent an email to Marjorie introducing myself and letting her know a bit about Beau without mentioning his name. I told her I was forwarding her email to him and that it would be up to him to see if they would work out. Then I forwarded her email to Beau. I was washing my hands of this thing as of this moment. I'd fulfilled my part in helping him like I said I would. What he did now was up to him.

Besides, apart from bringing that powder puff girl to the marina, he hadn't called, texted, let alone seen me since he'd pinned me against my office door with his damn mouth.

It was obvious he was embarrassed and didn't want to talk about it and deal with the fall out. Cowardly, but I couldn't blame him. I wasn't sure how I would react if we had to talk about it. It would be a shame for almost twenty years of close friendship to sputter out to an acquaintanceship within a few days over a mistake, but it wasn't impossible.

A mistake.

Was that what it was though?

Once the mimosas wore off, I knew I might feel pretty upset, but right then, I felt numb. No, not numb exactly. My emotions felt flat, sure, but physically? I'd relived that kiss a thousand times over and it never lost its potency.

I squeezed my legs together and looked toward the pool deck

and the sound of laughter and music, then at the elevator doors that would take me upstairs to cool, quiet, calm and a glass of cold water. Or maybe a cold shower.

Making up my mind, I punched the elevator button and headed for my floor. I needed to charge my phone anyway. Penny would bring my bag up for me if I didn't make it back down.

As soon as I walked through my door, I headed to the bathroom to turn the shower on, stripping myself of my cover-up as I went. I was slick with chlorine, sweat, and sunscreen and ended up stepping into the shower with my bikini still on.

Pulling my hair tie out, I tossed it toward the sink and let the cool water pound my scalp and shoulders, washing the sticky heat off me. I sighed with relief and lathered up.

If only I could relieve the tension that had been beating inside me since my episode with Beau. It was complete agony to know what his mouth felt like. I closed my eyes and let myself relive the seconds again, the force of his kiss, his lips, his hands, his body. As if the whole of him had been kissing me, not just his mouth.

The hot slide of his tongue.

Warmth pooled fast and hot between my legs, and I moaned aloud.

What if I hadn't turned away from him? I couldn't imagine we would have had sex in broad daylight in an alleyway, but he'd been hard. I'd felt him against me. Had he felt as desperate, as hungry as I had? What would I have seen in his eyes if I hadn't turned away?

I ached.

God.

My fingers tangled with my knotted bikini top behind my neck for a moment to take it off, then gave up unable to wait, and I braced a hand against the cold tile wall as the other slipped into my bikini bottoms.

In my mind's eye, Beau had me pressed to the door, his mouth

devouring mine and his hand sliding up my thigh and u
dress.

Damn, the dress I was wearing that day would have b
too tailored to allow that. I did a mental wardrobe ch
flowy dress. Wait, how about this bikini? Yes.

Wait.

Ugh. I moaned aloud, this time in frustration. I couldr
get out of my own head long enough to get myself off. An
so turned on.

Pathetic.

"Knock, knock? Gwen, you okay?" Beau's voice came fro
bathroom doorway.

20

GWEN

I screeched and whipped the shower curtain back, my heart pounding. "What the hell, Beau?"

I stopped short.

He was in black swim shorts that rode low on his hips and flip-flops. His beach towel was slung over one bare, muscled shoulder.

"Where's your shirt?" I snapped, trying for a towel just out of reach. "And what are you doing here?"

I glared at him.

"Um, which question would you like answered, exactly?" he said, laughing. "You invited me, I took it off, and I thought you were hurt in there? Not sure if I got all those in the correct order."

"I'm not." The towel tag got stuck at the end of the rail. "Hurt." I yanked. "Shit."

He handed me his beach towel instead. "Are you *sure* you're okay?"

I paused, realizing how completely idiotic I was being. But I was worried if he saw my face, I'd look flushed and out of breath and, oh my God, he knew.

He was chewing the inside of his lip, trying not to laugh, but his eyes were blazing.

"My knot was stuck."

"What?"

"My bikini top, behind my neck. It's stuck. I was frustrated, that's what you heard."

"Sure," he said and winked. "Need help?"

A lock of his unruly hair, in need of a trim, fell across his forehead. It leant an even more roguish air to his normal mischievous good looks. And he was definitely looking at me funny. Like he knew something.

I frowned to hide my embarrassment. "Everything okay with *you*? You're acting weird." Truthfully, I was so freaking happy to see him after the week we'd had. Maybe a few days apart was just what we needed, and things could go semi back to normal.

He shook his head, a smile playing around his mouth. "Nope. But hey, if it's your top, here, turn around let me help you." His fingers reached around my neck. "I guess we aren't going to the pool party."

"It's fine, I can do it." I swatted his hand away, then realized I had to set down the towel to have free hands. No big deal. I laid the towel on the vanity and fiddled with the knot. "Anyway, I was already there. You're late. Can you, like, go and wait … shit. I really can't get it undone."

Beau stepped into the bathroom behind me. "You look great in that bikini," he said, his voice gruff. "New?"

I swallowed, not even sure I could flush any more than I already had at being caught quite literally with my hands down my pants. "Yeah. Um, thanks." I risked a look at him in the mirror.

His brow furrowed as his fingers worked. Maybe it was just a friendly comment. "Jesus, why such a tight knot?"

"It's my biggest fear it will come undone in the pool and flash everyone." I laughed uncomfortably.

"And have those pretty tits make everyone's day."

My breath left me like a popped balloon.

Abruptly, Beau turned and walked out.

I mashed my lips together, then blew out a long breath. Running cold water in the sink, I splashed some over my face. "You want to go back down there?" I called with as friendly and unaffected voice as I could. As if the last thirty seconds hadn't happened.

"I just came to hang out with you, I don't mind what we do." His voice sounded strangled.

I snuck a quick peek out the door and saw Beau facing toward the window, hands covering his eyes and head tipped back.

He began to turn, and I darted back into the bathroom, fiddling with the knot behind my head and pretending I'd never moved. "How's Eileen recovering," I called.

"She'll probably have PTSD around all small dogs for the foreseeable future."

"Uh huh."

"Fuck it," I heard him say, and then he was back in the bathroom, standing behind me, catching my eyes in the mirror. "Hold your hair up," he said when he saw I was still struggling with the bikini top.

I licked my lips and slowly reached up one hand to pull my hair off my nape.

His fingers were warm against my skin. Scratch that, his whole body was like a furnace behind me.

Suddenly, both straps came slithering over my shoulders. I slapped my hands to my breasts to keep them covered.

Beau didn't move from behind me. "I can't stop thinking about seeing them." Instead both his hands settled on either side of me on the vanity and his reflection looked up from beneath lowered lashes.

Them? My breasts? Was I breathing? I couldn't tell. I felt faint, maybe I was breathing too fast. Or I was dreaming.

"What were you doing in the shower really?" he rasped from over my shoulder.

My throat felt clogged and my pulse skittered. "My bikini—"

"Try again, Gracie."

I tried to laugh, but it came out high-pitched and uncomfortable. "Don't be ridiculous. It's the middle of the day."

God, what did that have to do with anything?

He shifted slightly, and I jumped as he slid a fingertip down my spine and snapped the bra closure of my top. "You're still a little soapy. I guess you weren't done yet. In more ways than one. Can I help with that?"

I inhaled sharply and made a sound that sounded suspiciously like a whimper. "Beau. Is this some kind of joke? Back up."

"Gracie."

"Don't call—"

"Call you Gracie. I know."

I wanted to drown in the scent of him—clean skin, heady spice, the faint trace of wood varnish and burned sawdust. And the heat of him behind me. His bare chest could press against my back, and I swore I would hit nirvana.

Preservation kicked in. If I wasn't careful, I'd lay down my whole hand and he'd see how I felt.

"Look," I grumbled, feigning irritation. "Just because you got some harebrained scheme to kiss me earlier this week, which frankly," I spun around so quickly, he couldn't help but step back, giving me much needed personal space, "frankly was insulting—"

"Insulting? Excuse me. How do you figure that?"

I clutched my hands to my chest in an effort to keep my bikini in place. "Tell me it wasn't some misguided attempt to maybe try and add some sex into the whole maybe-you-should-marry-me-and-help-me-out thing. I know I made some comments about not wanting to marry someone who didn't want to sleep with me, but that didn't mean I needed you to experiment and see if you could—"

"Experiment? For fuck's sake, do you think I planned that out? I didn't plan on getting a hard on when I saw you naked and having the image seared into my brain for all eternity, and I sure as shit didn't plan on practically losing my mind while kissing you in some back alley. Like I said at the time, I don't know why it happened. But it did and since then I—"

"Oh, I remember *that* very clearly. '*I don't know why that happened,*'" I quoted him, effectively cutting off anything he was about to say. "'*It should never have happened.*' You looked horrified. So what the hell are you playing at right now?" I reached blindly for his towel and held it to my front.

"Stop," Beau said, pained. "Just stop." He blew out a breath and scrubbed a hand down his face. "I never said I didn't want to sleep with you."

My mouth dropped open.

"Okay, maybe I said that. But it wasn't what I meant."

I cocked my head to the side. "Oh, this should be good."

Beau took two steps back and leaned against the bathroom wall. Both his hands came up and held his head. It took all my effort, honed over more than a decade, not to let my eyes stray down his taut abdomen. Silk over steel. Was his skin as soft as it looked?

"Gracie."

I growled at him.

"Gwen," he corrected and held a hand up in apology.

I softened my expression. "Go on."

His eyes narrowed. "Wait. Do you *want* me to want to sleep with you? Is that why you're upset?"

"Argh. My God. Don't turn this around. If I wasn't trying to keep myself covered, I'd hurl something at you."

He chuckled but it was brief. "Why did you make me start calling you Gwen that summer?"

"What?"

"You heard me. And why does it bother you so much when I call you Gracie?"

Okay, he wanted to change tack and discuss names, that was fine and far safer.

"Because we were kids when you called me Gracie. It was like I was your big sister, or, or your babysitter or something, especially being older than you. Even though, man, you got so tall so fast and ... and I just wanted to feel like ..."

I felt my blunder before I mentally processed it, in the form of a rising tide of heat crawling up my skin and bringing my heart up my throat. It was all those mimosas I'd had, dammit, they'd loosened my tongue.

Blinking, I sought out Beau's expression. Maybe he didn't pick up on it. I floundered around for some innocuous sounding reason and decided to minimize a partial truth. "At the time," I emphasized, but with a casual tone. "At the time, you were getting all grown up. You looked super hot, and I just wanted to be seen as someone you might be attracted to, rather than your older sister, type, thing." I waved a free hand in the air dismissively. "I thought if you called me Gwen ... never mind. It was a phase."

"And now?"

"Now when you call me Gracie it just feels like—"

"That's not the *now* I mean. I mean *now* do you want me to see you as someone I'm attracted to. Are you sexually attracted to *me*?"

I half laughed. It was a squeak. "What?"

"You heard me."

"Why are you asking me this? Why now? What's the point?"

"If the answer was no, you'd say. I'm going to assume yes."

"God, you're arrogant. Fine! I have on occasion, yes. I mean it's only natural, we've been close for a long time, sometimes things might get blurred, whatever. Why is this all on me anyway?" I was babbling. "I mean, are you sexually attracted to *me*?" I asked as if it was the most stupid question in the world.

And the answer was most definitely, no.

No. Surely.

I'd know.

"Fuck, yes," Beau grated out and prowled closer. "I want to strip that bikini off you right now and bend you over the sink."

Holy shit. My stomach went into free-fall. I backed up, but my butt was already against the sink in question. But I was so shocked at the words coming out of Beau's mouth I snort laughed. I guessed the tension had to escape somehow.

"Damn," said Beau and chuckled, reverting back to the boy I'd always loved. "That sounded way better in my head." But then he shook his head and stepped closer still and took my hands where they were protecting my chest and held them down at my sides.

The towel dropped between us and my bikini top perched precariously, held up by the magic of two extremely alert nipples. Damn traitorous body, I thought, as my breathing got light and fast, my mouth dry and my nether regions achy and ... warm.

Danger, danger, my mind screamed.

I tried to think of something to break the tension or whatever it was that had seemed to highjack our hormones. "I think I can hear Mrs. Potts singing, *There could be something there that wasn't there before.*"

We both let out breathy laughs.

"Seriously, though. There's no animated movie quote to describe what I want to do to you right now," Beau said, his eyes intent on my barely covered breasts, "because it is definitely not PG."

"But ... but aren't we supposed to be looking for a wife for you?" I asked stupidly as Lieutenant Marjorie Smith briefly flitted through my head. I should tell him about that email.

"According to you, I'm on my own with that, right?"

Did I say that?

"Were you planning on retiring our friendship too?" His fingers came up and toyed dangerously with the hanging string strap that would peel the triangle clean off and expose me. "I seem to remember you saying something like that."

"No." I sounded choked and guilty. Because I had said that.

"Liar," he whispered and looked me in the eyes. His were warm, and blue, mischievous and deep. Like a hot spring on the ocean floor.

I licked my lips. "Beau ..."

"So if twenty years of friendship is all about to go overboard, why don't we just answer that question once and for all? Then we'll know."

Why was breathing so difficult? It was a basic human function that should require no thought.

I was getting light-headed.

And confused.

"W-What question?" It came out breathy. I could get a second job as a phone sex operator.

Beau's fingers gave a tug, and cool air hit my damp nipple.

We both stared at it, and I suddenly realized Beau's breathing was struggling as much as mine.

"Christ, Gracie. You're so fucking beautiful. I want ..." He pulled the other strap and my chest was bare.

I wasn't sure who moved first, or what made me throw every argument I'd ever had against showing him how I felt out the window, but I needed that feeling again. The incredible heat of his kiss that had been haunting me all week. I needed his mouth on mine.

The relief was like fresh water after days at sea.

But there was no quenching, the thirst raged on. Just like the first time, there was no gentle exploration—Beau's mouth took, and I gave, willingly.

His tongue slid against mine, and I felt it between my legs in a hot, sharp ache.

I grabbed onto him, clutching tightly, needing more, the sounds coming out of me, practically begging. Our chests met skin to skin, and I gasped into his mouth. Vague thoughts about why this was a bad idea tried to get in, but I was inside a protective forcefield of bliss and want.

Beau's arms clamped around my body, and I was airborne, attached to his mouth, which I wouldn't, couldn't give up.

Within moments I was falling back onto my bed, with Beau following me down. The weight of him settled on me, his hips between my hips. It was agony and ecstasy all at once. His lips had let mine go in the fall and I think the shock of our position hit us both. Beau gazed down at me, breathing hard, his eyes heavy-lidded and dark with arousal.

My body pressed up underneath him, my aching center unconsciously trying to find relief, and he groaned.

"God, Gracie." His body answered mine. "I'm so hard for you. This is crazy."

"Shh. I need you. Like right now."

It was madness what we were doing, but I tried halfheartedly to care and failed spectacularly.

Beau's mouth moved hot and wet down my throat, and I found myself clutching his arms and thrusting my chest forward. His lips trailed toward a nipple.

"Please," I whined.

"Please what?" he breathed against my skin, slowing his journey. His hands roamed over my skin, down my thigh and hitched my leg up so he could press against me. The coolness of my still wet bikini bottoms did nothing to ease the heat. If anything, the contrast made it worse.

I clutched his thick hair in my fingers, urging him lower, pulling him higher. I was a mess, crazed with so much want, that I didn't know what I needed. I growled and bucked him off me onto his back so I could tackle the waistband of his shorts. He landed with a huff and let go of me.

Then I paused, and just because I could, I ran my palms from Beau's shoulders slowly down to the waistband of his shorts.

He sucked in air as my hands got lower.

"Your skin is so soft here, I've always wondered."

"Gracie," he whispered and blinked at me. "What are we doing?"

I bit my lip and tucked my fingers in his shorts, pulling down.

BEAU

*S*he pulls my shorts down and I kick them off. Yet she makes no move to touch me.

"I don't know, Beau," Gracie says, her voice thin. She's kneeling next to me, her bikini top is around her waist, her tits are pert and just begging to be devoured.

My mouth waters. My cock aches. I think if I reach up to touch her, I'll see my hand shaking.

"Do we have to know what we're doing?" she asks. "Let's pretend there's nothing else but this moment, and when we're done we'll pretend it didn't happen. But let's have this. For now. No expectations. No consequences. Just sex. Simple. Surely you know how to do that, right?"

I sit up, sliding my hand across her jaw to her nape, tilting her head back. "It's you, Gracie. It's *us*. There's nothing simple here. All I know is that this is probably a very, very bad idea." I watch disappointment flare in her eyes. "An idea I have no intention of putting a stop to." I lean in and sip at her mouth. She tastes of oranges and cheap champagne. "And if we're just doing this once, I better make it count," I tease.

My hand flicks open the snap on her spine, and I fling the

damp bikini top away. Her tits fill my hands perfectly as I mold and weigh them, thumbs slipping back and forth across the tightened pink buds of her nipples. Her neck arches, her breathing gets erratic.

"You should know," she says, "that I don't orgasm easily. But this feels so good." She gasps as I lower my head and graze her with my teeth, biting down softly, tugging. "So if … I can't or something, you know … it's fine. It's still … good."

"Shut up," I mumble around her nipple and suck it into my mouth.

She giggles and whimpers. "That's good. God, that's good."

"Keep telling me what you like, and you'll be fine." I switch sides. I fucking *hope* she will. We're not even there yet, and I know that no woman's orgasm will ever be as important as this one.

I'm throbbing with need. Cool air on the moisture leaking from me tells me I'm already there, or could be with not much effort at all. It's like I'm sixteen again, getting hard every time I saw Gracie in a bikini. Rubbing one out twice a day in the shower. Ready to go off with a hair trigger. Think of something else, I tell myself.

"God, I love your tits. They are so perfect." Not helping.

"Talking, that helps. Turns me on so much." She pulls my head up from her chest and captures my mouth with hers.

Damn, I love kissing her. But I have goals. One of them is to peel her tiny string bikini bottoms from her body. As the material reveals the promised land, my attention is pinned. "You're bare," I say idiotically.

She nods. "Told you I waxed."

"You didn't say you waxed everything."

"Do—do you not like it?" She begins to press her legs together, but I grab her ankle. And then the other one.

"Don't," I rasp. "You're fucking perfect."

Pressing her legs apart, I pepper kisses up the inside of her thigh. She tastes vaguely of sunscreen and body wash. I want to see every part of her, but I want to make sure she's not embarrassed. "Hey," I pause, and she stiffens slightly, her hand over her eyes. "Look at me. Do you not like this?"

"Beau," she whines. "It's *you*. This … this is so intimate. Seriously, we should just be fucking right now and get it over with."

"Get it over with? Thanks."

"You know what I mean."

"Darling, it's better, down where it's wetter, take it from me," I sing softly and Gwen cracks up.

"You can't sing *The Little Mermaid* to me right now, I'll never be able to watch it again."

"I'm serious though, do you not like this when," the words get stuck in my throat and I force them out, "when you've done it with other guys." God, the thought of someone else in my place right now makes my stomach burn.

"I do. I—but … it's *you*."

"Yeah." My fingers drift up the inside of her thigh and back down. The skin on this part of her inner thigh is like silk. I repeat the motion and watch her belly quiver. "Yeah, it's me. And you trust me, right? I know almost everything about you."

"Apart from this," she says in a rushed breath as I almost touch her then drift away.

"But I want to. So badly." My hand drifts closer, and her hips buck. "I want to explore every part of you and taste every inch. What makes you feel good?" And I really, really need her to come. In a matter of minutes it's become my one goal, and today isn't over until it's happened.

"Tease," she gasps.

"Yep," I agree, happy with my decision to drive her as crazy as possible, and then I stroke her with a feather light touch, not enough to provide relief. She tries to press against my hand.

My fingers come away slick, and my arousal starts coalescing in the base of my spine. I'm dangerously close to just rutting with the sheet and blowing my load. As my fingers work her, getting firmer, getting bolder, dipping inside her, she's gripping the sheet, her head twisting one way and then the other.

I run my tongue up her thigh and she holds her breath. The closer I get, the more she tenses. I decide I can distract her and slip two fingers into her dripping center. She shudders violently, and I settle my mouth over her clit, licking and sucking in rhythmic feather light strokes.

I'm lost.

I'm lost in the taste of her. The feel of her smooth pink skin against my tongue and the salty taste.

I'm adrift in an ether that is focused on every sound she makes, every breath, every shudder, and has no sense of time or place. It could be seconds, it could be minutes, it could be more.

Her hands go from the bedding to either side of her, to my head, and back to the bed. She grabs my shoulders, she pulls me harder and then pushes me away.

"I don't … think … I can…" she groans as I slip two fingers in her again and press them upwards and drag them out. I repeat the motion. Again, and again.

She may not remember me stealing her Cosmopolitan magazines when she was in college, but yeah, I was paying attention. "Shut up," I tell her. "Get out of your own head. You taste fucking amazing and I'm not going anywhere. I'm doing this for me, not you."

And then I hear it, a light change in her breathing, a tensing that wasn't there before. I'd never have picked it up if I hadn't been so damned focused. I don't want to congratulate myself too soon, but oh God, the thought she might be about to come, almost sends me over the edge.

Focus, Montgomery.

I don't deviate once from what I'm doing. I let her pick the pressure as her hips begin to move.

"Oh God. Oh God, Beau," she chants, her voice a low grunt.

I've never heard such a tone to her voice. No longer embarrassed, it's all sex and need, and I know the sound of her saying my name like this will haunt me forever. "Oh … God." Her hips buck and pick up the pace, and suddenly my fingers are squeezed tight as she chases the feeling over the edge. "Beau," she screams my name.

God, I want to feel her orgasm with my cock before it's over. Before I even think, I'm poised at her entrance and I thrust inside.

"Oh fuck," I manage, my eyes squeezing shut. "Gracie." The feeling of being inside her is exquisite. It's tight and hot and where I should always be, and her orgasm is still going on, fluttering around my cock, and, holy shit. "Gracie." I'm an animal, pounding into her.

She grips me tight, holding on to me, saying my name in a whimper.

And then I'm there, the raging tide unleashed and barreling through me, and I'm emptying everything of myself into her.

THINGS RETURN SLOWLY, pricking into my consciousness. The sound of our breathing, the warmth of Gracie's body beneath me, her legs still gripping me tight. I can feel the exerted pace of her heartbeat beneath my own and smell the earthy scent of sex mixed with her body wash.

A feather light touch traces slowly up and down my spine.

I'm still inside her. And it hits me that we didn't use protection. I was so lost in wanting to be inside her, I didn't even pause. I know she's on the pill, but still, we should have discussed it. God, but it felt so good to be bare. So good to be inside her. So right, so intimate. So …

Jesus Christ, I just slept with Gracie.

BEAU

I'm lying on top of my best friend, cradled between her thighs. We're naked.

My whole body tenses.

Gracie's finger on my back stops tracing.

"Guess you're about to have the expected freak out?" she asks.

I lift up onto my elbows and try to relax. "I must be squashing you." Meeting her green eyes, I see amusement and a tiny bit of awe.

What just happened all comes back to me and it gives me something to focus on, other than the fact I just crossed the line so damn far. "So you came, huh?" I can't help asking like a smug motherfucker.

She nods, biting her lower lip and fighting a smile.

And damn if I can't help smiling too.

"Did *you*?" she asks cheekily and I bark out a laugh.

Then I add, "I'm sorry."

She frowns. "What for?"

"I know you're on the pill. And not that you would know this, but you should know I always use condoms. Always. It's been drilled into me by my father and my grandfather since before I knew what sex was."

"But not with me, huh?"

"No comment," I say because how can I explain that I've never in my life lost myself so completely with someone that I wouldn't have been able to say my name in that moment, let alone think about protection. I have no intention of examining why either. It happened, that was that.

I'm sure it has to do with the fact I feel so close her, that the connection had just hit harder. Deeper.

"So what happened to the pool party?" I change the subject. "Changed your mind?" A thought occurred to me. "Shit, where's Derek?" If I wasn't already softening, I would have shriveled. I glance over my shoulder, half expecting him to walk in.

"He cancelled."

"Oh." I feel relief quickly followed by irritation. "Lucky me." I lever myself off her and sit up, reaching for my swim shorts.

Her warm hand settles on my forearm. "Actually, it was lucky me," she says softly. "I'm glad he couldn't make it. I think it would have been the last time anyway."

"Why?" I glance at her.

She shrugs. "These things run their course."

"They do," I agreed.

We look at each other for a few moments. She rolls onto her side and props her head up. Her damp blonde hair has been drying during our wild encounter and it's the very definition of bed head. "You have sex hair," I tell her and pull one of the curls, letting it spring back. "So when we leave this apartment, this never happened, right?" I want her to confirm her rules again. "No consequences. No expectations. That's what you said, right?"

I already know from the clenching in my gut when I think about being inside her, that I want to do it again. But I can behave. I stuffed my sexual attraction for her in a mental box when I was a teenager, I can do it again. If she's adamant it doesn't change anything, I can do that. I need to do that because the alternative, that I might lose her as a friend, doesn't bear thinking about. How we play the next few minutes, the next few days and weeks, could change everything.

I can't believe I was so reckless.

She looks away.

"What?" I ask.

"I think the girls found you a solution. It's in your email. I checked with Derek, he knows her and he said it's a legitimate option."

My throat feels like it has a rock in it. I swallow, and it fills my stomach. I know this is what Gwen wants. For me to marry someone else, not her.

"Why do you want me to find someone else so badly?"

She frowns. "*You* want to. I offered to help. I'm just trying to help you."

"But why?"

"I want you to be happy," she says. "You've been wanting to build boats since my dad helped you build your first Pollywog."

"I still have that Pollywog."

She smiles and her eyes grow distant. She's probably remembering the times we'd go out with a six pack of beer and fish in the creeks until after dark. It drove both our fathers' crazy, but I'd built it myself. It was mine, and they couldn't take it away from me.

"So did us having sex answer your question?"

I must look confused.

She rolls her eyes. "Earlier in the bathroom, you said something about if twenty years of friendship was about to end, we should answer the question once and for all."

"Oh." I chuckled. "You had to know I had the hots for you when I was sixteen. I'd always wanted to know what it would be like between us."

She pulls the edge of the comforter over herself and lies back, covering her eyes with her forearm. "And?"

"And it was amazing. Obviously."

She breathes out slowly. "So is our friendship over then? Is that what finally made you make a move on me." Her voice is flat. "Is your curiosity satisfied now?"

"What? No, our friendship isn't over," I argue. Then doubts crowd in. God. "Is it?"

She doesn't move and doesn't uncover her eyes.

"Is it over for you?" I ask, my chest feeling tight, my deepest fears crowding to the surface.

She shakes her head. "No."

I grab her hand off her eyes. "You scared me."

She blinks and we stare at each other. Her green eyes are luminous, alive, and languid in equal measure. "But, we're both going to have to try hard here not to let it ruin everything," she says, mirroring my thoughts exactly.

"So what now?" I ask.

"Now I really need a shower. You may as well check your email. And we try to forget what happened here."

But now I know what I was missing, and it is going to be pretty fucking hard to forget.

I SETTLE in on Gwen's couch while she showers. It's a colossal effort not to go in there and join her. I mean, do we have to forget about it right this second? The truth is I haven't had enough. What if … I shake my head. *Get a grip, man.*

I replay my decision to come here today. I'd had enough of the weird week and not seeing her. I figured I'd see her with Derek at the pool party, and everything would slip back to normal.

Not once have I thought I might be jealous seeing her with someone else. I couldn't possibly be jealous. The last hour notwithstanding, there is no evidence over the last decades to indicate I would be. Then again, had Gwen ever really had a serious boyfriend? The immediate answer is no. I haven't had a serious girlfriend either. Neither of us have ever really been put to the test.

I guess we really do take up a large portion of each other's lives.

When I got here and she was making that ridiculous excuse about her bikini, she just looked so flushed, and so turned on, and so fucking sexy. My mind had gone there, and I couldn't reel it back in.

Scrolling through my emails, I try to concentrate and ignore the sound of the shower. I see the forwarded email from Gwen and click on it. Lt. Marjorie Smith does seem normal. I decide to send her an email right away before I talk myself out of it. I tell her I think her situation seems like it would suit mine. I explain my predicament and offer to match whatever background checks she needs that I've asked of her so we're both on the same page about the other. I can't believe this is my life. Marrying a stranger, that I haven't even met.

Then I Google Flathead, Montana and the place Gwen's email said offers proxy marriages. I can't believe it's legal, but sure enough, it is.

The shower turns off.

Visions of Gracie's slick, wet, body wrapped in a towel flits through my head. I clear my throat and force the thoughts away. But not before I feel a stab of lust in my gut that almost steals my breath. Squeezing my eyes closed a second, I shake my head. Shit. This is going to be difficult.

I look over the requirements of getting married. For a double proxy where neither of us has to be there, one member has to be in the US military. Done. How is this for real? I forward the website to Daisy, getting her email address from one of the emails she sent me from her account. She's a paralegal, she'll be able to double check the legality.

If it is, I think this could actually work. I wait to feel the bubble of excitement or satisfaction in my gut that tells me everything will be okay, that I could be weeks away from setting up shop, and it doesn't come. In fact, my stomach turns over more and more uncomfortably.

The rest of the emails from applicants aren't even worth the seconds spent speed-reading them. Each one makes me feel worse and worse. After the doggy sexual assault episode the other night I had preliminary phone calls with just two other women and rejected them immediately. Gwen can't accuse me of not trying. That was giving it a fair shot as far as I'm concerned.

"Hey, you want to go back down to the pool?" Gwen calls. "Just deciding whether to put on a swim suit or shorts."

So she's naked. Great. I wince. "What do you want to do?"

There's a long silence.

A silence I fill with wishful thinking of her asking me to spend the afternoon fucking her silly. I mean we've done it now. We've crossed the line. What would it hurt to do it again? And again? I'm so hard, I could hit a home run.

Which is impossible.

I'm never ready to go again so soon. I'm usually out the door, or asleep. But never ready to do it again.

I spread my legs and hang my head between them, careful not to give myself a black eye. Maybe I can get some blood flowing into my damn common sense brain cells instead of it pooling between my legs.

Gwen coughs.

I look up and make sure my hands are nonchalantly covering the rogue part of my body. She's back in her signature denim cut offs and a pale green tank that makes her skin glow and her eyes look like beach glass. Her blonde hair is smoothed into a low bun. I know she does this so her hair will dry straight around her face. I think after seeing it wild and wavy in bed, I know which way I prefer it.

"Uh. Actually, I should probably go down to the boat shop this afternoon," she says. "Dad is still not feeling well."

"Gracie," I start, my voice husky. But I'm not sure what I need to say.

Her lips quirk into an odd smile.

"What?" I ask.

"You're still here."

I stand, and my feet are moving before I realize I've made my mind up. "Yeah," I say and head toward her.

"I didn't think you would be. I thought you'd freak out."

"I *am* freaking out," I say calmly. "I'm freaking out," I take her hand and press it against me, making her breath hitch and her eyes flare, "because this doesn't seem to be going away." I lean down and press my lips to hers.

"Did your grandfather leave you his Viagra too?" she quips.

"Funny," I answer and kiss her again.

"This is a really bad idea."

"Terrible," I agree and slip my hands around her waist.

She clutches my forearms.

"But we've already crossed the line," I try out my argument. "While we're still here today, in this apartment ..."

She blows out a shaky breath and closes her eyes. When she opens them, I see sadness, annoyance, and longing. "No. Beau. Let's not make this worse. We've already complicated things enough. We can pretend we were caught up from all the craziness this week. We can pretend we were motivated by the panic of maybe losing our friendship. We can pretend losing your grandfather has made you crazy. We can pretend I was planning on having sex today anyway."

I narrow my eyes.

"We can pretend I had too many mimosas this morning." She shrugs. "But if we do it again, we're going to have to ask hard questions. And it's going to fuck everything up."

"Did you?"

"Did I what?"

"Did you have too many drinks?" I ask, letting go of her and stalking toward the balcony windows.

"I had a few. I wasn't impaired. I knew exactly what I was doing. But you know what I mean."

"*I* don't. I have no excuses, Gracie. For why I did what I did. I don't even know why I kissed you a few days ago. I didn't plan on it. I swear. And I didn't plan today." I rub a hand down my face. I feel lost, but I can't say that out loud. I feel like I'm on the cusp of making a massive mistake, though there's no clear right or wrong.

"I know." She shakes her head. "I don't have any excuses either," she says, but the words don't ring true.

"*Did* you sleep with me because you were already planning to fuck Derek today?" I don't mean the question to come out of my mouth so sharp. So callous. So angry sounding. But I hate what that thought does to me. The thought she was turned on and I just happened to show up. I look away before she can see anything in my expression. I have to let it go, I tell myself. I'm acting like a suspicious boyfriend. A jerk.

"No," she says. "Of course not."

"Sorry. That was a dick thing to suggest." I grit my teeth, and school my expression before I face her again. "I sent an email to Marjorie Smith."

"Oh." She nods. "Good. That's good. Seems to be a perfect solution."

"If all goes well, we could be married within a week. I had a look around on that website. They do a lot of work for the military."

"A week." She swallows so thickly, I can see her throat move from across the room. "That's, um, fast."

"Might as well get on with it, right?"

"Right."

23

GWEN

I turned the water scalding hot and then ice cold in an effort to ground myself. My body was sated, yet jittery with spent adrenaline.

Leaning against the cold tile shower wall, I replayed the last hour. God, the feel of Beau's mouth on me and the way he loved me with his mouth, his hands ... I shuddered in remembrance, hot and achy all over again. How had he known what I needed to hear? Trust ... and how it was just him, and I could trust him, how much he was enjoying it, how ...

"I'm doing it for me, not you, Gracie." The echo of his voice and his words wrapped around my gut. With those simple words he changed the whole dynamic to mirror our friendship. To my comfort zone. The place where I loved him. The place where he needed me and I willingly gave. Always. It was the same place that allowed me to help him find a wife even though I loved him myself.

In that one moment, he'd loved me too. Beyond the love of mere friendship. But he didn't know and didn't recognize it in himself. Sex had always been easy for Beau. He was so good at compartmentalizing that even though his women-he-had-sex-with category had just clearly blown up the women-I-am-only-friends-with category, *me*, I knew he would reinforce those boundaries and the episode would be relegated to an aberration. There was no way he'd shift his entire paradigm of thinking.

In fact, there was a high possibility he'd finally freaked out and already left the apartment. To be honest, it was why I took such a long shower. But even if he was still in my living room, I told myself, it didn't mean anything. The freak out could happen in hours or days, but I knew it would happen.

I'd seen it happen with other girls, as soon as they started to give even a tiny hint of being serious, he would shut the whole thing down. It was cold and it was absolute. And of course, they mostly always blamed me, though not in so many words.

I turned the shower off and headed into the bedroom. The sight of my rumpled bed made my belly fizz. I called out to Beau, asking about his plans to see if he was still here. When he answered back, I was surprised. Getting dressed, I gave myself a mental pep talk in the mirror to try and keep my guard up out there so I could minimize the effect his freak out and distancing would have on me when it finally came. I was going to have to work doubly hard to get us back on track.

If I could just get him to the marina the two of us could get busy working on the boat, and we'd be back to working side by side. That would help. I texted Penny to let her know I'd had to go in to help my dad and asked her to bring my bag up from the pool. It only held bottled water, sunscreen, and a towel, so there was no rush.

* * *

WORKING on the boat did help.

By four o'clock that afternoon, we were chatting and joking, and things had mostly returned to normal. I said mostly, because it was very difficult not to watch his hands and fingers sometimes and remember where they'd touched me earlier and how they'd coaxed an elusive orgasm out of me. For that matter, if I accidentally caught Beau concentrating on something, his brow furrowed, the pink of his tongue wetting his lips, I'd get a vision of him between my legs, so intent, so focused, even while his eyes had looked dilated and drugged.

Had he felt drugged on me?

Shit. It was like being soaked in gasoline with a lit match hovering near me about to send me up in flames.

Time, I thought. I needed time. Eventually, these memories of how he made me shudder and beg would fade. What wouldn't fade was how those feelings had permanently cracked the seal on place where I kept my feelings for him.

But I would ignore it.

I had to.

I looked up, feeling the weight of Beau staring at me.

He looked away, and I thought maybe I imagined it.

I sang along to Rod Stewart's entire *A Night on the Town* album as we worked.

We ordered pizza and took the two remaining beers out of the fridge in my dad's office.

"His *Blondes Have More Fun* album is way better," Beau challenged.

"That may be, but it's from another decade. You can't compare." I knew better than to tell him he was plain wrong. "You're better off comparing *Foot Loose and Fancy Free.*"

"You totally can compare. They could easily have been written in the same time frame."

"Says you. The sound is not the same. At all."

After the last strains of "Trade Winds," he pressed the eject button and slipped in another tape. As the upbeat but sexy beat began, Beau sang along and pretended his beer was a microphone. "*Mm-mm Sugar,*" he sang the opening and gyrated his hips. "*Mm-mm, Sugar.*"

I giggled. "Stop."

Beau didn't break character. Grooving around the shop, he pretended he was on stage in front of an invisible audience. He got totally into it, shaking his head, making lewd movements with his tongue and his hips.

I tapped my foot along to the beat, smiling and shaking my head at him. "Are you Mick Jagger or Rod Stewart?"

"Beau, baby. I'm Beau, the one and only. *If ya want my body, and ya think I'm sexy,*" Beau sang, trying and failing at Rod Stewart's husky sound, but not caring.

He was being so ridiculous and making such fun of himself, I couldn't stop laughing.

Eventually, I joined him and we kept dancing and singing and hamming it up.

"Give me a diiiiime, so I can call my mother," we sang. Beau slipped an arm around my waist and pulled me against him. It felt like someone opened a shaken up soda can inside my belly.

We finally got to the end of the song, laughing as we whispered along to the ending lyrics. *"If ya really need me, just reach out and touch me. C'mon, Sugar, let me know."*

I risked a glance up at Beau.

He was gazing down at me, his laugh slowly fading into something confusing.

A throat cleared.

"Dad!" I thrust Beau away from me.

My father was grinning as he walked in.

Beau trotted over to the old boombox and punched in the stop button just as the grinding guitar started on the next track.

"Lots of work happening here, I see," my dad said as I kissed his cheek in greeting.

"You know it," I said. "Best way to work."

"Rhys," Beau greeted and they shook hands, my dad squeezing Beau's upper arm affectionately at the same time.

My dad went to his office and changed, and then the three of us spent the final hours of the day working together. As evening fell, I became nostalgic, knowing there wouldn't be any more years of this, the three of us working here together. My nose burned and I blinked, the feeling of wanting to cry coming on too quickly. I glided over to the office aiming for the bathroom. Glancing over at Beau, I caught him watching me again. I knew he was feeling it too, coming to terms with the thought all this was ending.

"Rhys," Beau said, his gaze peeling off me slowly and refocusing on my dad. "Did Gwen tell you ..."

His words faded as the office door closed behind me, though I could make out that he was telling Dad about the marriage to Marjorie Smith and the loan paperwork.

I stayed still. The urge to cry passed, and I listened on the other side of the door.

My dad apologized again to Beau for springing it on him so suddenly, reiterating it was an offer he couldn't refuse. Beau reassured him he understood, and that Rhys didn't owe him anything.

I retreated into the bathroom and pulled myself together. Then I took a deep breath, and went back out to the shop floor.

"Hey," Dad said. "I was just telling Beau I need to deliver this boat by next weekend. Is there any chance I can ask the two of you to take it down to Fripp Island?"

"Next weekend?" I repeated needlessly. I didn't have anything going on, and my dad knew it.

"I can follow in the *Monty*," Beau added, referring to his grandfather's boat. He was the only one of his family to actually use it, and his grandfather had now officially left it to him.

"Sure," I agreed. I patted our current project. "If she's ready, it would be an honor to be the first one to have her on the water."

"I can tell the client you'll be there Saturday afternoon. He's coming down for the weekend. Wants to get his kids out fishing on it as soon as possible."

"There's weather coming in this week," Beau said. "But it should blow through by then."

"Great. It's settled. I'll let him know." My dad wandered back through to the office.

"Thank you," I told Beau.

He frowned. "Of course."

"It's just above and beyond. Especially now."

"It never used to be."

I nodded. Everything was different now that my father had decided to wrap up the business completely rather than letting Beau buy him out or transition into partner. I knew Beau too well to pretend it hadn't hurt him.

My father had to know that too.

Which was what made this whole thing quite strange now that I was really thinking about it.

"I'll close up," I told my dad. "You go on."

"I have to get back to Awendaw tonight," Beau said looking apologetic and conflicted. "I'm working on the house tomorrow, and I want to check on Eileen."

"I'll be fine on my own."

I waved them both off.

As soon as they were out of sight, I ransacked every filing cabinet in my father's office. If he was in some kind of debt or dangerous situation that was making him close up shop so fast, I wanted to know about it.

And if there was some reason he was shutting Beau out, I wanted to know about that too.

24

GWEN

I paced around my condo, avoiding the memories of my bedroom.

My search at the boat shop had turned up nothing in the paperwork that answered my question. If anything I had more questions because there were three orders for boats. Lucrative orders that my father would have had to turn down. But I'd opened my father's email and gone to his sent mail, comparing the dates from the orders and looking for an email refusing the work. There was nothing like that. In fact I'd found one email, letting a client know there was a waitlist and the project wouldn't be started until spring the following year.

Why would my father not turn down the work if he was closing the business? He must be though. He'd let all the staff go. It was hard to find highly skilled boat builders. There was no way he'd have let Jimmy go if he'd had a choice. Was he counting on Beau to take on the work? If that was true, it was thoughtful at least.

My father and I were going to have words.

And not only about that. On my dad's scribble pad next to his phone, I found a message from about two weeks ago to call Isabel

Montgomery back. Now that Beau had to get married, I'd bet she was making sure I didn't get my hooks into him. It was no secret she'd been condescending to my father too. He disliked her immensely. I was so glad he'd never painted Beau with the same brush. That woman knew no bounds. I needed to ask my dad about it and make sure he wasn't upset. She could be a real bitch, and I always felt guilty about it, even though I knew there was nothing I could do about the fact she hated me.

I could at least assure my dad that once Beau married someone, Isabel would have another focus for her judgment.

Entering my bedroom, I stripped for bed and brushed my teeth, refusing to let my mind roam to what had occurred earlier today. But as soon as I crawled between the sheets, the memories of Beau in my bed came crashing over me in waves. I gave in and relived every look, every touch, every feeling. It wasn't as satisfying, but after I'd brought myself to a shuddering release, I was at least able to close my eyes and drift into restless sleep.

I KNOCKED on Penny's door at ten a.m., holding two Colombian coffees from Armand's Deli. It was a hike for me to get there, but so worth it. And I'd needed to walk and clear my head this morning.

The door opened, revealing my bleary-eyed friend.

"I hope it's still hot," I said and thrust the cup at her.

"Thanks." Penny yawned, taking the coffee. Then her eyes suddenly got shifty and she glanced behind her.

"You have someone here?" I asked, amused.

"Mornin' luv," said Euan, striding out of Penny's bedroom. His hair was wet from a shower and he was pulling a t-shirt on and wearing the swim shorts I'd seen him in yesterday.

He came up and took Penny's cup, taking a sip and handing it back.

I didn't realize my mouth was hanging open until he reached over and placed two fingers under my chin and pressed up.

"The legendary British charm. What can I say?" He winked at me, then gave Penny a loud, wet kiss on the cheek. "Bye, luv. And thanks. Great way to spend my night off."

Penny was nonplussed, as if she was piecing everything together and hadn't quite gotten there yet. The penny had definitely not dropped, so to speak.

"Gwendolyn," Euan added with a smirk and stepped past me.

Penny yanked me inside and closed the door. "Omigod, omigod, omigod," she squeaked.

"Yeah," I said. "That was a surprise."

She flopped down on her couch.

Morning light streamed in through her balcony doors. Penny's condo was exactly the same floor plan as mine but flipped. All the finishes were exactly the same. Same cabinets, same carpet. Neither of us had ever painted the walls a different color than the off-white the builder had picked. It was a bit mind-bendy to be honest.

"Any good?" I asked.

She rested her head back. "Actually, yes."

I smiled. "Good. You want to tell me how that went down?"

She opened one squinty eye at me as I sipped my drink.

"I think I need a moment. Hey, you disappeared yesterday. Did Derek come after all?"

"Nope. He cancelled." I grinned.

"Yet *you* are looking *freshly shagged* too."

"Okay, look, I'm telling you because I'll explode if I don't tell someone, but then we need to forget it ever happened, okay?"

She sat up, her feet slamming down on the carpet, looking at me expectantly, excitement gleaming.

I pulled the corner of my lip between my teeth and scrunched my nose. "Beau and I."

Her mouth parted. "You're kidding."

I grinned and shook my head, then my smile faded. "So now I know. And it was …"

"Great?"

"Spectacular. But nothing changed. It can't. I don't want it to. We need to get Beau married so I can move on. I need to move on. Okay? Please?"

"What do you mean you don't want it to change?"

"I don't know. I'm just … we're out of time. I think this Lieutenant Marjorie Smith is going to work out. He'll be married within the week if all goes well. Then he'll have everything he ever wanted. And I'm happy about that. Truly." I sipped some more coffee, focusing on the bittersweet taste. "So happy that he'll be happy."

Penny sat quietly. She either wasn't listening or—

"You are so full of bullshit," she said. "So full."

"So full," I agreed. "It's a big weight to carry around," I deadpanned.

She slowly shook her head side to side. "I can only imagine."

"You have to let this be. Okay?" I begged her. "I don't want you guys getting more involved or trying to intervene. He needs to get his inheritance and this loan, and if you did something to derail him and he somehow found out, he'd blame *me*. I can't be responsible for him not getting this business started. It's bad enough I wouldn't marry him to help him out, I can't stand in the way of him finding someone else too."

Penny reached over and grabbed my hand. "Okay," she said. "I promise."

"And tell Sylvie, Daisy, and Alice too? Not about me sleeping with him, but that we have to step back and let this marriage happen."

She looked disappointed, but nodded. "I will."

"Thank you." I blew out a breath of relief. "So … Euan?"

She covered her eyes. "Oh my God. I know."

"Do you think you'll see him again?"

She turned her head toward me. "He's …" Her gaze drifted off as if she was watching a whole scene in her head. "We had fun. A lot …" her cheeks went deep red, "a *lot* of fun. But he's a player. I doubt it was as earth shattering for him." She laughed awkwardly. "I feel thoroughly used, in the best way. It was an eye-opener I can tell you. Those Brits are dirty bastards." She shook her head and went back to her coffee. "This is great. Thank you."

"You're welcome."

We both grinned into our drinks.

* * *

A FEW NIGHTS LATER, I called my dad at the boat shop to make sure he was there and not at home. He and Beau had been working nonstop on the finishing elements of the boat.

I told my dad I had a date, then I jumped in my Jeep and headed over the bridge to West Ashley. The *Mission Impossible* theme played in my head. Too bad Henry Cavill's mustache wouldn't make an appearance in my quest. I wondered what Beau would look like if he grew one. Probably a bit like Henry. They had the same jaw and the same soft, wavy, dark hair.

I pulled onto my father's concrete driveway and parked under the thick limb of a live oak, the Spanish moss drifting down like a curtain and tickling the roof of my Jeep. The spare key was where it always hid, in a small black magnetic box attached to the metal down spout.

I let myself into my childhood home, breathing in the scent of old wood, mildew, and plug-in air-fresheners, Eucalyptus edition.

The floor was refinished wood, my father having finally pulled up the pink carpet that had been there since he and my mom had bought the place in the early eighties.

My room was now his office, the walls still in soft pastel pink. Mom had painted the wall around the window with green hills and little bunnies when I was five. There was a unicorn and a rainbow too. A long, low filing cabinet covered up a good portion of the lower painting. I wondered if my father felt closer to the memory of my mother in here than he did in their room, simply from being able to see something she'd made.

I sat down in his rolling desk chair and quickly checked the drawers. Then I spun around and made a start on the filing cabinets. The end one was locked as always. It was where he kept our passports, birth certificates, wills, and insurance. I felt around in the back of the desk drawer for the keys, my fingers finding them easily, and then hurriedly unlocked the filing cabinet.

My father had never told me not to go into this drawer. In fact, I knew where the key was because he'd told me where it was.

A file with the marina address of the boat shop was the first thing I saw. My heart pounded and I began to sweat, but I convinced myself I wasn't doing anything wrong by being a bit nosey.

Opening the file, I found a thick, pages long purchase agreement, stapled together. I scanned the document looking first at the hefty price tag. I gasped. No wonder my father hadn't said no. I was almost relieved because I felt like I understood why everything was happening so fast. It was a once in a lifetime lottery ticket. He and my mother had gambled on that property and it had finally paid out. God, I was happy for him. I just wished my mom could have been here for them to enjoy it together. I knew right then, that my father was going to head down to central America and live off coconuts and beer like he'd always joked about doing. To be honest, now that I knew, I was surprised I hadn't seen a For Sale sign in the front yard of the house too.

I almost smiled and then my roaming eyes stopped. I froze on the name of the buyer.

Isabel Montgomery.

GWEN

$\mathcal{J}$ drove past the Montgomery home on South Battery four times, building up the courage to go and pound on that front door and demand an explanation.

By the time I pulled up to the curb in a no parking zone, I was fully fired up at the level Isabel Montgomery would go to to keep her grandson from pursuing his dreams. I knew I couldn't tell Beau, it would break his damned heart to see how close he'd come, and how she'd ruined it.

But I could sure as shit tell her how *I* felt about that. I marched up the stairs and pounded on the front door.

It opened to a tall, scowling man who looked vaguely like Beau but who was very, clearly *not* Beau.

"Gwen?" he asked, his scowl clearing. He was wearing jeans and a button down. Not the menacing suit from the other day at the funeral but still quite intimidating.

"Trystan."

He smiled and held his hand out. "Yeah. This is a surprise. Come in."

"Thanks." I shook his hand. "Is the dragon home?"

"Ah. Not here looking for Beau, huh?"

"No."

"She's upstairs, I'll get her."

I followed him in. "How are you enjoying Charleston?"

"I spent Sunday afternoon out at Awendaw with Beau, grilling shrimp, drinking beers, and pissing off the dock. I'm really taking to this whole Lowcountry life."

I raised my eyebrows. "Sounds like it."

"You should come the next time."

"I don't pee off the dock."

Trystan chuckled.

"Besides, we'll see if I survive a round with your grandmother first."

"What did she do this time?"

"Just trying to derail the rest of Beau's life."

He frowned slightly. "Right. Well, I'll go and get her. Make yourself at home." He motioned me to the drawing room and trotted up the stairs.

I stepped into the high-ceilinged room stuffed with antiques and ballooned silk curtains. I almost sat on the couch, but it looked hugely uncomfortable. Besides, I'd rather be standing when she got here.

"Gwendolyn," her voice came from the doorway.

I spun. "Mrs. Montgomery." She didn't loom as large as I remembered.

"To what do I owe the pleasure?"

"Pleasure?" I crossed my arms and focused on all the righteous indignation that brought me to her door. "I think we can just skip the pleasantries. Why are you trying so hard to stop Beau following his dream?"

Her face remained passive. God, she was good. "Whatever do you mean?"

I rolled my eyes. "Look I know you've never approved of my father and me, but you know Beau has dreams of boat building. You just can't stand all the time he's spent with us, the way he's eschewed your family. It would have been perfect for him to buy into my father's business, and he was so close to either that or starting his own, and you had to go and yank it all away by forcing my father into retirement."

"Forcing him into retirement? I did no such thing."

"And forcing Beau into some quicky marriage out of desperation," I went on. "Why? Why are you acting like such a bitch?"

I froze as the word came out. I'd never used that to anyone's face before. For a second I wanted to take it back, but seeing her lack of response, stiffened my resolve. Fuck her and fuckity resting bitch face. I said it. There.

I lifted my chin.

"Well," Isabel Montgomery said. "Can I offer you a drink? A cup of tea?"

"Excuse me?"

"I'm going to have one. Come and join me." She walked across the room and through another doorway toward where I assumed the kitchen was.

Against my better judgment I found myself following.

"Tell me, Gwendolyn," she asked as she filled a tea pot and set it on the stovetop. "Why is it that *you* haven't joined your father in his family business?"

What on earth did that have to do with anything?

"You like boats, right? You know so much about them. You work down at Sylvie LeClerc's little showroom?"

"So?"

"So why do that and not your father's business?"

"It's different."

"Is it?" She pulled two cups and saucers from the cupboard and two packets of tea.

"Yes," I doubled down. "It's selling luxury yachts with a massive company name behind you. People either can or can't afford them. And I like that they trust in the big name brand. It makes me feel part of something bigger. It's completely different. And it's my own thing. One has nothing to do with the other."

"Oh, but it does. It sounds to me like you don't trust your father's brand?"

"That's not what I said."

The tea pot whistled. She lifted it with an oven glove, pouring the hot water into two cups.

"*Why* didn't you want to work with your father and continue the family legacy?" she asked again.

"I told you why."

She handed me a cup and saucer and motioned me into a small parlor with a couch and chair. It was all done up in pink and green, like Lilly Pulitzer gone mad. She sat on the couch, and I sat on the chair and she waited.

Fine, I thought and shrugged. "I—I always thought Beau would work with my father," I found myself telling her. "That it would be *him* who took it over. He deserves it. He's worked so hard. My father adores him. He deserved it more than I did. He loves it more. Trust me. You should see some of his work." I felt weirdly emotional talking about Beau's passion. His talent. My eyes pricked. "He's truly an artist. He's a master. That's what makes this, what *you* are doing, so awful. He deserves the business. He deserves to have the name of my father helping him. He deserves to have his beautiful creations sailing the oceans of the world. I backed away because I wanted it to be his, and now you're taking it away from him. From both of us." God, I'd never admitted to myself why I'd stepped away from my dad's business. Damn her for making me face it. "Now thanks to your meddling, no one will carry on Rhys Thomas Boatworks."

"You love him."

"My father—"

"I meant Beau."

"Beau? Of course I do," I snapped. "He's been my best friend since we were teenagers."

"I should clarify. You're *in* love with Beau."

I exhaled. Who the heck cared if she knew? She was now one of, like, a gazillion people. There was no way in a million years she'd tell him though. She'd keep it to herself like a dirty secret. "Yes," I admitted. "So what?"

"Then why aren't *you* marrying him?"

"You may have a low opinion of me, but luckily I respect myself enough for both of us. So no, I'm sure you think I'd jump at the chance like the little gold digger you've always thought I was, but lucky for you I have enough self respect not to marry someone who doesn't love me like I love him. No matter what."

Isabel Montgomery snorted. Her lined face split open into a laugh, and I didn't recognize her. I'd never even seen her smile. But here she was laughing at me. And lucky her, she still had all her teeth. "Pride," she chortled inexplicably, almost looking impressed.

I set down my tea cup untasted and stood. I couldn't stand one more second with this cruel woman. As it was I felt like she'd stolen something from me. Telling her my secrets had made me feel vulnerable, like I was going to walk out of here with less than I'd walked in with, and I didn't like it. Now she was laughing at the fact I was in unrequited love with her grandson.

"You should know," I told her, "that even though you've tried to put him in an impossible situation, you are going to fail. He's getting married despite how you've tried giving him an ridiculous timeline, and he'll get his loan. And you won't be able to stop him."

She'd stopped laughing and was listening at least.

"He's marrying some woman he's never even met in a legal proxy marriage. You should be proud of yourself. Nothing like forcing people into loveless marriages for money. But that seems to be the way of all you blue bloods. I just hope for your sake, you've protected your family's assets."

Isabel's face fell and she looked shocked.

"Who?" she asked.

"I'm not telling you and risk you derailing him again."

"That's not—I'm not—oh dear." She reached for me. "Who?" she demanded.

I backed away. "The paperwork is already rolling." Beau told me by text he'd scanned and emailed everything Tuesday morning, I'd promptly gone back to bed, which made me an hour late for work. "He'll be married within a few days. I'll see myself out." I marched back the way I'd come. Trystan was nowhere to be seen, and I was grateful. I'd forgotten he was in the house, but the last thing I needed was for him to tell Beau I'd just harassed his grandmother.

"Gwendolyn, wait." She came after me, slow but determined. She looked so sad, I hesitated.

"Gwen."

"What?" I sighed.

"I don't dislike you at all. I'm sorry you think I do. Wait. No. I'm sorry I've made you feel that way." She amended her words to take on more blame.

"Is this a trick?"

"No. And I just want Beau to be happy."

"You have an interesting way of showing it."

"I've made a big mistake."

"Just one? Never mind. I wish you well, Isabel Montgomery. I hope you don't end up alone."

I left her muttering something about stupidity. Beau's, mine, or hers, I didn't care.

26

BEAU

*T*he days after I leave Gracie's bed are spent doing everything I can *not* to think about making love to her. The scent of her, the sounds she made, the way she said my name. Shit. I feel like the farther away I get from the event, the more I'm obsessed with reliving every single moment of it. And the afternoon right after we made love, at the boat shop, dancing around and singing to Rod Stewart, I couldn't stop staring at her as the realization that everything was changing was hitting me over the head repeatedly and how much I wanted it to stay the same. How much I wanted to keep her in my life.

I think of Trystan's harebrained suggestion about Gwen being in love with me. And it does something in my gut. A feeling I don't like. A longing.

I laughed at him.

I wouldn't now. Not because I think it's true, but suddenly I want it to be true.

What is romantic love, if not a combination of friendship, respect, and buckets of sexual chemistry? I've been avoiding it for almost twenty years, but there's no doubt I'm sexually attracted to my best friend. But even I can't say definitively that I love her. I mean "being in love" is the kind of thing that hits you over the head, isn't it?

But there's no way she'd be helping me find someone if she wanted me for herself, and I find the thought that she doesn't, crushingly depressing.

I spend the day with Trystan on Sunday and get so shit-faced I can't literally think about anything other than puking. I haven't done that since college days and realize at my age can no longer handle the hangover. Especially when all I want to do is lie on Gracie's couch and watch Disney movies and eat delivery food until I feel better. And maybe make her make those sounds again. Have her look at me in awe again, all flushed and panting.

But Gracie is off my menu.

On Monday, I spend the day scanning documents, going past the police precinct to pick up South Carolina Law Enforcement Division reports, one on myself for Marjorie Smith and one on her for me. I email everything to her and to the marriage event company in Montana. I'm going through the motions. I hear more about Marjorie's situation with her brother, and I focus on that when I start second guessing what I'm doing. I call the place in Montana and speak to the pastor. I know I've checked out the legality of what we're doing every which way I can and it's passed muster, but I still need to hear someone tell me. Maybe I'm hoping he'll tell me it's a joke. It's not. He tells me he has Marjorie and me slotted for Friday evening if all the paperwork comes through. It does.

All the rest of my time is spent helping Rhys Thomas finish the boat. I expect to see Gwen in the evenings, but she doesn't show up. On Tuesday evening her father tells me she has a date, and I feel like punching something. On Wednesday evening she can't come because she's going out with the girls.

One positive thing for Gwen that's come from my situation is that she, Penny, and Daisy have become really close. I'm glad she has some girlfriends, but I'm also ludicrously jealous.

I go home that night and watch *Beauty and the Beast*.

My grandmother repeatedly asks me to call off the wedding and not bring a stranger into the family, and I tell her I have no choice.

"You always have a choice, Beau," she says. "I'll cosign your loan."

She's never offered to help me in this way. I've never asked. And I won't be changing that now. I make sure to call Tom Middleton so he knows I don't want Isabel on the loan, in case she tries to put one past me.

Then Trystan comes to me and offers. Apparently, Grandmother thought I might take money from him instead.

The answer is no again.

* * *

THE RESULT of the week is that by the time I'm on the *Monty*, the sea wind in my hair and driving it from Shem Creek, around the Charleston peninsula, and into the mouth of the Ashley River to meet Gwen at the City Marina, I've never felt so despondent and alone.

The feeling of making a colossal mistake is almost suffocating me.

I try to chalk up the feeling as my worry about the weather system moving in, but I know we're ahead of it. We're leaving Friday evening now, having moved the whole trip forward, so we can deliver the boat first thing on Saturday morning and get back up here by the afternoon on Saturday when the weather is supposed to blow in.

Eileen, who's sitting next to me on the captain's chair, her ears flopping wildly and her whiskers blown back, seems to sense my despair. She keeps glancing at me, her eyes full of worry. I've never known a dog to have so much humanity.

She leans over and licks my arm. I smile. "Thanks, girl." She licks me again with a whine.

I look out over the water. Everything is calm. The sun is on a downward trek. It'll be a beautiful afternoon ride down the Inland Waterway. I wish Gracie and I could ride down together, but then we'd have to rent a car to come back and we always love the journey so we try to do it by boat pathways when we can.

What I haven't told anyone is that sometime on the journey down the coast, by myself, while the sun is setting, I'll become a married man.

* * *

AN HOUR LATER, Rhys Thomas's latest boat with Gwen aboard, her blonde hair tucked in a ball cap from the wind and sunglasses protecting her eyes is ahead of me cruising the Wappoo Creek toward the Stono River which will take us the back way around Johns Island.

The radio crackles with Gwen's voice.

"Measuring nine knots. Wind's picked up in the last twenty minutes."

I look at my gauge. "Roger, I see that."

Normally before we did this, we'd plan out our route better, but since we've hardly spoken this week that hasn't happened.

"Do you want to go out to open sea at Kiawah? Or do Wadmalaw and Edisto?" I ask.

"I'm worried about the wind picking up. Makes me want to stay inland."

I pull up the radar on my phone. "Yeah, but I'm tracking a small cell near Walterboro. I don't know where that's going to track out to, but we might be safer on the coastal side. Give us more time to get down there before it swings out."

"Roger that. Let's cut down between Kiawah and Folly. See what this little fishing boat is made of."

"You feeling secure on it?" The engine we put in this week is one of the most powerful available for a boat of its size. It can definitely handle deep sea fishing excursions, so running down the coast should be no big deal.

"Yep, the engine is purring."

"Gwen?"

"Yeah?"

I look ahead to her boat and see her look back at me.

This is fucking awful. Stilted, distant. We may as well be on different planets.

"Beau?"

"Gracie, I fucking hate this," I say.

There's no answer for a bit.

"What do you hate?" she asks, but at least she doesn't correct me over her name. And she seems to know I don't mean the boat ride.

"How can I go from feeling like I've never been closer to you one minute, to feeling like a stranger in our friendship the next?" I ask. I try to feel sorry for referencing what happened between us last Saturday, but I'm not. "Do you think about last week?"

"Beau, don't."

"Tell me it's going to be okay," I continue.

"It's going to be okay," she parrots.

"Is it?"

"I don't know, Beau."

"I've missed you this week."

She doesn't answer.

"Jesus. I miss you every second of every day. I feel like I'm about to lose you. And I can't stand it."

I watch the greenery slipping by. I look at the blue sky in one direction and the gathering clouds in the other. "Can you hear me?" I ask her when she says nothing.

"Roger that," she says, making me smile. Ahead she turns and focusses on where she's going.

My chest is aching, and I run through what I had for lunch that could possibly be making me feel this ill with indigestion. I rub a hand down my solar plexus and try and breathe deeply. "I can't stop—" I cut myself off, then release the button. Nothing good can come from me finishing that sentence.

"Beau?"

"Sorry. Nothing."

I look at my watch. Jesus, I could be getting married right this second. My skin prickles as a wave of nausea travels over me, sweat trickles down my temples even though the wind on the water has whipped the heat away.

My stomach turns over, the ache in my chest intensifying.

I'd never felt closer to Gracie, I'd never felt closer to anyone in my life than I did in her bed. I'd felt like a hero and like a desperate man. It was all the years of our friendship, our love, our respect and our adoration, because I really adored her, coalescing into a singularity. It was bliss and agony at once. The need to love her and please her and take her love in return. I can't believe I'll never feel that again.

I'll be married.

Even if she wanted, Gracie won't ever touch me like that ever again. Real marriage or no, I know how much she respects the institution. Even when her mother died, Rhys Thomas stayed married to her. "I married for life," he'd told me. "I love my wife. That doesn't stop because she's somewhere else waiting for me."

And suddenly I know without a doubt what my gut has been trying to tell me all week. That this marriage of mine will lose Gracie from me forever.

The thought is crippling. I exhale sharply and the wind steals it.

But the realization that comes next almost floors me.

I love her.

I love her.

I'm in love with her.

I am exquisitely, brilliantly, painfully, and uncompromisingly in love with my best friend.

And I am about to be married to someone else.

27

BEAU

'No service' glares at me from the top of my cell phone screen.

We are cruising merrily out the mouth of the Stono River. There's marsh as far as I can see in either direction to the left and right. Ahead is the horizon.

The afternoon sun is making everything glow. The sky looks so blue. The marsh so green. The sea iridescent.

People spend thousands on paintings of this view, and I'm going out of my fucking mind.

The bars on my cell phone are non-existent. Every few minutes one pops up, and my thumbs are a blur of panicked activity.

I have two emails in the outbox trying to go out.

One to Marjorie Smith apologizing.

One to the marriage event company in Montana calling the whole thing off.

I have their phone number and I try to call but it doesn't go through. I even try to send a text to the number on the off chance it's a cell phone and not a landline, but it comes back undelivered. I have no one else's number who can help me.

I am so fucked.

Fucking fucked.

We are about to hit the open sea and I can only hope that once we pass Seabrook, I can get close enough to land for a signal to go out.

I try the radio.

"Gracie, come in."

"Go ahead," she answers.

"Do you have a signal?"

"On my phone? No. Why?"

"No reason."

"Everything okay?"

"No. Not really."

"Beau?"

God, I want to tell her. But I can't over the radio. I need to see her.

And I'm also well aware she may not feel the same way. Trystan's viewpoint was one thing, but he doesn't know her. And there's no way she would have let me get this far without telling me how she felt, right?

Right?

"Beau? You are freaking me out. Are you okay?"

"Fine. I'm fine." My voice is a croak.

My cancellation of the wedding means I won't get a marriage certificate. I won't get a loan, and I won't be able to buy Rhys Thomas' boat equipment.

And I don't care.

The thought I could lose Gracie from my life is so much more agonizing to me that I cannot even understand how I've been so stupid. So blind.

I check my phone. Two bars, thank Christ.

I immediately open my email and the outbox is empty. Please God, let them have sent.

But there's nothing in the sent mail folder yet.

Maybe my server is having a problem updating since there's spotty service out here.

I crack open a beer and down the whole lot in one gulp.

"Congratulations to me," I say aloud, and Eileen cocks her head. "I may or may not be married. And I may or may not have lost the love of my life."

Alone with my thoughts and mistakes and not knowing the fall out of my actions is a humbling experience. Eileen is useless at offering any meaningful advice. But it doesn't stop me from explaining the whole sorry tale to her. To her credit, she's a great listener.

"Gracie, come in, over."

"Beau. Go ahead."

"Talk to me."

"Um. What about?"

"Anything. I want to hear your voice."

"Beau, you are seriously freaking me out. Are you having some kind of nervous breakdown?"

"You have no idea."

"Okay, that's it. We're stopping in Seabrook."

"No, I'm fine. Really. Just talk to me." I grapple for a subject. "Tell me about your date on Tuesday night." God, I don't want to hear about that at all. I wince.

"My date? I didn't have a date."

"Your dad said you did."

"Oh. Right. I told him I was on a date because I was actually breaking into his house."

"Um, I think we have static. It sounded like you said you were breaking into his house, over."

"Ten-four. That is exactly what I said."

I chuckle. "Um. Why?"

"Sorry to leave you in suspense, but have you looked port-side recently?"

I look to my left. Clouds were gathering ominously on the horizon. "Roger. I see them."

"Think we can outrun them?"

"Not if we stop in Seabrook."

"Roger. What about the storm in Walterboro?"

I look to the right, inland, and it doesn't look great either. Sheet lightning lights up the horizon in a series of flashes.

"I'm strapping Eileen down. I think we need to pick up the pace."

"I thought this weather wasn't coming in until tomorrow."

"You and me both."

* * *

EILEEN HATES BEING STRAPPED DOWN and cries pitifully. But the speed of the boat is such that I don't want to take the chance of us hitting a wave wrong. I could hold on. She could not. I'd put her down in the cabin, but that freaks her out even more. She needs to stay with her human in a doggy life vest.

The rain starts as we pass Edisto. The emergency weather radio emits a high pitched alarm with an alert from the National Weather Center who've just issued a small craft advisory. I know this kind of thing freaks Gwen out. As much as she loves boating and being on the water, she panics in moments like this. Normally we're together, and I can stay calm for her sake, even if I too am secretly worried.

"You okay up there?" I radio. "This came out of nowhere."

"I'm okay. We should cut in here and go around the back of the island."

"It will take longer than going through Fripp Inlet."

"It's safer. I need to get off the open water."

"Roger. I'm with you, let's get there in one piece."

The water is dark grey and frothing with white caps. And it's low tide, which means ever changing sandbars around here. At the speed we're going, they are a major hazard.

I know Gracie has to be scared.

"Gracie? I've got you. I won't let anything happen, okay?"

"Roger that, Beau. Thank you."

"One more thing, over."

"Go ahead."

I want to tell her how I feel, but the words seem so inconsequential right now. And what is she going to do with the knowledge anyway? For all I know I could be married. And if I am, she can never know how I feel. She needs to be free to find her own happiness.

"Watch for sandbars," I say. "If you go straight from here, we should be fine. And put your life jacket on."

"Roger that. Already on it."

* * *

IT TAKES another forty-five minutes in driving rain and a churning sea to get around past Harbor Island into the Inland Waterway. Then we maneuver between Hunting Island State Park where we used to camp on the beach when we were in our twenties, to approach Fripp Inlet from the other direction. We almost have to head out to open sea again before cutting into Old House Creek that will take us to the Fripp Island marina. I radio the harbormaster when I think we are close enough. It's best they know to expect us, in case something happens between here and there.

The visibility is for shit. My body is pumping pure adrenaline and my eyes are strained from trying to see through stinging rain to keep my eyes on Gwen.

I can barely see her, and I hope she's going the right way because wherever she goes, I'm headed too. Luckily her life jacket is bright pink.

Eileen is soaked and shivering, but at least she's stopped whimpering. I'm crooning and petting her as best I can while still maneuvering the boat.

Ninety minutes after the first raindrop, we're approaching the marina, and the rain finally slows to a drizzle

Gwen's voice crackles in over the radio to the harbormaster, and I hear him guiding her in.

The relief is overwhelming, but I try and keep it in check until I'm on stable ground.

The water is still rolling even though the rain has let up, so getting tied up in a slip is going to take a few tries. I put every buoy I have out to protect the hull from smashing against the dock and see Gwen has done the same. Then she's coming to help me. She's ditched her life-jacket and her sodden blue t-shirt is molded to every line of her. She's taken her hat off, or she lost it in the wind, I don't know which. Her hair is in wet ropes around her face. Her arms and legs are covered in goose flesh I can see even at this distance. Her lips are blue. And she has never looked more amazing to me.

Eileen yelps when she sees a human she recognizes.

"Poor girl," Gwen cries.

The harbormaster comes too, appropriately dressed in a yellow slicker. "Y'all are lucky to get out of this," he calls.

"Came down from Charleston. It came out of nowhere."

"These afternoon storms always do."

He grabs the bow rope I throw and Gracie grabs the stern. In moments, we're secure and I'm handing Eileen over to Gwen and following onto solid ground. Damn, it feels good.

The harbormaster holds out his hand and I shake it. "John," he introduces himself. "Y'all go up to the Bonito and get yourself a drink and get warmed up and dried out. I'll radio up that you were caught in the storm. With any luck they'll let you bring the dog in."

"Thank you," I tell him.

Then I look at Gracie. She puts Eileen down and straightens. I grab her and wrap her soaking body up in my arms, pulling her close. I just need to hold her. I press my face into her sodden hair, then her neck. Her body shudders against mine.

We stand there, and I don't want to let go.

"Gracie." My voice breaks.

"I was so scared, Beau."

I lean back and then take her face in my hands. Her eyes are half closed, and she presses her cheek against one hand. Her lips are blue and cold, but Jesus, I want to kiss her so much. Instead, I rest my forehead against hers. "I was too. So scared," I admit. "God, you're a beautiful sight. I'm just so glad you're okay. C'mon." I release her reluctantly. "Let's go get warmed up."

"We're supposed to sleep on the boat tonight." She grimaces as she folders her arms across herself with a shiver. "And I can't think of anything I'd like to do less."

Yeah, I'd had enough of the rocking too. "Maybe the sea will be calm later."

* * *

LUCKILY, a call from John nets us a spot inside, in a corner, so we can keep Eileen out of the way and charge our phones in the wall socket.

We do our best to dry ourselves with hand towels in the bathroom, and then we both order a shot of brandy and a dinner of fried seafood and hushpuppies. Wine for her and beer for me. Outside the window, the storm has blown through, leaving us with a spectacular sunset over the creek and marshes.

The world is washed clean and calm again.

"Hey, remember that weekend we came down with those friends from college and stayed on Hunting Island?" Gwen asks, sipping her second glass of white wine. Her lips have warmed, and her hair is drying wild about her face. It reminds me of her sex hair.

"I was thinking of that earlier today."

"When we were on the water just now? I don't know how you thought of anything apart from how not to die." She shudders, but she's laughing.

"I was thinking about you not dying too," I say seriously.

She smiles. "Anyway, we came a couple of times if you remember. Though the time we got a camp spot right on the edge of the beach was the best."

"We woke up and watched the sunrise. I remember."

"Everyone thought we were nuts to get up so early. Why don't we ever come and do that anymore?"

"I don't know. I guess we got jobs, and it seemed less easy to just get away."

"We're here now," she says, then her face falls. "But we don't have a tent."

"Actually, I think I have my tent from the last time. We all came down on the boat, remember I had to beg and plead with my grandfather to borrow it? I don't think I ever took the tent off." But just one tent. It's small. And suddenly I want very much to be in a small two-man tent with Gracie. And Eileen, but that's a small price to pay.

"Sleeping bag?" she asks.

"If I do, it'll just be one."

She bites her lip and looks down at her wineglass, her fingertip following a drop of condensation. I watch her closely. I can't hear, but I think her breathing just got funny.

It lights a flame inside me, and I feel myself hardening. But at the same time it makes my chest hurt.

Jesus, it's agonizing loving someone.

Can I be in a two-man tent with her all night and not touch her?

I think of all the wasted years I've had of knowing her, being with her, falling asleep on her couch together. It's a fucking tragedy.

I suddenly remember Trystan trying to explain how he felt about Emmy the other night. That happened to him after a week. I try to extrapolate that to the depth of feeling and history I have with Gracie, and I'm humbled beneath the magnitude.

"You okay?"

I realize I'm staring at Gracie in awe.

Mentally flailing, I try and make light of it. *"All at once everything is different, now that I see you,"* I quote.

Her eyebrow quirks up. "Okay, Flynn Ryder. You really okay? Quoting *Tangled* and acting all sorts of weird. Come to think of it, you've been weird all day."

"Um. Will you see if you can book us a camp site? I need to check my email."

"It's a long shot," she says. "Those beach sites are booked a year in advance."

"Cancellations happen. Especially with the weather we just had."

I click on my email.

I'm hoping for a miracle on every front.

28

GWEN

I second-guessed my suggestion to camp on the beach the moment it left my mouth.

Beau was about to be married any day now. There was definitely a line I wouldn't cross, even if it was a sham marriage. Beau and I would never be together the way we were last week once he was married.

But who was I even kidding? Even if he wasn't about to be married, I shouldn't have been wishing and hoping for anything, it was a dangerous road. But the truth was, today was scary as shit, and as he gathered me into his arms like he was terrified he'd never see me alive again, it did something to me. It gutted my heart but also turned me on from zero to white hot.

I knew he wanted me again. I could see it every time he looked at me. He didn't realize how his eyes strayed down to my lips. Down my chest. The way his eyes tracked my fingers as they stroked the stem of my glass.

Then he all but admitted it, with that Flynn Ryder comment.

But the question was, could I do it again, when I knew it meant more to me than it did to him?

We were each playing with different currency, and someone was going to be ripped off. He wouldn't mean it, but it would still happen.

But everything seemed to be working out. A beach site had just freed up. And wonder of wonders, Harbormaster John offered to drive us over the causeway to Hunting Island. We bought some bottles of water and a flash light from him as well as a promise to pick us up the next day. We collected our overnight bags and Eileen's food from our boats. Luckily, I'd stowed my bag in the watertight bench seat, otherwise I'd have had nothing warm and dry.

Beau found his tent and sleeping bag, five leftover beers, and two granola bars we'd probably save for breakfast.

"I'm so relieved not be on a rocking boat right now," I said as we struggled to set up the tent in the waning light.

"Me too. I've got this now, if you want to go to the wash house before it gets too dark?"

That was the good thing about camping here, they had a shed with toilets, showers, and running water. The campground seemed deserted, and I guessed the storm, plus the threat of more weather tomorrow had cancelled a lot of camping plans.

I gasped in fright when I saw what I looked like in the cracked mirror. My hair was crazed. Drying in the humid air after an afternoon of wind and rain hadn't been kind. I brushed it as best I could and tied it on top of my head, then took a quick hot shower, using my almost dry blue t-shirt to rid the excess water from my skin. Then I brushed my teeth and changed into a clean t-shirt and shorts. They were my shorts for tomorrow, but I could hardly walk through the campsite in a t-shirt and nothing else. I refastened my hair low on my nape, hoping it would continue to dry more smoothly than it had been.

When I got back to the campsite, Beau had already been to the men's shed. He was changed into a white t-shirt that molded to his muscles and soft jersey shorts.

He put out food for Eileen. She hardly waited for it to touch the plastic bowl he'd brought before she'd gobbled it all down. Seeing him care for that sweet little mutt always made my ovaries twitch. Even if I couldn't have him, I hoped one day, he would decide to have children.

He looked up, and a massive smile spread across his face.

"What's up, smiley?" I asked, laughing at him. "You auditioning for a toothpaste commercial?"

He shrugged and stood. "I'm happy."

"Good." I went to my bag and put my stuff back inside. Eileen totted back from doing some business in the thick vegetation and then curled around into a ball against Beau's bag at the opening of the tent. "She's exhausted." The sound of the waves crashing reached us in the quiet night. "Pity we don't have chairs to go sit on the beach."

"A little sand won't hurt us." He walked over and held out his hand.

Bemused, I put out my hand to his and let him take it and lead me down to the beach. "You gotta see the stars now that the storm has gone."

We stepped out from the tree line, and I looked up and gasped. "Wow."

"Quite something, huh?"

"Incredible," I breathed as I walked blindly forward, my head tilted back on my shoulders. "I could stare for hours."

Beau stepped behind me. His arms snaked around my waist, and he rested me against his chest. He felt good, and warm, and solid.

I dropped my head back against his shoulder, it was the perfect height, and heard his breath catch close to my ear.

"Gracie." He breathed and rested his cheek against my temple.

I wanted to look at the stars, but it felt so amazing being held like this against him that I wanted to close my eyes and pretend I was in a fantasy. The fantasy where he loved me as much as I loved him. I slowly circled my arms around myself so I could hold him and keep his arms wrapped around me. It was indulgent, but today had been scary and I needed this comfort. I wasn't afraid to ask for it. And it seemed he wanted to give it.

He breathed in deep against my hair, and it set goosebumps flaring up across my arms and neck.

"Gracie," he said again. I realized he'd called me this all day, and I hadn't once corrected him.

"Mmm," I hummed. My toes were cool in the wet sand from the rain earlier. The moon was rising, casting a white slash across the black ocean, and bathing us in soft light.

"I want to be free to build big, beautiful boats," he spoke softly. "Or small boats. Fancy boats and simple boats. Boats that withstand a ruthless ocean like the sea today and ones that will do nothing but sit in port and look pretty. I want *all* that. I thought I didn't have the luxury of wanting more than that right now. Except for one glaring thing. And that is wanting my best friend with me while I do it. It doesn't mean anything without you. This week has felt like everything is slipping away ... including you."

I squeezed his arms, letting him know I heard him. To remind him I was there. Still. I hadn't slipped away.

"It's a loss I wouldn't be able to bear, Gracie. I don't want all the other things without you."

"Beau," I started.

"Shh," he said. "Let me finish. I can't believe I thought it all so important."

"It is important," I argued and tried to pull away so I could look at him.

After a moment's hesitation, he let me.

I reached out and touched his cheek. His eyes flickered as I did it, like my touch affected him. Seeing it made my heart squeeze. "You were put in an impossible situation," I added, thinking of what his grandmother did, tears pricking the edges of my eyes.

"No. I made it that way. It doesn't matter if I start right away or wait and start in a year or two. I made it important. No one else." He shook his head. "And I was wrong. So, so wrong."

"What are you saying?"

"That the price is too high, if the price is you."

I licked my lips, as my mouth went dry.

His gaze pinned me. Intense. I was unsure where he was going with this. He was telling me something or asking me something important, but I couldn't hear it. "I—"

"I want to make love to you, Gracie."

My breath caught mid-inhale.

"I want to love you."

His fingers reached out and smoothed across my hairline, and around the shell of my ear, and on down the side of my neck to ring along the collar of my t-shirt. I couldn't draw a full breath.

"I tried to call off the wedding," he said.

"What?" I gasped.

"I don't know if I did it in time. God, I hope I did. But I know you'd never let me love you again. And the thought of that was too much."

"You gave up the chance to take over from my dad, to build your dream business, so you could ... m—make love to me again?" I shook my head. God, didn't he get it? Didn't he get how much I was sacrificing for him to get what he wanted. "Idiot, idiot!" I slapped his chest, and the tears that pricked my eyes earlier, burst down my cheeks. "You need to follow your dream. I need you to follow your dream. You following your dream makes me happy! What was this all for then?" I sobbed.

"My dream is *you*."

"What?"

"Gracie. My dream is you." He grabbed my hand that had hit his chest and pressed my palm against the same spot.

His eyes burned into me. "My dream is you. My dream has been you since I was sixteen years old. I've denied it, I've hidden it, I've ignored it, I've pretended it's something else. I can't anymore, Gracie. Now that I realize it, I can't keep it inside. I've loved you gently, fiercely, painfully, with friendship, and with passion. But I've loved you. I love you. I know you may not feel the same way, but marrying someone else is impossible. You have to see that. I'd rather never have anything than not have you."

I tried desperately to keep up with all the magical things he was saying. I wanted to tell him to slow down. That I loved him too. But then he might stop talking and the things he was saying … God, I wanted to hear them again. And again. For the rest of my life.

"You have to see there's no way I could marry anyone else now. Now that I know what I've been hiding from. I thought I wouldn't, shouldn't tell you how I felt. But I can't keep it inside me." He wiped my tears from my face. "Please don't cry. I'll always be there for you. No matter what. And if you can't find someone to have children with, let it be me. Please. Please, Gracie. Let it be me. You'll be an amazing mother, and you *need* to be a mother. Even if you adopt one day. I'll help you if you need me to. I'll marry you and I'll love you enough for both of us. And I'll be the best father I can be to our kids."

I couldn't breathe. The sobs wracking my chest precluded me from putting him out of his misery to let him know I felt the same way. I couldn't kiss him because I'd quite literally suffocate since my nose was now completely blocked. And he was starting to look at me with concern. Not that I blamed him. I was a mess. A mess who wanted to rewind and hear everything he just said again and again. A mess who still couldn't damn well draw a breathe to respond.

So I nodded.

The love of my life just gave me the most beautiful declaration of love I'd ever experienced, and I *nodded*. Then I shook my head. Then nodded again. Shit. I really couldn't breathe. This definitely hadn't gone anywhere as well as I hoped it would if I ever found myself in this situation.

"Gracie. Jesus. Are you okay? Breathe!"

29

GWEN

I managed one short struggling breath before I passed out, then banged on my chest and pointed at him.

"Like, I want to know what you're saying right now," Beau said as I struggled to talk and breathe. "But I'm afraid to guess."

"You need the Heimlich?" he asked.

I shook my head, inside I burst out laughing, but outwardly I was still a snotty convulsing mess.

"You want to blow your nose on my shirt?" he tried.

Then before I could answer, he reached behind his head and pulled his shirt off, offering it to me.

I grabbed it and pressed it against my face. It didn't help with getting more air, but it smelled of him, and hid whatever ghastly snot-isode was going on during the most important moment of my entire life.

Actually, it did help me calm down.

It also helped calm me when Beau wrapped his arms around me and pulled me against him, holding me while I ruined his t-shirt.

"I love you," I was finally able to say.

"Olive juice?"

"I love you."

"Elephant shoes?"

"I love you!" I leaned back and screamed up to the stars, laughing.

He was quiet, staring at me when I looked back at him.

"I do, Beau—"

"Say it again."

"I'm in love with you. That's why I couldn't marry you. It would have killed me to be some inconvenient wife you'd *had* to marry." I sniffed. Gross. Snot. But I persevered so he could understand. "I said no because you made it clear you weren't interested in a real marriage. You said you didn't want to sleep with me. You even said we could see other people. It would have killed me. I had to save myself. It was the hardest thing I'd ever done to turn you down, and then tell you I'd help you find someone else. But I wanted you to have your dream. I wanted you to be happy."

"Gracie …" His voice broke and my name came out as a whisper. An awe-filled whisper. "You love me?"

I nodded. "So much. For so long."

Now it was Beau's turn to get choked up. He blinked. Then blinked again and shook his head. Then his forehead sank down to my shoulder, his back hunched over as he held me.

I threaded my fingers through his soft hair and kissed his temple.

He turned his face into my neck and breathed against my skin. "I'm sorry I said all those things to you. I'm so sorry I fucked it all up."

"Shhh. It's okay," I soothed. My fingernails gently raked his scalp and he shivered.

"Gracie." His hands were warm as they roamed my back and then slipped under my shirt.

His mouth skated over my skin, against my ear, then down to

my collar bone, driving me crazy and setting my nerve endings on fire.

Hot hands skated up my spine, my bare, bra-less back.

I was consumed by the feel of this beautiful man who loved me. This man who knew everything about me, including all my snot, yet loved me anyway. It was overwhelming.

"Make love to me. Please," I begged.

I'd heard beach sex was a bad idea. Sand in weird places and all that. But we'd been standing, not rolling around. Besides, I needed him too much. I needed him to feel pleasure like I was feeling. To feel my love for him.

I sank to my knees.

"Gracie," he choked as I pulled down the waist of his shorts.

"Wow," I said with a laugh. "Almost knocked me out." He was thick and ready.

I looked up, he was looking down at me, eyes half-lidded. Like he was partly given over to the prospect of me giving him pleasure and also about to just put me on my back and take control. I looked down and saw a small bead of moisture. Reaching out, I slipped my finger over the tip of him and brought it to my tongue to taste.

He growled. "Holy shit," he rasped and leaned down to take my mouth with his. His tongue thrust inside as if trying to take back what I'd stolen.

Then in seconds he was sitting in the sand and he was sliding my shorts down my legs. I stood so he could push them off and then he yanked me to his mouth. "No, Beau. I wanted to—" his tongue flicked between my folds, then flattened out and sucked me into him making me gasp. His fingers gripped the cheek of my butt, and he flipped my knee over his shoulder opening me to him.

I almost lost my balance and had to hold his shoulder and grip his hair. He seemed out of his mind with need, like he wanted to consume me. I didn't even have a chance to get lost in my own head. He was relentless and demanding, and all I could hear were the echoes of him telling me how much he loved me. And all the ways he loved me and for how long, and then he was pulling me down astride him.

"Gracie," he said reverently right before he pulled me down onto him. He was hard and unyielding as he drove up into me. "Gracie, Gracie, Gracie."

My heart pounded. I held his head to my chest, kissing hair, his forehead. The feel of him inside me, filling me, knowing how much I loved him, there was nothing like this. I could never have guessed what it felt like to truly make love. To be made love to like this. With this kind of desperate need. I wanted to feel every second, every slide, every inch. I wanted him so much. I wanted more. But I didn't want it to end.

He slowed then, tilting his head up to me like he knew what was in my head. His eyes roamed my face.

I kissed his cheeks and his eyelids.

He gathered me close, his hands caressing down my back, up my sides pushing my t-shirt up, and then he was leaning me back and flicking his tongue over my nipple. "Good. That's good." I gasped. His teeth scraped gently and I shuddered. He switched sides, sucking softly but firmly. It was as if I felt it between my legs. I arched for more and he gave it.

My hips were moving, sliding back and forth languidly. His fingers dug into my hips and he forced me down harder, held me so he could thrust harder.

I gasped.

"Touch yourself," he whispered. "Please."

I hesitated, but slipped a hand between us, two fingers sliding over my damp and swollen flesh, trying to find the perfect spot.

His eyes strayed down, and his breath hitched, his lip catching between his teeth.

Down my back I felt his hands roam, over my butt, between the crease. I shuddered.

His breathing grated. "Gracie." He looked up at me. "Can I touch you there?"

My skin grew tight. Too tight for my body. I nodded, nervous. Goosebumps broke out in ripples across me.

I looked into his eyes and he watched me unflinchingly, and it all coalesced.

In seconds, too soon, I was drawn tight, cinched into exquisite agony and then flung and spun apart.

My eyes closed, even when I tried to keep them open, and a cry tore from deep inside my chest.

"Oh God," Beau growled and held me tight, bracing me against the force of his thrust.

Then his head was buried against me, his body shaking. I held him still as he rode it out, still riding the pleasure myself. I pressed kisses to his head, his hair, his face when he lifted it.

"I love you, Beau."

"I love you too, Gracie." He blinked up at me slowly, and wiped my cheeks of fresh tears I hadn't even felt sliding down my cheeks with the magnitude of what was inside my heart. "Whatever happens," he whispered. "I want forever with you, and I'll do whatever it takes to make it happen."

WE FELL asleep on a spread open sleeping bag inside the small tent, wrapped around each other, Eileen curled at our feet like a furnace.

I hadn't forgotten what Beau had said about being unsure if he stopped the wedding in time. I couldn't help but feel terrible for Marjorie Smith and her brother. She'd been so close to a solution, and if she'd filed paperwork with her superiors and then pulled it and then did it again with someone new, Beau could have really messed everything up for her.

I made a decision then and there to follow up with her and see if I could help her.

I awoke with the first bird chirp in the morning. Leaning up on my elbow, I looked at Beau's sleeping profile, his features relaxed, his eyelashes resting against his cheekbones, looking all sexy and shit. He had light stubble across his jaw that made my fingers itch to reach out and feel. His brown hair was mussed and curled, reminding me how much time my hands spent in it—raking, clutching, grabbing and smoothing. His bare chest rose and fell, and I resisted the urge to lay my cheek against it to feel his skin and hear his heart.

Eileen was still curled up. She opened an eye then pretended to still be sleeping. She was not a morning person. From the pale light I could see filtering across the tent, I figured sunrise was moments away.

Sunrise!

I nudged a sleeping Beau.

He was snoring lightly, and in his sleep he rolled toward me. Feeling someone next to him seemed to slightly rouse him, and he immediately hauled me against him, caging me with his arm. He let out a long contented and rumbling sigh.

I decided to be more proactive about his consciousness and, slipping from his arm, rained kisses down his torso until I reached my goal.

Ten minutes later, a satisfied Beau was sitting next to me on the beach, and I was smirking with pride. The air was already humid. We ate a granola bar each and sipped cool beer for breakfast.

Eileen hobbled down to join us.

The sun pierced the clouds and climbed slowly out of the water, casting shards of light toward us.

When I'd looked my fill, I turned to find Beau staring at me. "I can't believe I almost lost us," he said. "Can you forgive me for being such an idiot?"

I took his hand, and our fingers threaded together. "Of course," I told him. "And you're not an idiot. *You are my greatest adventure.*"

He grinned. "Thanks, Mrs. Incredible."

"Um, that's Elastagirl to you."

And then another idea began to take shape, and the more I thought about it, the more excited I became. I tried to school my expression.

I had some calls to make, emails to write, and texts to send.

BEAU

*N*ot knowing if I'm a married man or not has to be up there with one of my life's most peculiar moments.

As soon as we make it back to Fripp Marina, I check my phone. The service is still for shit, so I have no high hopes I'll get my emails, but there are no texts either. The man who bought the last ever Rhys Thomas boat is nice enough. I can tell he's a bit miffed Rhys didn't deliver it himself. But I show his two young boys all the features—the rod holders that were custom made, the USB ports, the slide out laptop desk, the speakers, the removable liners of the two coolers, and eventually he forgets to be upset.

I give him my number in case he needs anything refinished or fixed, and then I meet Gracie back on the Monty. She elected to wait for me there, citing some urgent need to get online, though I'm sure she had as much luck as I did earlier. We set out by ten a.m. and retrace our route from yesterday. It's calmer today, even though I know there's more weather scheduled for later. It looks like it blew to the north though. As we pass Kiawah, my phone pings with several incoming texts and emails.

My insides whoosh with nerves. Gracie whips to look at my phone, then our eyes meet.

"Hey, listen," she says. "Before you check anything, I need to tell you something. I went by my dad's place last week—"

"When you said you broke into his house instead of going on a date?" I joke.

Her nose scrunches, but she doesn't smile.

"Okay, what?"

"You know how last night, I said I didn't blame you for getting into this marriage thing because you were put in an impossible position?"

"Yes?" I draw out the response, not sure where this is going.

"Well, it was done on purpose."

"What do you mean?" My eyes narrow.

She licks her lips, her green eyes looking pained. Her fingers come up and squeeze my hand.

"Gracie."

"Look, I can't stand to hurt you. But by telling you this, it's impossible not to. You need to know because it's going to come up, and I know about it. And I don't want you to think I knew and didn't tell you. But I did know. I found out. So I know. And now I'm telling you." Her run on sentences cause her to run out of breath. But by the concern she's demonstrating, I know I'm really not going to like what she has to say. "You need to know," she reiterates.

"Gracie, please tell me. I can cope with anything as long as it's not anything to do with you not loving me."

"I love you," she says. "Always. Here goes. Your grandmother was the one who bought my dad's building. Who forced him to close within one month or the deal expired."

That was *not* what I was expecting.

"She offered him a stupid, *stupid* amount of money. He couldn't say no. He really couldn't."

"Why—" I swallow heavily. "Why would she do that?" My thoughts career. "When?" I croak.

"Right after your grandfather died. Before the funeral."

"Do you think she knew what was in the will?"

"Yes, I do." She nods. "Maybe not specifics. I think she thought you were about to inherit and would buy into Rhys Thomas, and she moved quickly to take that option off the table."

The pain in Gracie's eyes takes my breath. Her pain is for me, which is truly humbling.

I'm shocked at this assessment too, of course. I shake my head. "There's no way. She wouldn't do that."

"Beau—"

"No," I snap, and Gracie recoils. "Shit. I'm sorry." I grab her hand as she removes it from me. "I just mean I've spent time with her recently, and I don't think she did this." She *can't* have. The way she spoke with me about wanting me to follow my dreams. It makes no sense. I tear my gaze away from my best friend and stare out at the blue horizon while I replay the conversation in the kitchen less than two weeks ago.

"Well, I've spent time with her too."

My gaze snaps to hers, and she nods.

"I went to see her the same night I found the paperwork. To confront her," she adds. "You can ask Trystan, he was there, I—"

"What did she say?"

"Well, she didn't deny it. And Beau, I saw the documents with my own eyes."

I suck my lips between my teeth and scowl ahead.

Inside, I feel cast adrift as if everything I once believed in is awash at sea. But I have to remind myself, I was always a prisoner in that family. And I stayed. Trystan left, but I stayed. And there were many times I was a willing captive.

I love Charleston.

Love this salty, sultry, sticky part of the world.

Love the quirky characters that you can love and hate.

Love the brackish waters and the green marshes.

Love the dilapidated plantations and the splendid ones in equal measure.

Love the slave cabins preserved for us all to remember how far we've come.

Love the Spanish moss draping from the trees that is neither Spanish, nor moss.

I've never wanted to leave.

And working with Gracie's dad, Rhys, has given me more than I ever would have found on my own. Not least of all his daughter.

I love his daughter. God, do I ever. Now that I see it, it feels like my chest is unraveling at the speed of light, trying to let the whole universe in.

Swallowing thickly, I realize I will have to explain everything to Rhys Thomas. Explain my intentions toward Gracie and hope I don't seem like the buffoon I've clearly been. The thought of proving myself to Rhys is far more terrifying than a misguided old woman who's tried to derail a plan that I've realized isn't that important anyway. Not in the grand scheme of life and love.

I smile.

Then I laugh.

Gracie frowns at me, confusion swimming in her jade eyes.

My laugh gets deeper, and I lean forward and take her mouth with mine. The taste of beer lingers, along with her mint chapstick. I'm drunk on her. "You know how last night, when I said none of it mattered without you?" I ask when I release her mouth.

She blinks up at me.

"That's still true. What Isabel did or didn't mean to do, or why, doesn't matter, does it? Even if it did put me in panic mode where I made some hare-brained decisions," I concede at her incredulous look. "There are things I am unbelievably grateful for. One is you. And the other, is, well, … you. And the fact your dad got a retirement payout he more than deserves."

"But—"

"Hey. I'm going to do it anyway. I'll build boats. It may take longer. But I *will* do it. Maybe you'll help me." I catch the speculative glitter in her eye. "Maybe you won't. But you'll *see* me do it. And Isabel can be happy for me. Or not."

Gracie's mouth quirks, and she's fighting a smile. "That's good," she says finally. "I'm glad."

We are less than a mile offshore, about to turn in between the barrier islands of Kiawah and John's Island, but there's not a vessel near us. I pull the throttle slowly toward me, slowing the boat.

I won't be able to drop anchor, or just drift, we're too far out, but … "Hey." I snake my arm around Gracie's waist and pull her so she's standing between my legs. I kiss her deeply.

"Just get us back home," she manages two minutes later, when it's clear if I go on much longer we may end up on the evening news, either because the coastguard caught us *inflagrante* or because we are officially missing persons who let their unmanned boat get pulled out to sea and got lost.

"Roger that," I say and push the throttle forward.

The emails are waiting for me, I know. But right now, I feel like I'm holding a lottery ticket and if I check the numbers I might realize I lost.

* * *

WE PULL into Shem Creek and glide up to the dock my grandfather bought several years ago where the boat lives during the summer months.

Gracie's dad is pulling into the gravel parking lot in her Jeep, having timed our arrival perfectly. So much for a goodbye kiss.

"How'd it go?" he calls.

"Great. He's a big fan," I tell him, climbing off the boat with Gracie's bag.

Gracie catches my eye and smiles as she sets Eileen down to do her business.

"You two patch things up?" Rhys asks.

"I didn't realize there was an issue," I deadpan.

He raises his eyebrows at Gracie.

She shrugs and avoids my eyes in front of her dad. "Whatever. Good to see you, Beau. Enjoy the rest of your weekend." She bends. "Bye, Eileen, my sweet booooboo." Then she slings her bag into the Jeep and hops in.

Damn that girl.

I grin like a maniac and pull out my phone.

You're in so *much trouble*

I see her Jeep pull to a stop at the end of the marina road.

Gracie: *Bring it on, sailor.*

Can I see you later?

Gracie: *Maybe ... ;)*

Her Jeep pulls away.

My truck sits waiting for me. Eileen is wondering if we're headed home. But I have full cellular service, and I need to look at my emails. I can't put it off any longer.

Worst case scenario—Marjorie and I get the marriage annulled. But Gracie is going to feel like everything between us is sullied. I know her. I *know* that's how she'll feel. She may not be a regular church goer, but she was brought up Catholic. And not only that, but Marjorie needed someone to help her out. For good reason. And now I'm pulling out of the deal.

There's no clean way out of this.

Get it over with, Montgomery.

I sit right down on the dock in the blazing sun and open my emails.

There are three emails from the marriage event company in Montana, two in response to my frantic email yesterday and one originated from them with the subject line: *Please confirm urgently.* The time stamp doesn't help. I don't remember when I tried to email them or even what time my emails finally went through.

Below their first email is one from Marjorie. The subject line reads: I'm sorry.

My heart pounds, and I click open the first email.

* * *

I RECEIVE what I think is the best possible news, that Marjorie postponed the wedding. At around the same time I was having a nervous breakdown out at sea, something had caused Marjorie to do the same thing and call off the wedding. Apparently, there were questions about whether we knew each other in real life, and she couldn't go through with the lie.

The relief that surges through me, almost makes me light-headed like I narrowly missed being hit by a bus.

I immediately text Gracie and ask to see her.

GRACIE: *I can't see you until Wednesday. I'm so sorry!*

THE TEXTS BEEPS THROUGH, and it feels like a kick in my stomach. I'm so damn confused.

She can't see me? Or she won't?

Doesn't she want to know whether I'm married or not? Uncertainty slithers through me.

Are you mad at me for some reason?

GRACIE: *Mad? Of course not.*

Okay. I miss you.

GRACIE: **Smiley face* I miss you too. I'm so sorry I'm so busy.*

THIS FEELS BIZARRE. But I remember how much I didn't pick up on her moods when I got my news about the inheritance and asked her to marry me. As much as I know my best friend, it's definitely become clear to me there's a whole side to her she's able to keep hidden.

Either that, or now that I'm in love, it feels like my chest is flayed open and vulnerable to every slight, both real or perceived.

Dammit, I feel like my chest would ache if the wind blew wrong.

Why do people look for this their whole lives? I don't get it. It's uncomfortable as shit.

Are you having second thoughts? About us?

GRACIE: *No! I mean, are you?*

. . .

NEVER. *But I need to see you.*

GRACIE: *I can't. Will you trust me?*

* * *

ON SUNDAY, I go to Alice's on my own. I chat with Euan, who asks me if I've seen Penny. "Penny?" I ask.

"Yeah. Penny who lives in Gwen's building."

Oh. "What about her?"

"Nothing, man. Nothing. Forget I asked." He sticks a tooth-pick between his teeth and wanders down the bar.

"Where's Gwen?" Alice asks.

"Busy. I think. I don't know. Have *you* seen her?" I tack on hopefully.

She shakes her head. "No, actually. But according to Sylvie, they've been crazy on Mr. Canopolis' boat."

Mr. Fuckopolis.

"We took up so much time last week at find-Beau-a-wife-central," she goes on, oblivious to my scowl. "She's probably catching up. Sorry that wedding thing didn't work out, by the way."

I frown at Alice. "I'm not. You do realize I'm in love with Gwen, right?"

She smiles wide. "I do. It's just so damn good to hear you say it. Especially since I've known how she feels about you, for like—"

"Fucking ever," Euan chimes in.

I drop my head and bang the bar top. "And why didn't anyone tell me?"

"You weren't ready," says Alice with a shrug.

I raise my head and glare at Euan. Surely guys stick together on this kind of thing.

He takes the toothpick out of his mouth and points it at Alice. "She's right."

"It's fucking miserable," I moan and drop my head back down.

Alice cackles.

I miss Gracie so much. Sunday is our day. Sunday evening is our evening. I glance over at the pool tables. We should be doing that.

But we're not.

BEAU

*T*he next two days are agony. And about fifty times a day, I have to talk myself out of calling Gracie and just demanding to see her. There is no boat to work on to keep my mind occupied. I tinker around on a project at Awendaw. I text Trystan and check in on three of the projects I was working on for Montgomery Homes and facilities, but he assures me they are being handled and thanks me for organizing them so well because they are the only projects worth pursuing at the moment.

My grandfather would be proud. I grimace.

I'm very definitely avoiding my grandmother, though. That much is clear. She has summoned me for dinner on South Battery and left "umpteen" messages on my phone. The truth is, I'm annoyed she was right that I should have called off a marriage to a complete stranger, because seriously, *what in the actual fuck was I thinking?* And I'm even more annoyed about the fact she's bought Rhys Thomas Boatworks and has yet to admit it. Though to be fair, since I'm avoiding her, she hasn't had a chance.

On Monday, I step out onto the wide porch of the plantation house at Awendaw and I call Rhys Thomas.

"Beau, my boy. I miss you around here. You want to come and help me pack up the shop? Jimmy and the guys just got down here to help for a couple of days, I'm sure they'd love to see you."

I clear my throat. "I'm sorry I'm not there." I squint into the canopy of live oaks, hoping he can hear the sincerity of my statement.

"Eh, it's fine. So to what do I owe this call?"

"I'm in love with your daughter, sir," I throw it out of my mouth before I second guess myself. "And I don't know when, but I'm probably, at some point, going to ask her to marry me. I wanted to ask you in person, but on the off chance I see her before I see you, I wanted you to know." I drag in a quick breath and rush on. "I may not ask her, I probably won't, because I don't want her to think I'm just doing it because I need a wife. But I'll want to. In fact, I may not ask her for years," I fib. "But just in case. I'm sorry it's taken me so long to realize how I feel about her. But please know, I've always thought she was amazing. Always had the utmost respect—"

"You have my blessing."

"Sorry, what?"

"You have my blessing. I don't know what took you both so long. Been watching y'all for nigh on twenty years. But don't make me wait much longer, okay?"

My breath is caught in my chest. "Thank you, Rhys. Your blessing means a lot."

"You've always had it, Beau."

"Thank you, sir." I take a moment to compose myself. "You heard from Gracie?"

"She's here right now. You looking for her?"

My heart pounds. "I am. Can I have a word?"

"Sure. Hold on. She was just talking about inviting you out on a date." There's a muffled sound. "Gwendolyn Grace Thomas," I hear Rhys yell. "Phone for you."

I pinch the bridge of my nose while I wait.

"She says she's busy. But she'll text you."

"She—"

"Bye, Beau."

The phone goes dead and I stare it. What is going on right now?

GRACIE. *I'm freaking out. You avoiding me?*

GRACIE: *No. Kind of. I was avoiding leading on a married man.*

I'M NOT married

GRACIE: *I heard*

AND?

GRACIE: *Can you trust me just a little longer? And, I have truly been busy. I'm sorry. But also, I was thinking ... we've done everything backwards. I want to go on a date.*

I BARK out a laugh borne of relief. Jesus. If she'd just pick up the damn phone or read my texts I would date the shit out of her. I would take her out for breakfast, lunch, and dinner. Instead, I type:

YOU KNOW how bad I am at dating right?

. . .

GRACIE: *Beau*

I CAN ALMOST SEE her roll her eyes, and it makes me grin.

A BIT hard to date when you're avoiding me. Can I take you out to dinner tonight? Please?

WHAT I REALLY WANT IS TO crawl into her bed and wrap myself around her.

GRACIE: *I'm busy tonight. I do have plans for us on Wednesday evening though. It's a bit fancy. Do you have a suit or tux? I'll text you the details.*

I BREATHE OUT.

Eileen sighs too as if she can sense that my entire being that's been strung tight for days, has suddenly begun to uncoil.

THAT'S TWO DAYS AWAY. I miss you. God, I sound so pathetic right now.

GRACIE: *No, you don't. I'm glad you miss me. I miss you too. This has been agony for me too, but it will be worth it, I promise.*

I DON'T KNOW what Gracie is doing, or why, but I close my eyes and relive the moment she told me she loved me. I believe in her love down to the depths of my soul. And I know I'd wait for her as long as she needed no matter how much it was killing me. But, if she's going to make me wait another two days to see her, and wants me in a suit, I'm going to give her a damn suit. And I'm not wearing the same one I buried my grandfather in.

I drive into town and visit Berlin's on King Street. They tell me they'll have a suit ready for me by Wednesday lunchtime. It'll fit me like a glove. She's probably dragging me out to one of those fancy cocktail parties on a mega yacht Sylvie makes her do for work.

Sylvie tells Gracie it's because they need to network with potential clients, but Gracie tells me it's because Sylvie's looking for a husband. Gracie always brings me along so people don't hit on her, and I like to go because I nose around the boats, looking at all the bells and whistles and get inspired in my own designs.

But after that work function, I'm going to take her out for a proper date. I'm going to wine her and dine her and then take her home and make love to her all night long.

I drive up to Summerville and visit my mom and tell her about Gracie. Of course she's ecstatic, she adores Gracie. Then despite my protestations, my mom tries to make me take her engagement ring from my father. I don't have the heart to tell her I'm not planning on marrying Gracie just yet. I need some distance between my life with Gracie and this whole inheritance and fake marriage fiasco. I'd hate for Gracie ever to think for even one second I was marrying her because I had to. What I don't do is go by the boat house to help Rhys. I know I'm avoiding going to the place I basically lived while growing up.

* * *

ON WEDNESDAY AFTERNOON I head into town and swing by grandmother's, but she's out. Trystan is nowhere to be found either and isn't responding to texts. He's not at the office nor the house. Though I think he might be with Emmy since he's finally convinced her to give them a shot. I stop in at a cafe Gracie loves and do some more tweaks to my business plan. At four I text Gracie.

WHERE SHOULD I MEET YOU? *Should I pick you up at your condo?*

GRACIE: *I'm helping Dad right now, I'll change there, so meet me at the boat shop around 7?"*

I COLLECT my suit which is pale gray and head back to the house on South Battery to shower and shave. Grandmother isn't home, but clues in the kitchen and the smell of her floral perfume tells me she's been home since I popped in earlier and gone out again.

I pair my suit with a white button down and for once in my life comb my hair.

All the preparations I'm making for a date with my best friend make me painfully aware I'm nervous as shit. It's Gracie, I remind myself. No big deal. But in the intervening days since our amazing night on Hunting Island, the whole thing is starting to feel like a dream. She's been so elusive since we got back, I can't help part of me thinking maybe she's second guessing our leap into this new territory.

* * *

IT'S STILL over eighty degrees at about six-forty-five that evening. I look for a spot in the city marina parking lot, which is a feat since it seems abnormally busier than usual. Finally, I wedge my truck up against the chain-link fence at the end of a row since I don't have a passenger who'd need to climb out. I slip on my suit jacket again, cursing the kind of event that would make someone wear a suit in this heat.

I pass Alice's truck and wonder if she's down here visiting Gracie or Rhys. Looking up, I see her down near the boat shop, her blonde hair up and in a pink dress. It's a bit of an effort to go to, but maybe she has the hots for Gracie's dad. Though I don't know who would have the heart to tell her he was still in love with his late wife. I wave, and she must not see me because she turns and darts back into the boat shop. Weird.

Approaching the boat shop, I grab the door handle and haul open the metal door. Eileen comes hopping out to me through the opening.

What on earth? "Hey, girl," I croon and crouch down to her. I frown, knowing I left Eileen out at Awendaw this morning. "What are you doing here?"

She has a ribbon around her neck with a piece of paper rolled up.

I slip the paper out of the loop.

Beau
Will you marry me?
Say yes,
All my love, Gracie

My breath catches, and I look up.

Rhys Thomas opens the door. "Well?" he asks with a grin. "She's in here waiting for an answer."

Getting to my feet, my chest feels tight. Marry, Gracie? In a heartbeat.

"Yes. So very obviously, yes."

Rhys pats my shoulder, then pulls me into a hug. "C'mon in."

It's dark inside after the bright sunshine, and I blink several times to adjust, but then suddenly lights blaze on, strung from every rafter and every corner, lighting up the whole space. And there are people everywhere, taking up all the space that used to house the boat and boat lift. Trystan strides forward in a suit, and I realize Rhys is wearing one too.

"Congratulations on your engagement, Beau," says Trystan. Behind him I see various friends. My mother. God, my mother is here with my stepfather. My eyes immediately seek out my father to see if they are in the same room. And he's here in front of me, shaking my hand. Grandmother's here. Wait, Isabel's here?

I'm so damn confused as to what is going on right now. My collar tightens and I begin to sweat. Where the fuck is Gracie? "Where's Gracie," I ask Rhys between greeting people, my eyes scanning left and right. He says he'll go find her, and disappears.

Alice. Penny. Euan. Jimmy who used to work here. Sylvie. Even our housekeeper Magda and her husband Jeremy. My sister, Suzy who I haven't seen in weeks is hugging me and whispering in my ear how happy she is, and she can't believe I didn't tell her. There are the Rathbuns, the Ravenels, the Middletons, the Maybanks. People I've known my whole life, including Father Peter. Weird. There's music playing. We've somehow managed to move toward the back of the warehouse.

I grab Trystan. "Tell me this isn't an engagement party without my fiancée. Where the hell is she?" My panic is climbing to epic proportions.

"It's not your engagement party," he says, an eyebrow cocked.

The music changes and goes up several notches. The throng of smiling people start splitting into two and forming a walkway. As the last person steps aside my heart crashes through my chest.

Gracie is standing at Rhys' side, her arm through his. She's in a long cream gown, and her hair is up with a large white flower. Speaking of flowers, she's holding a bunch of flowers. And she looks so beautiful smiling at me from across the room, my throat closes up.

"Breathe," Trystan says quietly at my side. "Seriously. Now is not the time to pass out. By the way, I'm your best man. I hope you're cool with that?"

I tear my eyes from Gracie and blink at him, realizing I'm standing with Trystan at my side, Father Peter just behind me, and holy shit, I'm in the middle of my wedding.

32

BEAU

*G*racie is beautiful as a bride. I take the deep breath, that Trystan prescribed and then burst into a chuckle. I shake my head in disbelief that Gracie has just pulled this off.

She can't get to me fast enough, and I practically wrestle her away from Rhys, making everyone laugh.

"Hey," I whisper, looking down into her green eyes that look liquid under all the lights and emotions swimming in their depths.

"Hey, yourself."

"The answer is yes, by the way. Yes, I'll marry you." That earns a chuckle from the gathered group.

"How do you spell love, Pooh?" Gracie asks me.

I mash my lips together as if I can stop myself grinning so much, but it's impossible.

"You don't spell it, Piglet. You feel it." My mouth descends toward hers.

"Whoa there," interrupts Father Peter. "Ahem. We didn't get to that part yet."

"He's always been impatient," snaps my grandmother, and

everyone is shocked into silence before someone snorts a giggle and laughter erupts around the room again. There are a few sniffs too, and I look up to see my mother wiping her eyes. She's not the only one.

Father Peter begins the ceremony, and I know I'll have no recollection of all the prayers he utters. I'll only remember a few key moments. The part where Eileen brings Trystan two wedding bands which he unties from her neck ribbon and hands to us, the part where we say "I do," and most clearly, the part where Father Peter declares us man and wife and I grab Gracie and make out with her so passionately everyone starts whooping and yelling at us.

"Hey, that's my daughter," yells Rhys.

"That's my wife," I call back.

I turn my attention back to her. "You look stunning."

"You clean up quite well yourself."

I look around. People have seemed to realize we need a second to ourselves, and they are milling around toward a table heaped with drinks and food. A live band is tuning up. "How on earth—I can't believe you set all this up. This is why you couldn't see me."

She bites her lip. "I wasn't sure you'd go along with it at first, but then I realized you wouldn't do it if I gave you a choice. I know you too well. You're worried I'm rushing into it to help you. And I am. But it's the rest of our lives, Beau. We may as well start now. And this way you get to fulfill all the stipulations to your grandfather's will." She shrugs. "And I get to marry my best friend whom I love beyond all reason and never, ever want to be without."

"This is … this is amazing. I'm speechless. And you look … wow." I sweep my gaze over her bared neckline and down the long line of her fitted gown.

"It was my mother's," she says.

"It's beautiful. You're beautiful."

There's a tap on my shoulder, and I turn to find Trystan, and with him is a petite redhead with twinkling blue eyes.

"This must be Emmy," I say and hold out my hand and she shakes it. "I've heard so much about you."

"Emmy this is Beau and his wife, Gwen," Trystan introduces us.

"Aaaaah," Gracie squeals. "Sorry, hearing myself introduced that way is going to take some getting used to. Nice to meet you." She takes Emmy's hand.

"Congratulations to both of you, that was the most interesting wedding I've ever been invited to. Do we call it a surprise wedding? I didn't believe Trystan when he told me." She nudges him and he smiles down at her, then kisses her on the nose.

There's another tap on my shoulder, and the look on Gracie's face makes my gut clench.

"I need to talk to you both," says Isabel Montgomery.

* * *

"I'D LIKE TO APOLOGIZE," Isabel says to us as soon as the office door closes us in.

"I'm sorry, what?" I ask.

Isabel wrings her hands. She's wearing a pale green linen skirt suit and her pearls. "Congratulations, Beau."

"Thank you, but why the apology?"

"Can't an old woman apologize? I'd particularly like to apologize to you, Gwen. I know I don't show it, and I'll try to do better, but I'm extremely fond of you."

Gracie tilts her head. "Um. Okay. Thank you."

Then Grandmother looks at me. "I know it seemed like I bought this building out of spite. But really—"

"Let *me* explain," Rhys said from the door.

"Dad?"

Isabel and Rhys trade a glance.

"The thing was," he begins. "I thought—"

"We both did," Isabel interjects.

Rhys nods. "We both thought that if Beau had good reason to be forced to get married quickly, he would naturally pick *you*, Gracie. And it would finally make you both admit your feelings and well, we'd be doing this. A wedding."

"And then I said, 'no.'" Gracie bites her lip.

"For good reason, I might add," Rhys says proudly. "No offense, Beau."

"None taken." It's the truth after all.

"I *told* Isabel you wouldn't get married under those circumstances. For convenience. I was right. As usual."

"Naturally, sorry Gwendolyn, I disagreed," Isabel says. "I thought you'd always maintained a friendship with my son out of a bid to get close to him and our family. But recently, I realized even if that were the case—"

Gracie stiffens next to me.

"Grandmother," I say in a warning tone.

"Hold your horses and let me finish. Even if that were the case," she looks at Gracie, "and I'm not saying it was, it also didn't bother me quite as much as I thought it did. When I found out what Robert had stipulated in his will, I was as shocked as the rest of you. And I didn't want Beau to become fish food. I considered Gwendolyn the lesser of two evils."

"Wow. Thanks for that ringing endorsement." Gracie snorts, and I take her hand and give it a squeeze.

Rhys scowls. "And we know what my reaction was to that, don't we?" he snaps at my grandmother, some earlier irritation clearly being brought back to the surface.

Isabel clears her throat. "I apologized," she says to Rhys imperiously. "And you accepted, if you'll recall."

"Yeah, yeah," Rhys grumbles.

"And now I've apologized to you, Gwendolyn."

It isn't much of an apology. But it's typical Grandmother, leaving a sliver of 'I told you so', in case she turns out to be right.

But really I just want to focus on the fact the Gracie has just become my wife.

Holy shit.

I stare at my best friend, incredulous.

"Fine. I accept your apology," she's saying to my grandmother graciously, even though she'd be well within her rights to tell her to fuck off. "Now do you think we can go back and enjoy our wedding. Alice is catering. I think we all need a drink. And Beau needs to make a speech."

I shake my head. "I what?"

"Kidding," she says and squeezes my arm. "Just making sure you were listening."

"I'm not done," says Grandmother. "This is a valuable piece of real estate and as much as this scheme was thought up to find a way to force you two together, it is a good investment. But there's no rush. I see no reason why things can't continue on. And Rhys agrees."

My skin chills. "Are you saying the boat shop can stay here?" I ask, carefully, daring not to hope too much.

Rhys purses his lips. "I still want to retire. But Beau, I've got orders. You and Gracie both know how to manage all my filing systems. And my customers will still be getting a Rhys Thomas boat. And perhaps you might consider Thomas-Montgomery as a future business name?"

Gracie slips her arm around my waist and presses herself to my side. It's like she knows the shocks of the day might be quite a lot to take in.

"I would ... be honored. Sir." I nod. It's all I can manage.

Rhys extends his hand and I take it.

Of course he pulls me into a hug and slaps my back. "I love you, son. Take good care of both my babies."

"Will do."

"Who's that woman with Trystan?" Grandmother asks. She's distracted herself from our manly display of affection by peering through the office blinds. "They are together, but not talking. They keep looking at their phones and smiling and winking at each other. It's very bizarre."

"Oh, that's Emmy. That's how they met," I tell her. "Through their phones. Trystan says they have entire conversations with each other over text, even when they are in the same room."

Grandmother shakes her head. "You young people are just so odd. I can't imagine trying to date in this day and age."

I open the office door and we all file out to whoops and cheers.

"Speech!" someone yells and hands me a beer.

I lock eyes with Gracie. "Fine," I say loudly and turn to the room. "I'll say a few words."

Gracie winks at me.

"Women are dangerous and expensive ..." I begin.

THE END

Thank you for reading Beau and Gwen's Story

Read the hilarious and sexy story about how
Trystan and Emmy met in
ACCIDENTAL TRYST

The next in the Charleston series will be
IMMATERIAL GIRL
coming 2019

Join my reader group mailing list so you never miss a release:
http://eepurl.com/dk9N75

Or text NATASHABOYD to 31996
from a US based cellphone

Have you read my romance EVERSEA?
Would you like a free copy?
Go here to claim your free book
This does add you to my *New Release News* email list which you
can unsubscribe from at any time

ALSO BY NATASHA BOYD

The Butler Cove Novels
Eversea (Eversea #1)
Forever, Jack (Eversea #2)
My Star, My Love (An Eversea Christmas Novella)
All That Jazz
Beach Wedding (Eversea #3)

Deep Blue Eternity /*The Recluse*
(*A standalone contemporary romance*)

The Charleston Series (unofficial series title)
Accidental Tryst
(*A Romantic Comedy*)
Inconvenient Wife
Immaterial Girl (*TBA*)

and a standalone Contemporary Romance
set in the South of France coming 2020

ALSO : Ever wished your favorite romance author would write a "bookclub" type book? Well, I did! *The Indigo Girl* a historical fiction (or should I say, *herstorical* fiction?) novel is available now in hardcover, ebook and audio. It's based on a true story and it's a woman's story you don't want to miss. I am so incredibly proud of this book, and the honor of being able to tell this incredible young woman's story. I do give talks about it at libraries, museums and schools. You can check my Website to see where I will be discussing it next .

My next romance is coming in 2020, and is set partially in Charleston, SC and The French Riviera.

BLURB

Josie Marin thought she was getting a promotion, but instead explodes her career. In a state of shock, she impulsively takes up a friend's offer to nanny for a little girl on a mega yacht in the South of France. Even though she can't stand boats, this seems like fate giving her an opportunity to lick her wounds in a bucket list paradise while she figures out how to get her life back.

But this little girl she's arrived to look after has a daddy. A widowed, hot, young, billionaire of a daddy. A man who is both France's economic king and their tragic broken prince. He's the French paparazzi's dream fodder. And if there's anything that Josie needs less than having to be stuck on a yacht, no matter how luxurious, it's an inconvenient and highly-combustible attraction to her new boss.

Everyone thinks Xavier Pascale's is a playboy, a wastrel, and has an empire built from family money. But no one knows how his father's cheating destroyed their family and almost bankrupted their legacy. Nor do they know how his first wife broke his heart and her own life, leaving him emotionally wasted and trying to raise a daughter on his own. Now he's closed off, wary, and utterly untrusting of this American girl who's passing herself off as a nanny when she has zero experience.

The first time he saw Josephine Marin, he felt it like a faint-earth tremor along a catastrophic fault line.

He should send her home.

He really should.

Add to Goodreads

ACKNOWLEDGMENTS

Thank you as always to my amazing husband and two beautiful children who support my career every way they can. Thank you to my two critique partners Al and Dave, and to my amazing editor Judy Roth.

And to my readers, thank you for your continued support, it means the world to me. I love that you trust where the story needs to go, and where I need to go.

With all my love, this book is dedicated to you, I wouldn't have a career without you.

With love,

Tasha x

ABOUT THE AUTHOR

Natasha Boyd holds a Bachelor of Science in Psychology. She has lived in Denmark, Spain, South Africa, Belgium, England and wrote most of the Butler Cove novels while residing with her husband and two boys on Hilton Head Island, SC, USA—complete with Spanish moss, alligators and mosquitos the size of tiny birds. She now splits her time between the "Lowcountry" and Atlanta, GA.

Text NATASHABOYD to 31996